THE FATE OF A FLAPPER

THE FATE
OF A
FLAPPER

A MYSTERY

SUSANNA CALKINS

MINOTAUR
BOOKS
NEW YORK

First published in the United States by Minotaur Books, an imprint of St. Martin's Publishing Group

THE FATE OF A FLAPPER. Copyright © 2020 by Susanna Calkins. All rights reserved. Printed in the United States of America. For information, address St. Martin's Publishing Group, 120 Broadway, New York, NY 10271.

www.minotaurbooks.com

Designed by Omar Chapa

The Library of Congress Cataloging-in-Publication Data is available upon request.

ISBN 978-1-250-19085-7 (trade paperback)
ISBN 978-1-250-19086-4 (ebook)

Our books may be purchased in bulk for promotional, educational, or business use. Please contact your local bookseller or the Macmillan Corporate and Premium Sales Department at 1-800-221-7945, extension 5442, or by email at MacmillanSpecialMarkets@macmillan.com.

First Edition: 2020

10 9 8 7 6 5 4 3 2 1

To my guys—Matt, Alex, and Quentin

CHAPTER 1

The black delivery truck pulled up to Mr. Rosenstein's drugstore, its movements stealthy and smooth as it parked, not a squeaking brake or rattling screw to be heard. Its shadow from the dropping sun stretched across the sidewalk, just touching the store's glass windows, which displayed mortars and pestles, vials, soaps, and soda bottles.

At the sight of the truck Gina Ricci halted midstep and buried her nose in a florist's storefront display about fifty feet away. The florist shop was new to the street—another business masking Signora Castallazzo's operations. As Gina pretended to admire the fall blooms, she pulled a silver compact out of her handbag and angled it so that she could discreetly observe what was happening. Deliveries could be a dodgy business—better to wait until everything had been safely unloaded and the truck had departed before making her way inside to the speakeasy below.

Two men in brown overalls with gray caps pulled low

over their eyes slid out of the passenger side and walked around to the back of the truck. Their builds were similar, but one was much older than the other. Father and son, maybe. The driver remained at the wheel, his elbow protruding from the window. The engine, Gina noticed, was still idling.

Two of Signora Castallazzo's right-hand men stepped out of the drugstore, their movements coordinated and purposeful. The first man was Little Johnny, a large Russian fellow whose nickname was at odds with his size. He gestured to the deliverymen to open the truck's back doors. Not surprisingly, Mr. Rosenstein, the thin, bespectacled chemist, was not on hand to receive the shipment. The Signora controlled all deliveries received at the drugstore, as well as at the tearoom on the other side.

As the men began to unload the crates onto an iron hand truck under Little Johnny's watchful eye, Mr. Gucciani, or "Gooch," remained a few steps away, his sharply tailored suit jacket loosened, with his hand close to his hip. He was looking up and down the street, and she saw his gaze settle on her for a moment. He held up his hand to her before dropping it back to his side. *Wait.* She gave the barest of nods to indicate she understood. His eyes traveled past her, and he craned his head. He then said something to the other men that Gina couldn't make out.

Angling her mirror in the other direction, Gina inhaled sharply. A black Model T was inching its way down the street, stopping directly behind her. Shifting her body slightly, she could see two men in dark suits inside staring intently at the truck. One man pointed, and the other man nodded. Both men's faces were grim. They could be Drys—the federal agents charged with arresting anyone found illegally selling, manufacturing, or distributing alcohol intended for consumption. The local cops didn't police Prohibition; they only arrested drunks if they were publicly disorderly or committing a crime. If treated gingerly, they were usually willing to accept a payoff—or even a drink. The Signora, Gina knew, kept them close. The Drys, on the other hand, were a different breed altogether. Passionate in their pursuits, they could be dogged in their quest to suppress the alcohol trade.

Gina stiffened, fighting the instinct to hide inside the florist shop as the passengers got out of the truck.

Don't run, she told herself. *Don't ever run.* She'd learned the slogan her first day on the job, and so far, remembering it had served her well.

She smelled another bouquet, wondering if she should go wait in the tearoom, which served as another front for the speakeasy.

"Newspaper, miss?"

Gina glanced down at the boy who'd materialized at her side. Dressed head to foot in gray clothes flecked in mud and grime, he looked to be about ten or eleven. Across his slight chest he wore a cloth satchel marked *Daily Tribune*. Inside the satchel were three or four newspapers that he'd not yet sold. An uncut cigar peeked out of his vest pocket. Knowing these newsies, there was probably a flask of bourbon tucked away as well. His gray cap was tugged low over his forehead, but not so far that she missed the desperate look in his eyes. "Just a penny."

"Scram, kid," she said. She peered past him. Would they ever finish the delivery? "I already got a paper waiting for me at home."

"Real exciting news, miss." Not to be deterred, he held out the newspaper so she could read the headlines. BOMB HURLED THROUGH LAKE SHORE ATHLETIC CLUB WINDOW. And below it, in smaller but still eye-catching text, NINETY-FIFTH BOMBING IN CHICAGO THIS YEAR.

The delivery was starting to look like it was going to take a while. *Can't stare at flowers forever,* she thought. She pulled a penny out of her beaded handbag and handed it to the newsboy. "Now beat it, would you?"

Grinning, he scurried away to continue his hustle else-where. Opening the paper, Gina leaned against the brick wall between the florist and the tearoom entrance and began to read about the bombings. Ninety-five bombs detonated in Chicago this year alone. Pineapple bombs, black powder bombs, dynamite, Molotov cocktails . . . there seemed to be no shortage in the ways people sought to terrorize one another. Bootleggers and businessmen alike, even a college quarterback, of all people, had been threatened by bombs. The side effects of skills learned during the Great War.

Gina continued to page through the paper as she waited. In a Colorado penitentiary, hundreds of inmates had taken part in the largest prison riot ever seen in the United States. On the North Side of Chicago, a housewife had murdered her husband for mocking her cooking. "Well, he did put her down in front of their friends," Gina muttered to herself, perusing the piece.

She flipped to the last few pages of the paper, skimming

over the features and advice columns. A review of Heming-way's *A Farewell to Arms*. Fashion guides for slimming clothes for heavy women. Articles about dieting. CHOCOLATE COM-PANY SAYS, "EAT MORE SUGAR TO STAY SLIM." And as always, Doris Blake's advice to modern women on how to be attrac-tive to more traditionally minded men.

She glanced at her watch. Almost five thirty.

One of the men got out of the Ford and advanced toward the drugstore, holding up a badge. "What's being delivered today?" he asked. He didn't sound anything like the Irish cops she was familiar with—probably not from Chicago.

Without missing a beat, the older of the two delivery-men replied, "Balms. Oils. Some cosmetics for the ladies. Hand lotions. All produced at our factory in Des Plaines." He pointed at the side of the truck. "Boscoe's." He showed the man a clipboard, which had the delivery orders typed out.

The Dry pointed at one of the crates in the middle of the stack. "Mind opening that for me?" His tone was friendly, but Gina could see his body was tense. The other agent, still in the car, had leaned forward.

The younger deliveryman licked his lips and glanced at Little Johnny. The Signora's man just jerked his head toward the crowbar. "Do it."

They all watched as the man moved the top crate aside and positioned the crowbar above the middle crate. With a sharp wrenching sound, he pried the lid open.

Taking the crowbar into his own hands, the Dry pushed aside the layer of straw that had lined the top of the crate. Reaching in, he picked up one of the vials and uncorked it, taking a deep sniff, his expression not changing. After recorking it, he dropped it back inside. He reached in deeper this time, pulling out another bottle. Once again he took a sniff, then dipped his finger inside and touched it to his tongue for a taste. This time he grimaced. "Someone would need a death wish to drink that stuff," he said, not cracking a smile.

Little Johnny grinned as though the man had made a joke. "*Ja.* Just so," he said. The deliverymen echoed the laughter. Only Gooch stayed silent.

The Dry gave the straw another half-hearted poke with the crowbar and turned back to Gooch. "Carry on," he said. "We'll wait."

As the crates were being loaded, the Dry had them open another one. Once again he did the same thing—selected a random vial, uncorked it, tasted its contents, and then stepped back. He did this two more times. All the while the drivers in both cars were keeping careful watch. Finally the Dry grunted something that Gina didn't catch, and headed back to the waiting car.

As soon he slammed the car door shut, the federal agents drove away, leaving the deliverymen to reload the crates back onto the hand truck and wheel them into the drugstore. Once inside, the crates would be pried open by Benny, Mr. Rosenstein's shop hand, and the shelves would be restocked with tonics, balms, cosmetics, and other sundries. Later, assuming all went well, the crates would be transferred downstairs to the Third Door, where their false bottoms and secret spaces would be revealed, exposing the specialty liquors reserved for the more discerning of the speakeasy's customers.

"This place is getting hot," she heard the older delivery-man say. "Mr. Boscoe won't like it."

Gooch stood next to the man. "If Mr. Boscoe has a problem, tell him to take it up with us directly." As always, there was a lethal undertone to his deep voice.

Shrugging, the men hopped back into the truck and drove off. Before he followed Little Johnny in, Gooch looked straight at Gina and jerked his head toward the drugstore. She could almost hear his voice. *Get a wiggle on, toots.* He went back inside.

Gina had not gone two more steps when someone grabbed her elbow. Whirling around, she instinctively adopted the fighting stance her brother had taught her when she was a kid. Working at the Third Door had quickened her reflexes and toughened her up.

Rather than the lecherous man she expected, she faced a middle-aged woman, with a mucky toddler clutching her skirts. A kerchief covered her grayish-brown hair, and a drab brown dress engulfed her shapeless form. Behind the woman she spied the newsboy from earlier, now looking more sullen than cocky as he poked the ground with a stick.

"What do you want?" Gina asked, dropping her fists but not her guard. "I don't have any money."

"I'm not a beggar, miss," the woman said proudly, her English tinged with a Polish accent. "You work in there, don't you?"

"The drugstore? Yes."

The woman made an impatient sound. "The moonshine parlor. I know you do."

Gina glanced down at her light fall jacket, which covered an ordinary day dress. She would change once she was inside. How could the woman have known?

The newsboy spoke up then. "I've seen you. You've gone in one of them stores, and then you don't come back out."

"Excuse me. I'm going to be late," Gina replied, feeling a bit uneasy. Even though the Third Door was one of the most poorly kept secrets of Chicago's Near West Side, she knew the Signora wouldn't like her talking openly about selling alcohol. The Feds' presence during the delivery had unnerved her, too. A constant reminder that the Drys could bust up their place at any time. She'd be out of a job, or worse.

She shuddered. She couldn't even imagine what her papa would do if she ended up in jail or out of a job. Especially not now, with his palsy growing worse every day, further limiting his ability to bring in much income.

"Please, miss. I don't mean you no harm," the woman pleaded. "It's my husband. He spends all his time in there, spending every penny he earns. My children are hungry and without proper clothes on account of his drinking." She put her arms protectively around her daughter. "My rent is due and we're facing the street. I don't want to go to the mayor and rat this place out, but I beg of you, send my man home. Back to where he belongs."

Gina looked down at the two kids, who looked back up her. The boy stuck his tongue out, but the toddler gave her a sunny smile, displaying several missing teeth behind her chapped lips. "What's your husband's name?"

"Stanislaus Galinsky. His *pals*"—here she grimaced—"call him Stan."

An image of a rough-hewn regular jumped into her thoughts. Gin and tonic. Ale when they had it. She'd been working at the Third Door over nine months now, and she'd gotten to know the regulars. Stan stuck to himself, at least; not a handsy guy. Still, drinking away his earnings . . . she shook her head.

"I'll see what I can do." As the woman began to thank her, she added more sternly. "Mrs. Galinsky, I can't promise you anything. You understand me?"

Gina turned away then, not wanting to look at the woman's downcast face or the pitiful appearance of her children. She'd tell Gooch to kick the bum out. Of course, they couldn't keep him out for long; or even if they could, he'd stake out another spot. She shook her head again. Such was the way of things.

CHAPTER 2

Once inside the Third Door, Gina quickly went to the women's salon and changed into a red silk concoction, a new piece. Madame Laupin's latest creation. An unexpected gift from the Signora.

Gina smoothed her hands over the fabric, admiring its soft sheen and beautiful movement, once again marveling at the life that was hers. Who would have thought, ten months ago, she'd no longer be doling out soup and washing dishes in a dingy, run-down kitchen? Now she was selling ciggies and drinks and getting tarted up every night. She boldly applied a bit of lipstick that was nearly as scarlet as her dress and surveyed the result with satisfaction.

After touching up her mascara, she headed onto the speakeasy floor. Her main job was to sell cigarettes, gum, and candy, only serving cocktails when the other servers were dancing or when the joint got too full for the other girls to handle.

Moving too quickly, she nearly collided with Lulu, the cocktail waitress with the frizzy red hair, who was perpetually late to everything. "Hey, doll!" Lulu called, blowing her a kiss on her way to change. "Looking good!"

A few men who were already there gave her an appreciative glance, even as their female companions turned their guys' faces from her.

They needn't worry, Gina thought. *I'm not looking for a sheik.*

Besides, the Signora had made it abundantly clear that they weren't to date the patrons, or at least not set anything up while on the clock. Still, Gina fluffed her hair a bit and widened her smile. The tips had certainly helped make sure her papa had meat three times a week and she could pay all their bills on time. The windfall she'd received back in January following the unexpected death of her cousin Marty Doyle had improved their situation somewhat, but money was still tight.

The memory of Marty still made her wince. She'd barely known him before he was murdered, but she'd been shocked to learn that he had bequeathed her his possessions, including all his photography equipment, because she was the only surviving issue of his favorite cousin, her mother, Molly O'Brien. He'd also paid six months out on his lease, which covered a one-bedroom flat with kitchen, as well as another flat that had been converted into a working darkroom. She'd been pleased to discover that both flats were situated in a building above the speakeasy, although a bit less pleased to discover that the Signora was her landlord, and Little Johnny's mother lived in the flat below. Still, she couldn't complain, given that the Signora had graciously extended the already reduced lease for another year.

Gina had half-heartedly gone through Marty's old

things, giving some of his clothes to her papa and selling a few items when she could. She really didn't know what to do with everything else. Some days before work she'd come over to develop photographs and make herself coffee and cookies, but the space had mostly stayed empty. She'd also enjoyed using Marty's equipment, learning the art of photography on her own after some initial lessons back in February. The Signora hadn't hired anyone to be the speakeasy photographer after Marty's untimely death, and Gina was still hoping to develop her skill enough that the Signora might hire her on the same terms she'd given him. She'd toyed with the idea of moving in, but she couldn't stomach the thought of leaving her father on her own.

"Gina! Come get your tray!" Billy Bottles called, setting the wooden piece at the end of the bar. It was the bartender's job to fill it with the most commonly requested ciggies, papers, and tobaccos, as well as a few necessities like a cigar cutter and a lighter. There was even a small box for her favorite Wrigley's gum and mints.

"Thanks, Billy," she replied, smiling at the white-haired bartender. He just grunted in reply. As a surly guy, he muttered a lot. Like Gooch and Little Johnny, he had deep-rooted connections to the Signora, and he'd been working as the Third Door's bartender since it opened a few years back. A whiz with cocktails, he took great pride in his work, sometimes coming up with his own concoctions. He did have a bit of a temper, especially if someone didn't like a drink he'd made. That anger had never been directed at her, though. Maybe because he'd known her papa when he was young, back when he'd been known as "Frankie the Cat."

Carefully, Gina fastened the strap so that the tray rested comfortably at her waist. Since January, she'd gradually learned to position the tray so that it wasn't so heavy on her neck and shoulders, although the strap still pulled on her neck hairs at times. A few months ago she'd painted the word *Smokes* on the tray, all in curlicues, with bright red paint, which she felt gave it a bit of character.

She moved to greet a handful of regulars descending the stairs, but Jade had already beaten her to it. "This way, Mr. and Mrs. Henderson," Jade said to the couple, giving Gina a cool look as she led them to a corner table. *Mine*, Gina could almost hear the Caribbean-born singer say, in the slightly taunting way she had. "Brought your friends in, I see?"

"We told them about your singing," Mrs. Henderson gushed, causing Jade to smirk at Gina. "Told them they simply *had* to hear you," her husband added.

There had been a bit of a thaw between the women over these last few months, but Jade was clearly the Signora's hot-to-trot green-eyed favorite and always lorded it over the others. Not that Gina blamed her—Jade's beautiful voice deserved something better than the second-rate audiences who came to the Third Door. On occasion Jade performed over at Louis Armstrong's joint in Bronzeville, the Sunset Café, but that had yet to turn into a regular gig. As Jade had resentfully told her once, her skin color meant she couldn't headline at some of the fancier clubs and theaters outside of Chicago's South Side. However, at the Third Door her popularity was unmatched, and she had many regulars wrapped around her finger. Right now, both couples had laid some extra dollars on Jade's tray.

"I'll give you some real razzle-dazzle later," she said, slipping the cash from view. She strutted past Gina, queen of the walk.

A loud guffaw from the other end of the bar caught Gina's attention. A group of men was huddled there, and in the middle was Stan Galinsky, the newsboy's papa, still yukking it up with his pals. She curled her lip. All of them drinking away their weekly paychecks. How many others had mouths at home waiting to be fed? She'd never given it much thought.

Instead of pointing Stan out to Gooch as she intended, Gina marched over to the man, planting herself squarely in front of him. "You're Stan, right? Stan Galinsky?"

The other men stopped talking at her approach, looking her up and down with a mixture of interest, admiration and annoyance.

Stan looked up at her, his eyes bleary and bloodshot, a stupid grin revealing the wrinkles across his face. "Aw, sweetheart, I'm taken," he said, causing the men around him to laugh. "Though my wife might not be too happy to see me right now."

Gina frowned. In his cups even before dinnertime. "Your wife is outside the drugstore. Waiting for *you* to come out."

"Petra can keep waiting," he replied, still slurring his

words. "Just gonna harp and carry on like she always does. Right, fellows?" He looked around at his pals, who all slapped his back and guffawed.

"You got that right, Stan!" they called. "Show her what's what!"

"Your *kids* are up there, too," Gina said. "They're waiting for their papa to come home."

A flicker of shame danced in his eyes before he turned away. "Lemme alone," he slurred. "Or I'll tell the Signora you're trying to drive away her customers. She wouldn't like *that*, would she?"

That's true, Gina silently agreed, taking a step back. What would the Signora do if she warned off a paying customer? Usually it was up to Gooch and Little Johnny to run the bums out of the speakeasy, but they'd only do so if someone was picking fights, pawing at the women, or had blown through their dough.

"I'll take some Marlboros," one of the other men called to her. "Just so long as you don't tell *my* wife."

Gina handed the man his cigarettes, plastering a smile back on her face, trying not to think about the tearful woman waiting for her wayward husband to find his way home.

By seven o'clock, the Third Door was hopping. Stood to reason. On a Friday night people had bucks to burn. Or, just as likely, they'd come out hoping to find someone willing to blow some scratch on them.

Most of the tables around the dance floor were occupied, and a few couples were already dancing as Neddy Fingers tickled the keys of the piano in the corner. As usual, a few women were casually positioned around Ned, hoping to catch the slender playboy's attention.

A few more people were seated at the bar, chatting or idly watching Billy make concoctions of all sorts, adding honey to some, bitters to others, and garnishing a few with mint, cherries, or orange slices. At this time of the evening, Gina had noticed, most of the drinks were a little frothier and more imaginative, Billy Bottles' way of disguising the terrible taste of the gin. Later in the evening the drinks would start getting darker and more bitter, as if everyone were getting too fried to care what their drinks looked or tasted like.

As she moved around the room, she noticed that a man seated alone by the wall seemed to be watching her. His hand was wrapped loosely around his whiskey tonic, and as she approached, she could see that his fingernails were carefully trimmed and buffed.

"Cigarettes, cigars, candy, mints? If you don't see something you like, I can go see if Billy's got it in stock."

"Oh, I see something I like," he said, grinning at her slightly, giving her the once-over. He was probably in his early thirties, slender, very well dressed. He had Irish features—dark blue eyes, black hair. Very handsome.

She shifted impatiently. "On the tray?"

"Sure, Gina." He pointed to a cigar. "I'll have one of those."

"You know my name?" she asked, as she cut the foil on the cigar. She'd never seen him before.

"I pay attention," he replied, taking the cigar and holding it out for her. Before she could light it, he set it back down, his jaw tightening as he caught sight of something over her shoulder. "Ah. I'd love to chat more, but I need to take care of something first. If you'll excuse me."

Putting the cigar in his vest pocket, he downed the rest of the whiskey in his glass and stood up.

Gooch was standing there. "The Signora is ready for you now, Mr. Morrish. Follow me."

Gina narrowed her eyes, watching as the men disappeared from the speakeasy floor. *Wonder what that's about?* she thought. She knew the Signora had her hands in a lot of pots and was always finagling with others to expand her means and reach. Though it was hard not to speculate about all the backroom meetings, Gina knew enough not to ask questions and she most definitely knew to keep her mouth shut.

Two men had seated themselves at a high table by the bar when she wasn't looking and appeared now to be waiting for service. Seeing Lulu about to head over, Gina tapped meaningfully at her delicate silver art deco wristwatch. Catching the gesture, Lulu returned her empty cocktail tray to Billy before disappearing to the ladies' salon. Time to get ready for her first set.

"Good evening, gents," Gina said to the two men. She ran her fingertips lightly across the contents of the tray. "Care for a smoke?"

"From you, doll, I'd buy anything," one of the men said, giving her a dimpled smile that most women would probably find charming. With his wavy blond hair and even features, he had the look of a man who usually got what he wanted. "Modernos for me. How about you, Dan?"

"It's Daniel, George," his companion replied. He looked up at Gina. "I'll take Modernos as well, thank you. Plus two sidecars."

They placed the money on Gina's tray, but only Daniel added a tip. A whole extra dollar. Not with the lecherous air of expectation but rather with the ease of someone used to tipping expansively.

After lighting the men's cigarettes, Gina put their drink order in with Billy, keeping an eye on the whole floor. Everyone seemed settled in with their smokes and drinks, as they tapped their feet to Ned's quick-fingered version of "If You Knew Susie (Like I Know Susie)."

A petite woman dressed in gray and silver emerged from the direction of the ladies' room and approached Gina, sliding a beautiful evening bag off her wrist.

"What a lovely bag," Gina said, admiring the loops of shimmering deep red beads and intricate silver handle.

The woman gave her a pleased smile. "Thank you. My father gave it to me a few years ago. It's my favorite." She opened the clasp and handed Gina a dollar. "I imagine my friends have already ordered. I'll take a bourbon rickey. You can bring me my change with my drink."

"Sure thing," Gina said. "I'll be over in a sec."

As she waited on Billy to finish the drinks, Gina turned her attention back to Daniel and George, studying them with a practiced eye. Ever since she'd started learning the craft of photography earlier in the year, she'd taken to looking at the details of people's faces and clothes more closely, thinking about what it would be like to photograph them. While both men wore expensively tailored suits, Daniel had a slightly more finicky air, still buttoned up and starched, while George looked a little rougher but more relaxed. If she had to guess, given the way Daniel had bestowed the tip, he'd been born to wealth and privilege, while George had not.

The drinks ready, Gina carried them over, placing small cocktail napkins on the table before laying down the glasses. Not every customer scored a napkin, but since Daniel had tipped her so well she thought he might appreciate the gesture.

"Thank you, darling," George said to her. He clinked his glass against his friend's. "Bottoms up, Dan! Here's to the booming stock market and making our clients—and us!—oodles of cash! That means a new Duesenberg for me!"

A Duesenberg! It was hard not to feel impressed. Gina had never ridden in such a fancy car. After laying down the bourbon rickey in front of the woman, who'd rejoined her friends nearby, she continued to listen in on their conversation even though she knew little about the stock market. There was something compelling about George's unabashedly joyful sense of greed that both intrigued and offended her.

Daniel took a deep gulp, grimacing. "Too many people entering the market who don't know what they're doing. Too much borrowing. Too much speculating! They're going to ruin everything."

George snickered. "Your trust fund is showing, Dan. The more in the market, the merrier, I say."

Daniel drained his glass. "Haven't you seen the reports?

Some experts say that the market could crash if we don't slow down. We have to keep the riffraff out."

"Better not let the boss hear you say that!" George replied, setting his glass down hard on the oak table. "Look, Dan, I just approved three more loans today. Stocks will keep going up and up, mark my words. So long as the banks don't close, we'll just keep raking in money!"

"Tut-tut. So vulgar, George."

"Looks like you need another drink! Hey, darling," George called to Gina. "Keep 'em coming, would you, honey? It's been a good day, and I think it's gonna be even a better night."

Gina gave them the disdainful smirk she'd perfected in the last few months and moved away. She'd given these stinkers enough of her time already. On to the next.

Over the next hour, more customers descended the stairs, allowed down in couples and small groups. First a pair, then another pair, then another three, all dressed to the nines. Feathers, silks, satins, beads, boas, headpieces—everyone sparkly, shiny, and ready for a boozy grand time. Their entry was determined by Little Johnny, who was upstairs monitoring the green door off the alley. The passwords varied, but those in the know were aware that tonight's password was Elephant's Elbows. Though the passwords seemed a bit silly at times, they served a vital purpose, creating a sense of camaraderie in a forbidden world, and ensuring an urgency to keep the secret from those who would expose and betray them.

As Gina refilled her tray with more rolling papers, tobacco, and mints, she could overhear two women seated by the bar talking and giggling loudly, clearly trying to capture the interest of some men around them. One of them was a dainty brunette, pale with delicate rosy cheeks. In her fluffy brown hair, she had pinned an elaborate silver butterfly headpiece that matched her silvery dress. From her neck hung an elegant black opal on a silver chain that set it all off divinely. The other was a slender blonde with bobbed hair, dressed in a sleek teal and black number. Both women looked like they came from money.

The blonde nudged her friend. "Jeepers, Fruma! Vidal's here! You didn't invite him, did you?"

"Oh, no!" Fruma exclaimed, sounding genuinely concerned. "Addie, what's he doing here?"

"He's looking around. Maybe he hasn't seen you. Quick! Go to the ladies' room."

"Bah!" Fruma replied. "Too late. He saw me. He's heading over."

Her attention caught by the conversation, Gina watched as a man with slicked-back hair strode across the room, ignoring all the prancing and trotting couples scattered across the dance floor. He stood in front of the women, his hands thrust into his trouser pockets. "Hey Fruma. What's shaking?"

"What are you doing here, Vidal?" Fruma asked, toying nervously with the opal around her neck. "You know we're not engaged anymore."

He pulled up a chair, to the obvious annoyance of both women. Reaching across the table, he seized Fruma's hand.

"Darling! I've missed you so much. You haven't returned any of my calls! I've been so worried. I took a chance that I'd find you here tonight." He looked accusingly at Fruma's companion. "Adelaide! Have you been passing on my messages?"

"Get lost, Vidal," Adelaide said, sniffing. "Can't you see Fruma doesn't want to see you?"

Vidal's face grew dark with anger. "Hoity-toity, think you're better than me," he said, looming over them in a menacing way, causing both women to cringe.

Gina raised her hand in the air, her spangled bracelets catching the light of the grand chandeliers above, trying to get Gooch's attention.

Except it wasn't Gooch who noticed the women's predicament—it was George, the stockbroker. He strode across the floor and positioned himself between Fruma and Vidal. "Ladies, is this man bothering you?"

They both nodded, their eyes large and star-struck by their hero. Daniel, Gina noticed, continued to drink at their table, unconcerned with the fracas. George stood up straight, trying to loom over Vidal, having only one or two inches on the man. "Sir, I believe these women said they didn't wish to be bothered. I suggest you leave them alone."

"What's going on here, Gina?" Gooch asked, materializing at her side.

Gina cocked her head toward Vidal and spoke in a low tone. "That guy there—his name is Vidal—is bothering those two women. That other guy is just sticking his nose in."

Gina stepped back as Gooch handily maneuvered the interloper to a table on the other end of the dance floor.

Before he walked away, the bouncer wagged his finger in the man's face. *Speak to these women again and you'll be sorry.*

"Guess the fun never stops here. Are they regulars, Gina?" Mr. Morrish had returned to the table he'd occupied earlier, his meeting with the Signora evidently concluded. He'd been watching the confrontation with interest.

"Not regulars," she replied. "We get all kinds here— some looking for different kinds of fun." She studied him. He still seemed watchful, intent, contemplating the two women giggling at Vidal, who was now situated on the other side of the dance floor. "You got what you needed?"

He gave a short laugh. "Not quite," he said, and pointed at his empty glass. "Right now I'll take a sidecar."

When she returned a few minutes later with his drink, he took a sip and grimaced. "Sorry, this won't do. I'll take a whiskey tonic instead." Gina put the barely touched drink back on her tray.

"Hang on a sec, Gina. How about you and I continue where we left off earlier?"

"Wh-what do you mean?"

He pulled the already-cut cigar from his vest pocket and held it out for her to light. After he took a puff, he looked straight into her face. Their sudden proximity made her cheeks flush. She didn't date a lot of men—although there was Roark, whom she hadn't seen in weeks. She didn't want to think about him now.

Mr. Morrish seemed amused by her reaction. He touched her arm before she could step away. "You happy here? The Signora good to you?"

"Quite happy," she said, wary of his sudden intimacy.

"Bad things go down here, Gina. You've got to know that. A girl like you—" He paused.

"What? What about a girl like me?"

"Well, let's just say it would be a real shame if something happened to a girl like you."

Gina froze. *Was that a threat or a warning?*

He dropped his hand then, breaking their odd contact. Then he smiled. "I'll be around. Don't you worry."

CHAPTER 3

"Hey there, bearcat," a man's rough voice murmured in her ear, as she was putting in Mr. Morrish's drink order with Billy. "You're busy tonight."

Her heart beat a little faster as she turned to face Roark, looking up into his warm hazel eyes. She'd met the exserviceman and former police officer back in January, when he was unofficially looking into Marty's murder. They'd had coffee a few times, and some nights he had driven her home after she was done with her shift. Never out for dinner, never for drinks. He had taken her to a movie once, though, back in July. It was *On with the Show*, the first all-talking and all-color film. They hadn't gone out on a date again since. There was a distance underlying their mutual attraction that she wasn't sure what to do about.

Roark hadn't been around so much in the last few months, either, ever since he'd been hired to take crime scene photographs for the nation's first forensic lab. The mayor had called for the lab after the horrendous St. Valentine's Day Massacre occurred back in February, and Roark was

one of the men charged with getting the lab in order. He'd
never talked much about his time either on the force or when
he was a lieutenant in the Great War, but both experiences
had left him scarred and wounded in different ways. When
she'd met him, he'd been using a cane to walk, but as he had
healed, his vibrancy had returned. Seeing him now, it was
hard to imagine he'd ever seemed weak.

For a moment they regarded each other, something unspoken passing between them.

"I haven't seen you for a while," she said, taking in his
straight, muscular form.

"No. It's been too long." He looked in the direction of
Mr. Morrish, who appeared to be watching them from his
table. "Far too long, I'm thinking."

Gina's cheeks warmed. Had he seen Mr. Morrish's attentions to her?

"How's the lab going?" she asked, changing the subject
as she balanced the sidecars carefully with two gin rickeys
on a tray.

"Fine, fine. Some cases starting to come through," he
said, excitement lighting his face. "I think the lab is really
going to make a difference in bringing criminals to justice."

"That's keen, Roark." She smiled at him.

"Say, Gina," he said, stepping closer. "There's something
I need to discuss with you."

"Oh?" she replied. "What is it?"

He looked around. "Not here. Not now. Let's get together soon. Privately."

She took a deep breath. "I'd like that." Seeing Gooch

beckon to her, she stepped back. "I've got to get back to work."

"All right." He gave her a half-smile. "Also, Gina—"

"What?"

"Red looks real good on you."

"Keep an eye on that bunch," Gooch said after she walked over, a smile still stamped on her face from Roark's unexpected compliment. Following the bouncer's gaze, she could see that a single boisterous group had formed out of the earlier pairs and trios at the end of the bar, as drinks were tossed back with abandon. Most of the action seemed to surround George, who kept ordering rounds of drinks—although Daniel seemed to be the one who paid for them. Fruma and Adelaide, the red-cheeked brunette and the elegant blonde, were now actively cozying up to the men.

As Gina watched, Fruma gave a loud shriek of laughter and swayed a bit in her chair, leaning in toward George. Gina could see that the woman's ex-fiancé was still watching from across the room, a bitter look on his face. Fruma glanced at him from time to time before returning to simper over George, who was seated close to her other side.

She's determined to make her ex-fiancé jealous, Gina thought.

"She's zozzled all right," Gina said, replying to Gooch. "I'll check on them."

She sidled over to the group. "How's everyone doing over here?" Gina asked, placing the empty glasses and wet cocktail napkins on her tray.

"Doin' just fine," Fruma replied, shaking her empty glass.

"I was about to tell you all a story! A fantastic story! Now where was I?" she asked, looking at the others with extra-wide eyes. "Oh, right, I jumped out of an airplane. Probably set a record, too!"

Adelaide rolled her eyes. "Come on, Fruma. Not that old yarn again." She leaned toward George in a conspiratorial way, but without bothering to lower her voice. "She tells it every time she gets sloshed."

"Well, now I'm *very* interested. How'd an itty-bitty girl like you manage to do such a frightening thing like jump out of an airplane?" George reached out to stroke Fruma's bare arm with one finger. "Tell us more."

Adelaide stood up. "I think we should go—" she started to say, before getting drowned out by groans from both Fruma and George.

"Don't be such a flat tire, Addie. Don't you think she's such a flat tire, Georgie Porgie?" Fruma giggled, fully leaning into George.

George smiled at Adelaide. "Come on, darling, don't be a square. Have a drink. Danny boy here will get it for you, right, Dan? One for me and Fruma, while you're at it."

"It's Daniel," he said, downing his drink before standing up next to Adelaide. "Keep me company, would you? George is on a mission."

Adelaide tossed her head, looking angry. "Fine. I'll have whatever you're having. Right now, I need to powder my nose."

Adelaide's comment reminded Gina that she needed to check on the ladies' room. One of her least glamorous tasks. She'd

heard that fancier places had private attendants, but the
Signora viewed such indulgence as an unnecessary expense.

When she entered the room, only Adelaide and the brunette with the red evening bag she'd admired earlier were
in there. Crinkling her nose, Gina began to gingerly pick
discarded hand towels from the floor and toss them into the
corner basket. She could almost hear the indignant voice of
her late mother. *Who raised these women to throw their used towels on
the floor like this?*

Adelaide was fuming. "Can you believe that Fruma?"
she asked the other woman. "I saw George first, and Fruma
took him from me!" She disappeared into one of the stalls.

"Oh, that's a shame," the other woman said soothingly.
When Gina caught her eye in the mirror, she winked. "She's
in a state," she whispered. Not surprising, given the rounds
of drinks that the group had tossed back. She raised her
voice so that the other woman could hear her. "Did you call
dibs on George, Addie, and Fruma ignored it?"

"Yes, and it's not the first time she's done that, either!"
Adelaide called back. "Alma, I know she was only going
after George to make Vidal jealous! She didn't care I wanted
him!"

"He's not worth it," Alma replied, straightening her
bangs in the giant gilt-edged mirror. The effort seemed stiff,
as if she were not a woman who usually spent much time
prinking and preening. Gina opened the linen closet containing freshly laundered hand towels and began to restock the
small baskets on the counter. A nice scent after the smoke
and perfume of the speakeasy floor.

"Oh, but George is so handsome! I mean, you can't *marry*

a George, but he's a fun enough chum," Adelaide said. "Besides, he says he's got a Duesenberg."

Alma rolled her eyes good-naturedly. "That *is* the most important evidence of quality," she whispered to Gina. To her friend she called, "Addie, I'm heading out now. See you in a bit."

After Alma left, Gina continued to tidy the jars of soap, just about finished with her tasks. Adelaide didn't say anything else until she emerged from the stall a few minutes later. After washing her hands with the lavender soap, she began to primp, making exaggerated expressions at herself in the mirror. "I should be in film, don't you think?" Adelaide asked, smoothing her shiny blond hair, openly admiring herself. She seemed less angry than before.

"Definitely," Gina replied, hiding a smirk. That was another easy lesson she'd learned at the Third Door. Just agree with the drunk patrons, no matter what ridiculous things they said.

As Adelaide continue to gaze at herself in the mirror, she frowned as if something had just occurred to her. "Can I tell you something?"

"Are you asking me or her?" Gina replied, pointing at Adelaide's reflection in the mirror, trying to lighten the mood. She didn't want the woman getting all riled up again.

"What?" Adelaide asked, confused. It took a moment for her to catch Gina's joke, and when she did, her grin stretched into a great bellowing laugh. "'Are you as-asking me or h-her?'" the woman repeated, practically crying through her barks of laughter. "No, I was asking *you*." She giggled again, then stopped. "What was I telling you?"

"That Fruma wanted George for herself," Gina guessed. "And that you're going to get him back."

"Fruma wanted him for her—hey! Wait a minute! Who told you?" Adelaide asked.

"She did," Gina replied, pointing at Adelaide's reflection.

Adelaide began to laugh, but then started sneezing. Drops of red appeared in her nostrils.

"Hey, your nose is bleeding," Gina said, stopping mid-laugh. She handed Adelaide a tissue. "Are you all right?"

"Oh, it happens," Adelaide said, holding her head back. "I think I'll just start wearing red. Don't you think that's a good idea? Except I don't look so good in red. Not like you." She dropped her used tissue on the floor.

Irritated, Gina picked the tissue up, wishing she could give the woman an earful. "Should I get your friend?" she asked instead, in as pleasant a tone as she could muster.

"Nah, I'll be fine," Adelaide replied, leaning over to kiss the mirror, leaving crimson marks where her lips had touched the glass. As she did this, a beautiful amethyst and jade necklace swung free of her bodice. Before Gina could admire the jewelry, Adelaide had already tucked it back inside her dress, so that only the elaborate silver chain around her neck was visible.

"See you later, darling," she said, throwing her reflection another kiss. "Gonna go reclaim my guy."

"You do that," Gina muttered, taking a half-hearted swipe at the mirror to clean the lipstick mark away. She'd learned the hard way that people didn't really belong to each other, but Adelaide could figure that out for herself.

Adelaide, Gina saw, had returned to her friend's side. Fruma was still batting her heavily mascaraed eyes at George, practically sitting in his lap. Obviously Adelaide had been unsuccessful in her plan. Her earlier giddiness in the ladies' room seemed to have washed away, replaced now with irritation.

"I got your drink," Daniel said, indicating the sidecar on the table.

"Oh, Addie! I may have drunk some of yours already. Maybe I'll just finish it up." As she reached for the glass, Fruma's face started turning a bit green. "Oooh, I don't feel so good."

"I think we'd better get you home," Adelaide said, putting her hand under her friend's forearm and tugging her upward. "Come on."

"I can take you home. I've got my car outside," George offered, before proudly adding. "A Duesenberg. Model J." He was practically sticking out his chest when he mentioned his automobile.

"I've got my car, too," Daniel said, apparently having grown emboldened by the drink. His look toward Adelaide was strained but hopeful. "A roadster."

"We're sticking together," Adelaide said firmly. "George can take us both home."

"Sure thing," George said, downing the last of Adelaide's drink and putting his arm around the drunk woman's waist; she moaned a bit as she buried her face in his expensive jacket. When they turned, Gina could see that Fruma did not look well. If she made it home without getting sick in the man's car, it would be a miracle. Daniel looked peeved as he followed his friend and the two women up the stairs and out of the speakeasy.

A few rounds of shimmies, shakes, and sparkles later, Gina was finally able to slip away from the speakeasy main floor for a quick break. She stole through the back entrance and through the tunnel where great barrels were stored, and then up an old ladder to the alley outside. Even though she'd witnessed a murder out here once, months ago, she still liked to get away from the smoke and the noise and the general goings-on. She popped a piece of Wrigley's spearmint gum into her mouth. The Signora frowned on the girls chewing gum, said it made them look like cows.

She checked her dress to make sure she had not gotten it dirty when she climbed through the window. *Red looks real good on you*, Roark had said, causing a flush to rush to her cheeks.

She checked her watch. She'd already been gone about ten minutes. She only had another ten more. When the wind blew, the rank air in the gangway assaulted her nose. Gagging a little, she wandered down the alley toward Polk, trying to clear her head. She didn't go so far that Little Johnny couldn't see her in the mirrors they'd rigged up in the alley a few months back.

Hearing a step behind her, Gina whirled around to see who was there. About ten paces away, a man was lurching from side to side, moaning and clutching his stomach. A great drunken mess. She was about to run away when the man passed under one of the few streetlights that dimly lit the alley, and she recognized him.

"Finally leaving, Stan?" Gina asked, before silently adding, *Ready to stop being a deadbeat?*

Seeing her, he stopped. He put one hand on the brick wall on the other side of the alley, and the other he kept at his stomach. "I should have listened to you," he said, slurring his words. "Drank too much. My darling Petra is gonna—" Here his face changed and he looked like he was going to heave. Gina kept her distance.

"—gonna kill you. Yeah, Stan. She probably will. And you'd deserve it, too."

"At least I got paid today," he said. He patted his vest pocket and pulled out his wallet and peered inside. A bewildered look crossed his face. "Hey, where'd all my money go? I must have been robbed."

"No, Stan, you weren't robbed," Gina said. "You drank away your earnings. Looks like all of it."

Unexpectedly, tears filled the big man's eyes. "I love my Petra. I love my kids." He looked around, completely confused. "How am I gonna face her?"

"I don't know. You gotta. Don't stop anywhere else. Go straight home. You get me?"

"Yeah, I get you."

Annoyed, she watched him stumble down the street and into the foggy night. She could almost hear Ned crooning, *"Me and my shadow . . . strolling down the avenue . . . all alone and feeling blue . . ."*

The bouncers could have sent him home earlier, but Stan should have known his limit. And who would pay? His wife and kids. Prohibition was truly exhausting at times.

CHAPTER 4

The harsh double ring of the telephone yanked Gina from her sleep. Stumbling from her bed and down the corridor, she peeked in at her papa as she passed by his bedroom.

Still asleep. That was good. At least the ringing hadn't disturbed him. Although, on the other hand, that probably meant he'd taken more sleeping medicine than usual to stave off his many aches and pains. Not so good. She was going to have to call in the physician to check in on him. She sighed. Another expense when they were just getting by.

The insistent *brr-brrrng* caused her to hasten her step. Who was calling so early on a Saturday morning? Probably a wrong number. Still, it made her nervous, even though knowing her papa was safe made her a little less wary about who might be on the other end. They'd only had their own phone for the last few months, installed and paid for out of her earnings.

Passing into the living room, she glanced at the grandfather clock in the corner of the room. Eight o'clock. She'd only been asleep for about five hours, then. It had ended up

being a boisterous evening, and she hadn't left the Third
Door until close to two a.m.

She swooped to grab the gleaming black candlestick
telephone before it could ring again and seated herself at the
padded oak telephone table. She held the mouthpiece about
an inch and a half from her mouth. "Hello?" she said.

"I need you," a woman on the other end replied, forgoing a greeting. Gina recognized the strident economical voice
of Nancy Doyle, a policewoman and her late mother's older
cousin. They'd gotten to know each other reasonably well over
the last few months, although they were still a bit cagey and de-
fensive with each other. Nancy was a peculiar bird, though lik-
able in her own way. Given the widespread corruption among
the cops she witnessed on a daily basis, Nancy stood out, a
strange beacon of integrity in a torn and tattered world.

"What?" Gina asked, pulling up her knees to stretch her
nightgown over her bare feet. "Why?"

"I've got a job for you."

"Let me just get breakfast for my papa. He's still sleeping, and—"

"No time," Nancy interrupted. "There's a dead body,
and I need some pictures. Now. Bring your Kodak."

"A dead body?" Gina asked, sitting upright. "Who
died?"

"One of my neighbors. I'll explain when you get here.
Right now, I need you to hurry, before the police get here. We
don't have much time." Without waiting for her to reply, her
cousin rattled off an address a few blocks away. "Don't be long."

With a click, she hung up, leaving Gina still holding the
phone in her hand. Frowning, she set the receiver back in its

cradle. "How odd!" she said out loud. "Does she really want me to come take pictures of a dead body?

Scribbling a note for her father in case he woke up before she returned, she grabbed her camera and two rolls of film from her bedside table. As she scurried out the door into the beautiful October morning, it was hard not to wonder about what she'd encounter when she arrived at the scene.

Walking at a near-trot, Gina reached the address that Nancy had given her in less than ten minutes. The house was another two-flat, similar to the one she had lived in with her papa her whole life, but was a little grander and more elegant.

Nervously, she approached the house, not sure what to say when she reached for the brass knocker on the door.

She didn't have to worry long. Just as she clapped the knocker, the curtain behind the glass panel moved, and Nancy swung open the door, evidently having been keeping watch. She beckoned to Gina and, with a quick surreptitious glance up and down the street, shut the door behind them.

"Took your sweet time, didn't you," Nancy grumbled. She had already donned the starched no-frills gray dress she wore like a uniform, a habit she'd developed during her twelve years on the force. As usual, she had pulled her hair back into a mostly tidy bun worn at the base of her neck. In her midthirties, Gina's cousin was a woman who had no interest in being anything like the flappers and modern women around her.

"It wasn't even ten minutes!" Gina protested, still panting from her five-block exertion.

Nancy's sniff revealed everything that had to be said about excuses. "This way."

After they passed through an enclosed porch, Nancy led her through the parlor and into a small second corridor that led to two closed doors. She opened the first of these doors, which led into a woman's bedroom.

Gina stopped short when she entered the room. A figure was sprawled across the bed, on top of a bright green coverlet. Though a light blue blanket covered much of the body, she could see a woman's arm jutting out awkwardly, along with a shapely and silk-stockinged leg.

"W-what happened to her?" Gina asked, stepping closer, trying to keep her stomach from lurching.

"Just take the photographs, would ya? We can talk about it later," Nancy said, sounding impatient. "Cops will be here any minute."

"I've never really done this before—"

"Come on, just take some pictures from different angles. The body and the rest of the room. Okay?" Then, with some begrudging courtesy, Nancy added one more word. "Please."

The word "please" got to Gina, particularly since it was not a word that her cousin used very often.

"How'd you know about this?" Gina asked, taking out her new pink Vanity Kodak and carefully loading the first roll of film into the camera. Despite its gorgeous and silly appearance, with its spaces for a lipstick tube and mirror, it was quite a serviceable camera that took excellent photographs. She looked around. "Why aren't the cops here? It's been a while, hasn't it?"

"My neighbor called me. I'd given her my number a while back, since we're on the same block and all that. She sounded half out of her mind on the telephone. I came over to see what was going on and found this mess. I made her call the police when I saw you arrive. Didn't want to delay anything too long, you understand. So you gotta hurry. They'll be here any minute."

Gina didn't really understand at all, but she began to study the room's light and shadows with a serious eye. As she began to take pictures of the body and the room, she pulled back the drapes in the window and turned on several lamps so that the corpse would photograph better.

"Just gotta remember to put that back in place before the cops come," Gina muttered to herself as she worked. She knew enough about criminal cases to know that detectives still expected to work a crime scene that hadn't been touched. "I won't touch anything else."

"I thought you said *you* were the cops," a woman behind them said, sounding suspicious. Her blond hair was tousled, her eyes were rimmed in red, and she wore an expensive-looking black silk bathrobe that was wrapped messily around her. The woman looked vaguely familiar, but Gina didn't have time to ask any questions, turning her attention back to taking photographs of the room and the body.

"We are," Nancy said. "I just want to get a jump on those slowpokes." Then, in a more speculative tone, she added, "I wish we could see under her blanket."

"Oh, I can move it," the woman said. Before either Nancy or Gina could stop her, she had stripped the blanket off, a look of revulsion crossing her face as she stared down at her roommate's body, still clad in a shiny evening ensemble. Clearly, the woman had not yet readied herself for bed when she died.

"You shouldn't have done that," Nancy said blandly as she leaned over to look more closely at the corpse.

"Well, it's how I found her," the woman replied, sniffing back tears. "I just thought it was more respectful to cover Fruma up a bit, you know?"

Fruma! Gina forced herself to stare down at the dead woman's face. The face was purple and distorted. Virtually unrecognizable. Yet her curly brown hair was memorable.

Gina glanced back at the roommate, with her messy blond hair, pale cosmetics-free face, and tousled demeanor. Out of context Gina hadn't recognized her at first, but memories from the night before came flooding back. Both these women had definitely been at the Third Door last night. Adelaide and Fruma.

"What's wrong?" Nancy asked, her voice sharp and demanding. "Why aren't you taking more pictures? You didn't run out of film already, did you? The police photographer usually brings backup rolls. Didn't you?"

Gina closed her mouth and bent her head over the camera, not wanting to bring any attention to herself. Adelaide did not seem to have recognized her yet, most likely because she was still in shock. Or, equally likely, because people don't remember the faces of cigarette girls, particularly when they are busy photographing a crime scene the next day. Probably better to keep this to herself until she could discover what was going on.

"Just brought two rolls," she muttered to Nancy, allowing her long bobbed hair to obscure her face from Adelaide. "That's all I had on me at home. And it's not like you gave me any time to run to get more. Now if you'll excuse me, I want to make the most of my shots."

Fighting a wave of nausea that surged up from her belly, Gina angled her camera to get a picture of Fruma's face, studying the dead woman's features more closely. They were fixed in an expression of terror. A dreadful ending. Additionally, there were black marks all around her eyes and cheeks, most likely from her mascara. Had the woman been crying when she died? The thought caused a chill to run up and down Gina's spine.

Looking closer, Gina also could see some white powder near Fruma's nose, as well as in the drool that appeared to have dripped from the woman's mouth. She sniffed. Fruma smelled of strong perfume, smoke, and something more acidic. Vomit, maybe? "What happened to her?" Gina asked, still keeping her face somewhat obscured from Adelaide's scrutiny.

"I don't know!" Adelaide wailed, sinking back into a purple chair in the corner. "I just found Fruma like this, about a half hour ago. I had come to see if she wanted any breakfast. I was making eggs and sausage, and I thought she might be h-hungry. This is awful!" She put her face in her hands and began to weep in earnest.

Despite the woman's incredible distress, not surprisingly, Nancy made no movement to comfort her. "Was she sick?" Gina asked.

Adelaide stopped wailing and seemed to try to regain her composure, although her eyes were still dilated from shock and fear. "Fruma had too much to drink last night, I do know that. I heard her getting sick. I thought I heard her crying at one point." She gulped. "I should have checked on her."

"Why didn't you?" Nancy asked.

Adelaide looked guilty. *Because you were mad at her*, Gina thought. Without thinking, she snapped a picture of Adelaide, hoping she wouldn't notice.

Then she turned back to the body. "What's that on her face?" Gina asked. She pointed to the traces of white powder on the woman's upper lip and by her nose before taking another picture.

"Sleeping potion?" Nancy leaned over and sniffed. "Did she usually have trouble sleeping?"

"I don't know," Adelaide said, wringing her hands. She seemed really confused. "Yes. Maybe. I'm not sure."

Gina thought about other powders she'd seen Mr. Rosenstein grind up at the pharmacy. "Maybe it was some sort of headache medicine?" She looked around. "I don't see any vial or bottle. No cup for water. We should check the kitchen. Or the bathroom."

"I've never seen her take any medicine, not even when she had a headache," Adelaide replied. "She never seemed to need the stuff. She was strong like that."

"Maybe it was something else," Nancy said, still peering closely at the woman's mouth and nose.

"Maybe—" Adelaide started, but then stopped, looking frightened.

"Maybe what?" Nancy asked. "Go on."

"Fruma was funny last night. Not ha-ha funny. Odd."

"How do you mean?" Nancy pressed.

"She was moody. Sometimes up, sometimes down,"

Adelaide replied, sounding more eager now that she had something useful to share. "Despairing even. There was something that had been bothering her, I know that."

"What was it?"

"Well, she'd recently broken off her engagement, for one thing," Adelaide said, still seeming a bit dazed. "She had seemed glad to be rid of him, but maybe she was more upset than I knew."

Gina snapped another picture, thinking about the interactions of the two women the night before as she listened. Fruma had been mostly in good spirits, not despondent like Adelaide was describing. Still, she'd been fried when they left; maybe her mood had turned for the worse after they left the Third Door. Drink could certainly do that to a person.

She also remembered her conversation with Adelaide in the ladies' restroom. *I called dibs. Then Fruma decided she wanted him for herself,* she'd said. Then her final words before sashaying out. *Gonna go reclaim my guy from Fruma.*

She wanted to probe Adelaide's account, but she didn't want to reveal her identity to the woman until she'd had a chance to speak with Nancy in private. For now, it seemed better to stay quiet and listen to Adelaide's explanation.

Adelaide had begun to cry again. "Oh, I should never have gone to bed. What kind of friend am I? She was suffering, I just know it. Maybe she wanted to do away with herself. Took an overdose?"

"Suicide?" Nancy asked, considering the body, peering down at the substance on the woman's lips and nose. "Hmmm... Could that powder be cocaine, not a sleeping potion? Or heroin maybe?"

"Is there a note?" Gina asked, when Adelaide didn't answer.

"Let's look around," Nancy said. She and Adelaide looked around the room, rifling quickly through the dead woman's dresser, desk drawers, trunk, and wardrobe. As they did this, Gina quickly put in the second roll and took a few more photos. She didn't really know what she was doing. She looked around. *What else?* She wondered. *What else would a crime scene photographer focus on?* Sighing, she took a few more shots of Fruma's inert form, hoping she wasn't missing anything important.

"Nothing," Nancy sighed. "She's not likely to have hidden a note. Suicides leave their notes in plain view, when they leave them." She smoothed her hair in a habitual way. "Doesn't rule out an overdose, of course. She takes a dose, falls asleep, gets confused, takes another dose. Then, before you know it, she's overdosed. I've seen it before."

The bragging quality to Nancy's words caused Gina to look at her sharply. When Adelaide huddled again in the purple chair, Gina sidled back over to her cousin. "Nancy," she whispered, "*why* did you ask me to take pictures?"

"Because I'm tired of those ninnies on the force cutting me out of all the interesting investigations, that's why," Nancy hissed. "I should be a detective by now. Or at least a sergeant."

Gina began to take pictures from each corner of the room as Nancy continued to grumble. "I mean, look at Alice Clement! She was one of the first women on the force, and she made detective thirteen years ago!" Nancy pounded her fist into her other hand. "I've got nothing to show for my twelve years on the force. Street beat, brothels, docks—

nothing big. Nothing that will put me on the map. Nothing that will get me noticed."

In the distance they heard the police sirens. "All right, Gina, time for you to skedaddle," Nancy commanded. "Out the back door, if you would."

Gina hurried about, making sure she had her camera, case, and film canisters all safely tucked away. She was almost out the door when she remembered to pull the drapes closed and turn out the lamps she'd turned on earlier.

"Better put the blanket back in place," she added, before heading toward the kitchen. "There a back door this way?" she called.

"Yes, but it's been jammed for a while now." Adelaide replied. "You'll have to go out the front door."

"They'll see me!" Gina exclaimed. The sound of the sirens was definitely closer.

"Well, don't let them," came Nancy's terse reply.

Gina had just made it a few steps down the street when the police car carrying several uniformed men drove by her. She couldn't help but glance at it, before casting her gaze back to the ground. Unfortunately, the man in the backseat was looking out the window, right at her. Roark. No doubt coming to photograph the scene at the request of the police. He swiveled around to stare at her, but she didn't look up. She half expected him to stop the car and ask her what she was doing, but when he didn't, she continued to move quickly down the street.

CHAPTER 5

As Gina pushed open the door to her other flat, the one above the Third Door, she breathed in the familiar aroma of the chemicals used to develop film and make prints. Another smell, an essence really, always lingered in the air, too, and Gina had never been able to quite capture what it was. She thought it might have been the scent Marty had worn before he died, back when he was still the Third Door's official photographer, or perhaps it was just a remnant of the cigarettes he used to smoke. Marty's bequest had shocked her, but she'd certainly enjoyed having her own space, even though she knew that nosy Mrs. Lesky, Little Johnny's mother, who lived in the flat below, kept tabs on her whereabouts.

Since she still had quite a few hours before she would need to bathe and dress for her next shift at the Third Door, Gina changed into one of the older dresses that she kept at the flat, in Marty's old bedroom closet. It was worn and frayed, and it didn't matter if some of the harsh chemicals got splashed on it.

Moving into the flat with the darkroom, Gina carefully

laid out all the materials that were needed for the first part of the developing process. After about twenty minutes, she'd finished developing the film and hung the strips from a cord over the bathtub while they dried. She'd learned to be much quicker and efficient when she developed the film, so it didn't take her very long at all.

She then moved back across the hall to where Marty had lived, plopping down on the living room sofa. Over the last few months, Gina had been gradually making the flat a bit more cozy, even though she still liked using Marty's things. It helped her feel close to the cousin she'd hardly known. She pulled out the Sears and Roebuck catalog, beginning to make lists of things that she might order for her papa. Now that she'd had a steady income for a while now there were things she wanted. She'd already ordered him some new shoes and herself some more developer's paper and a waterproofed apron for when she made the prints.

As she flipped through the catalog, she came across the home study pages. *Grammar made easy. Mathematics made easy. Bookkeeping made easy.* Everything made easy. *Speeches for the man who must make a speech.* None of that seemed particularly interesting. A few books on developing personality—*How to win men over with your personality. No thanks*, she thought.

Her perusal of the catalog was interrupted by a sharp rap at the door. She peered through the pinhole, finding Roark standing there, a deep scowl on his face. *What do I say to him?* Gina asked, feeling a bit panicked. *What's he gonna say to me?*

Bracing herself for an onslaught, she unchained the door and let him stride in.

"I saw you at the site of a police investigation this

morning," he said. His tone was curt, measured. She couldn't
tell if he was angry or not. "What were you doing there?"

She shut the door behind him. "You saw me on the street,
taking a walk near where my cousin Nancy Doyle lives."

"You were visiting her?" When Gina didn't reply, Roark
continued. "Look. I know you were at Fruma Landry's
apartment. Don't bother denying it. What I don't know is
what you were doing there."

Gina folded, giving up the pretense. It seemed pointless to
lie, particularly since he'd probably find out the truth sooner
or later anyway. "Nancy called me around eight a.m. Asked me
to bring my camera. She asked me to photograph the scene."

"What?" he exclaimed. "Why *you*?"

The question stung. "Why not? I'm plenty good enough."

"Settle down, bearcat. You are plenty good enough."
Without asking, he began to study some of the recent photographs that she'd left spread across the table. "You're definitely getting very comfortable with the camera." He smiled
at her then, with the funny twisted smile that made her heart
lurch. Then his jaw clenched. "Tell me why Officer Doyle
asked you to photograph the scene. Be straight with me."

Gina sighed. "She wanted her own set of photographs."

He looked exasperated. "In heaven's name, why?"

"Nancy just wanted in on the investigation. The men on
the force keep her off the good cases."

"So she decided to go around them. Not a great way to
build up trust."

"Do you blame her?" Gina frowned. "She's been on the
force, for what, ten years? Fifteen? Does she ever get included
in the big cases?"

He shrugged. "Maybe not. I do blame her for bringing *you* into the case. We don't even know cause of death yet—it could be a criminal case. And even if its not, this is police work. Civilians shouldn't be involved in cases like these. *You* shouldn't be involved and she should know better." He was looking angry again. Standing up, he went and looked out the window. There was not much of a view, just the buildings across the street. Then he turned back to her, a stern question in his eyes. "How did *Nancy* know about the dead body before the rest of the police?"

"She lives on the same block. The roommate, Adelaide, called her." She thought about Adelaide's dazed expression. "She seemed out of it when I was there."

"The neighbor called Nancy? That's not good. Looks like she was going around the law. Nancy, too."

"Nancy did call the cops. *Almost* right away," Gina protested, surprising herself by defending Nancy's actions. "Are you going to tell on her? Tell the other cops that she asked me to take photographs before they called the police in?"

"I don't know yet. I'm still a bit steamed."

Gina decided to change tactics, hoping to convince him that they weren't adversaries. "Do you know what happened to the woman? Fruma Landry?"

Roark sat back down in the chair opposite her. "What do you think?"

"I have no idea," Gina replied. "Except she had white powder on her face, around her nose and mouth. Was it a sleeping potion? Or even cocaine? Perhaps she suffered an overdose. That's what Nancy thinks."

"Do you agree?" He seemed genuinely interested in her opinion. That trait always surprised and warmed her.

"No, that doesn't seem right to me. After all, Miss Landry was still wearing an evening gown. You'd think she'd have put on a nightgown, put on face cream, do her hair in rollers, that kind of thing, if she were getting ready for bed. Only then would she take a sleeping potion, I would assume."

"Yes, I'd assume the same." Then his eyes narrowed. "Wait, how did you know that she was still in her evening clothes? Her whole body was covered by a blanket when we arrived on the scene."

"The roommate pulled back the blanket before we could stop her." She paused, remembering the moment she saw Fruma's distorted tear-stained face. "I didn't touch anything." *At least, I made sure I put them back the same way I had found them.*

"For heaven's sake." Roark scowled. "I hope you at least took photographs of the room when you first got there!"

"Yeah, I did." More softly, she said, "Miss Landry looked like she'd been in pain when she died. She'd been crying. I saw the mascara on her cheeks. The roommate said she'd been despondent. Said she'd broken off an engagement recently."

"Suicide?" he asked, interest overcoming annoyance. "I wonder."

Gina considered the woman's dress, her position on the bed, and then her vivacity at the Third Door. "That doesn't feel right to me either. And there wasn't a note. I know that there's not always a note, but still, that doesn't seem quite right."

"No, I agree. Particularly since we found a small handgun in the top drawer of her vanity. Loaded. If she'd wanted to kill herself, why not just take a bullet?"

Gina nodded. That made sense. "Could she have just choked on her own vomit? Maybe drank too much? Would that explain the flecks of white around her nose and mouth?"

"Yes, perhaps. The coroner will let us know," Roark said. He seemed to be weighing whether or not to tell her something. "Though there's another possibility altogether."

"Yeah? What's that?"

"She may have suffered from alcohol poisoning. It was obvious she'd been out and about, having a good time the evening before. Drinking who knows what, who knows where. We'll know soon enough, when we get the coroner's report."

"Alcohol poisoning?"

"Yes, we're thinking her sickness was compounded by any drugs she took when got back home. We know she'd been drinking that night. The roommate didn't say where they'd been, but I don't think it will be too hard to figure out. Bad batches of hooch happen all the time. Whether it was cocaine or heroin, that drug might have reacted badly with whatever she'd been drinking. The lab chemist told me that."

Gina sat back, trying to recall everything about what the two women had said and done at the Third Door the night before. She remembered how Fruma had looked decidedly green when they left. She'd assumed at the time it was from drinking too many sidecars. *Had* she drunk some bad alcohol?

Certainly there were stories in the news, practically every day, about people dying from alcohol poisoning. People would take all sorts of stuff to get squiffy. Wood alcohol, grain alcohol. Rubbing alcohol. If a substance had alcohol in its name, people would drink it. She knew that Mr. Rosenstein kept powerful emetics, mustards, and other solutions on hand, in case anyone accidentally poisoned themselves with rotgut. *It's too bad that Adelaide hadn't known such a cure existed*, Gina thought, *if in fact that was the cause of Fruma's death*. She hadn't even checked in on her, when she knew her roommate was not well. Gina rubbed her cheek. Something to ponder later.

"Did you see Miss Landry at the Third Door, Gina?" Roark asked, pulling her back from her musings. "Do you remember her? Given your gin joint's proximity to where they lived, it stands to reason that she might have been there."

For a long moment she thought about telling Roark everything she knew, but then she stopped, thinking about the Signora. Did she deserve a heads-up first? "I'm not sure," she hedged, a wash of shame flooding over her at the lie. "I was busy."

Roark scowled. "You did seem 'busy.' I remember." He stood up abruptly and took a half-step away from her.

Jeepers! He's really angry! What did he mean by that? she wondered. *That's what he said last night, too.* "You seem busy."

She remembered then how Mr. Morrish had been practically holding her hand just before Roark arrived. He must have misunderstood. "Roark, I—"

"You need to give me those photographs, Gina. As well as the negatives."

"What? No! I won't! You can't make me!" She stood up, too, and planted herself in front of him.

Roark stared down at her, holding her gaze. She took a deep breath.

"I'm not going to force you, Gina," he said finally. "I just need to see your prints. Check them against mine. There could be something there."

She couldn't give them away. Not after she'd promised

Nancy. Still, she understood why he wanted to see them. "I'll make you a set."

He inclined his head, acknowledging the compromise. "Gina, do I have to remind you that you shouldn't even be involved? This is a police matter."

When she didn't reply, he opened the door and stalked out without another word. She could hear his footsteps as he walked quickly down the corridor. *What had he wanted to talk to me about?* She had forgotten to ask, and right now she was too miffed to care.

As Gina made the prints later, she studied everything through the enlarger, before varying the exposure and light to make a variety of different prints. She'd found that playing with light and shadow did much to provide perspective, as did just physically manipulating the prints so that she could look at them this way and that.

Gina considered Fruma's pose in death. *What had happened to her? Was it just a drug overdose? Had she killed herself?* she wondered.

Unfortunately, suicide and the single woman were not strangers, though at the Third Door, Fruma had seemed more indignant than sad. Otherwise she'd been giddy in her conquest of George. Perhaps she had become depressed as the evening had progressed. Who knew what had happened after they had left the Third Door. What about that scene with the jilted fiancé, Vidal?

Had Fruma been despairing over their breakup? It was hard for Gina not to remember her own dark days after David had practically left her at the altar a few years ago.

The guilt and shame she'd experienced when learning about his philandering had been immense, even though her anger had eventually worn away any sense of regret she'd felt over the broken engagement. So she couldn't blame Fruma for wanting to show the world that she was feeling peachy keen, even if there was much darkness swirling below the vivacious exterior. No one wanted to play the role of jilted lover.

Gina turned her attention back to the photographs. Fruma hadn't gotten under the covers; she hadn't put on a negligee or even pajamas. More important, there wasn't any medicine or sleeping potion near her, and certainly no note had been discovered. No, it seemed likely this overdose, if that was what it was, had not been planned.

She studied Fruma's hand on her stomach, which she'd clearly been clutching when she died, and remembered how Fruma had looked sickly when she was escorted out of the speakeasy. Roark had said the coroner suspected that she might have had alcohol poisoning. Had she gotten some bad alcohol at the Third Door? If so, the whole operation could be shut down.

Should she tell the Signora? She had a strong sense of loyalty to her employer, which had grown these last few months. The Signora was like a steel statue brought to life, and Gina had come to appreciate the woman's hardened demeanor. Still, it seemed best to keep this to herself, at least for the time-being.

That night, after she put dinner in the oven for her papa, Gina dialed Nancy's number. "I have some prints for you."

"Good," Nancy said. "My shift goes to eleven o'clock tonight. Can you bring them by my place in the morning? Say at ten a.m.?"

Gina stared at the telephone. "Your place?" She was unable to mask the surprise in her voice. Nancy had never invited her to her home before.

"Yes," her cousin replied. The telephone crackled in her ear, mirroring Nancy's impatience. "I'll see you then."

"Wait a second, Nancy," Gina said hurriedly, before her cousin could hang up. "I wanted to let you know. Adelaide and Fruma were at the Third Door last night. I didn't want to say anything in front of Adelaide because I didn't want to scare her off. But that's where they got zozzled."

"Oh yeah?" Nancy sounded interested again. "I figured as much. Knew they had to have been somewhere in the area. That's good." She paused. "What about Miss Landry's mood? Was she sad? Did she seem like she wanted to kill herself?"

"I'd say good spirits for most of the night. Definitely squiffy when she left, though. Only Adelaide was out of sorts. Although—" Gina paused, trying to recollect everything that had occurred.

"What?"

"Two things. A man had bothered Fruma earlier in the evening before Gooch gave him the what's what."

"Yes, Adelaide mentioned that," Nancy replied, sounding intrigued. "What else?"

"I remember that they were flirting with some men there. I didn't get the feeling they'd known the men beforehand," Gina said. "Then later, Fruma kept trying to explain something, but the men kept laughing at her and she didn't like it. Something about jumping out of an airplane! I really couldn't follow what they were saying."

She scratched her head. "Wait, one other thing. Later, when I was checking the ladies' room, I heard Adelaide say that Fruma had stolen her guy. Some man named George— one of the two they'd just met. I guess she had called dibs."

There was a long silence. "She called dibs?" Gina didn't know if Nancy's incredulity came from not having dated much or from not spending enough time around heartless women.

"Yeah. Adelaide said it wasn't the first time that Fruma had taken a man away from her, either."

"Could Adelaide have been talking about Fruma's fiancé?"

"Perhaps. I'm not sure. I do think that Adelaide was irritated with Fruma, even though I think she was trying to hide it. I remember thinking at the time that Adelaide seemed jealous, wanting Fruma to keep away from that guy George."

"Hiding her irritation?" Nancy hmmm'd again. "Then what?"

"I remember that all four left together. Early. Maybe around eleven."

"Okay. That it?" Always the impatience.

"Well, you should know that Roark stopped by Marty's flat just as I was finishing developing the film. He *did* see me this morning outside Fruma and Adelaide's flat. He was with the coppers."

Nancy's voice grew wary. "Yeah? What did *he* have to say?"

"Well, he was plenty mad. Said you shouldn't be trying to get the jump on the cops"—here Nancy just snorted—"or dragging me into it."

"Tell him to mind his beeswax."

"Yeah, I will," Gina said. "He did tell me that the coroner thought it might have been alcohol poisoning. Although I remember Adelaide drinking the same drinks as Fruma, and she seemed fine."

"Right, it would be odd if only Fruma was afflicted, then. That Adelaide wasn't sick, too."

"They're going to run some tests at the forensics lab," Gina said. "The coroner's report should explain—"

"I'm not going to wait until we get the *coroner's report*"—Nancy nearly spit out the words—"to investigate a suspicious death. Maybe Fruma did die of alcohol poisoning, or maybe it was an overdose. For all we know, she had some sort of heart problem and the whole thing is just natural causes. What if it *is* something else? The trail will grow cold, and the leads will disappear if we wait. See you tomorrow morning. Ten sharp. Don't be late."

The click indicated that Nancy had hung up, leaving Gina once again staring into the mute phone.

CHAPTER 6

Gina hurried down Morgan Street toward the Third Door. It had taken her a little longer than she would have liked to get dinner prepared, and Papa's palsy seemed a bit worse recently. Before she had left, she had had to find their upstairs neighbor, Mrs. Hayford, to see if she would come down and keep her father company for a while. There was a good chance that Gina would be late for her shift, which might cause the Signora to dock her pay.

About to turn down the alley, she found herself stopped by a youngster who had planted himself firmly in her path. It was the same newsboy she'd bought the paper from yesterday. Stan's son.

With a pang, she handed him a penny. It was hard not to feel a little sorry for him; he looked so fatigued. He handed her a neatly folded paper, one of three left in his bag, then stuck his tongue out at her.

"Hey, what gives?" she asked. "I paid you. We're even Steven."

"My ma's mad at you."

"Oh yeah? Why's that? What did I do?"

"My papa came home sick last night, something terrible. He can't even get out of bed. Ma's so mad! Says someone should have sent him home. She asked *you*."

"Well, I'm sorry to hear he's still sick. He's gotta sleep the bender off." Gina tried to push past him, but he edged in front of her again. "Sorry, kid. I gotta go."

"Papa was gonna take me to your joint. Buy me a proper drink," the boy said. "When I had a few more years on me." He looked disappointed. "He told me this morning he's never setting foot in the Third Door again."

"Well, your mama's probably glad about that," she said. Seeing the boy's downcast face, she asked. "What's your name, kid?"

"Jakob."

"Look, Jakob, I'm sorry your papa's sick. Still, that's on him that he got so piffled," Gina said, bending over to look him in the eye. "Sometimes drink just doesn't agree with a man, and a man should know his limits. That's on him. I'm sure he'll be better soon, when the drink wears off."

"Maybe the sick won't wear off," Jakob said, tearing up a little. "You don't get it, miss. Neighbors who stopped by this morning said they've never seen anything like it. My ma's real worried. We can't afford the doctor."

With a pang she remembered how Stan had plodded off down the alley, groaning. Had he been sick then? Maybe he'd stopped off somewhere afterward. Of course, sometimes the force of alcohol came later, a deadly one-two knockout punch when a person was least expecting it.

"Now he'll never take me in there," Jakob said, kicking the ground.

"Oh, relax, kid, these gin joints are all over the place. They'll still be around when your papa is ready to take you. Prohibition's not ending anytime soon." She pushed past the boy then and knocked on the green door with the eye-level metal grille.

As Little Johnny let her inside the speakeasy, an uneasy feeling stole over her, the strangeness of the day making her feel weary. It was hard not to think about Fruma's dead body on the bed, still dressed in her glad rags. Last night, Fruma had seemed so vibrant, so full of life, and now she was just... gone. If she'd died from alcohol poisoning, as Roark had suggested, perhaps Stan had been poisoned, too.

An hour or so later, Ned began to play the prelude to "Ain't Misbehavin'," a solo piece for Jade. Exhibiting her usual dramatic flair, Jade strode across the dance floor, dressed in an orange gown that was interwoven with shining silver swirls. Madame Laupin had outdone herself with this incredible beauty. The dress clung to Jade's figure seductively but still managed to come across as sophisticated and glamorous, the way the Signora preferred her girls to appear.

For a moment Jade surveyed the room from her position on the middle of the speakeasy floor, coolly waiting for her audience to settle down. Then, when the room had stilled, Jade gave Ned an imperious nod and began to sing with her rich, throaty mezzo-soprano. Her voice almost always brought a tear to Gina's eye, it was so beautiful. Not that she would ever tell Jade.

As Jade sang, a couple looked out over the balcony before grandly descending the stairs.

"Is that Louise Brooks?" a woman near Gina whispered loudly to her companion.

Gina looked more closely. Sure enough, the woman was the spitting image of the film star, down to her crooked black bangs and the funny gap in her teeth. Certainly there were times when famous starlets, baseball players, and musicians would stop by the joint. However, this newest arrival was not that actress—Gina had paged through enough of the *Variety* magazines the girls would leave strewn about the ladies' dressing area.

"Oh, Vern, this place is quaint," the woman said loudly to her companion, a slightly balding but still handsome man in his thirties. "I thought it would have a little more hustle. Nothing like New York, that's for sure."

Jade, whose green eyes had been half closed while she was crooning, opened catlike as she glared at the woman.

Gina moved quickly to intercept the couple. "Good evening," she said quietly. "Welcome to the Third Door. May I show you to a table while Jade is performing?"

The man gestured for her to lead the way.

"Oh, I don't like this table," the Louise Brooks lookalike said, her whiny complaint interrupting Jade's big finish and earning her another baleful glare from the singer. "We're in the mood to be *seen*," the woman said with a sly look to her date, clearly oblivious to the offense her chatter had caused Jade. "Aren't we, Vern?"

"Sure thing, Harriet," Vern replied, slipping a dollar onto Gina's tray. "Get us a better spot, would ya, toots?"

As Jade sauntered off the floor to great catcalls, Gina expertly closed her hand over the bill and slid it into her bodice. When she started back in January, she wouldn't have known what to do, but now she just winked at the piano player. "Say, Ned, how about getting this place jiving again?"

Obligingly Ned switched over to "Yes Sir, That's My Baby," causing women to shriek and hop up from their chairs, dragging their dates and gal pals onto the dance floor.

"Great, Harriet," the man said to the woman. "Let's grab a spot."

Harriet still didn't seem impressed with the selection. "I want *that* table," she said, gesturing toward a table where two bespectacled College Joes were nursing their gin rickeys. "It's closer to the piano."

Gina could see that the woman would not be easily appeased. "Hang on a moment," Gina said to the couple, and then sauntered over toward the men. "Say, fellows," she said. "Why don't you drink up and ask those young ladies to dance?" She nodded at two College Bettys, tapping their feet and swaying their hips. "They're gonna start fox-trotting together and you'll be out in the cold. Now's your chance!" The two men looked at each other and obligingly downed their glasses and slouched over to the women.

Gina toweled off the table with a small cloth she kept tucked in her tray, then turned back to the waiting couple. "Here you go."

Vern nodded appreciatively and slid his eyes over her body in that familiar way that men had. "Thanks, doll. We'll have a Ward 8 and—what do you want, Harriet? A Mary Pickford?

Harriet puckered her lips. "You know how to make them here, right?"

"Oh, yes, of course," Gina replied. "Billy Bottles is the best."

"For Chicago, maybe." Harriet nudged her friend. "We're used to New York cocktails, aren't we, Vern?"

Vern shrugged. "Drink's a drink, I guess."

"I also need some smokes," Harriet said, batting her eyes playfully up at him. "Marlboros."

Vern pulled out a quarter and dropped it on Gina's tray. "You heard the lady." To Harriet, he added, "I just need to step into the men's room for a moment. Don't run off with another guy while I'm gone."

"You got it, toots," Harriet called as he walked away. She took the pack from Gina, the smile dropping from her face. "Not so fast. I need a light. First I gotta find my holder. I don't want to ruin another pair of gloves."

"Of course," Gina said, trying to maintain her patience as she waited for Harriet to rummage through her beaded handbag and retrieve an elegant silver and turquoise cigarette holder. Unfolding the stick, she slipped a cigarette into the slot at the end and held it out to Gina to light.

After the cigarette was lit, Harriet grabbed Gina's wrist. "Say, have you worked here for a while?"

Gina pulled her hand free. "Almost ten months," she said, rubbing her wrist. "Why?"

"Then you must know Lawrence Roark. I heard he comes here a lot. I was hoping he'd be around tonight."

What does she want with Roark? Gina wondered, a pang of jealousy shooting through her. There was something about the way the woman purred when she said Roark's full name that bothered her. No one used his first name, and she'd never known why. "I haven't seen him," Gina replied, not wishing to betray her bothered thoughts. *At least not since this morning, when he was mad at me for interfering with police work.* When a customer at another table beckoned to her, she added, "Sorry, gotta go!"

"Don't forget our drinks," Harriet reminded her.

Gina suppressed the wave of irritation that rose at the woman's condescending tone. When she put the drink order in with Billy she said, "Feel free to take your time. That one can stand to cool her heels."

"Gina," Roark said, "I need to talk to you."

They were standing near the piano. Roark had just entered the speakeasy and headed straight toward her. His eyes were intent on her face. "I never got a chance to tell you something yesterday, and with Fruma's death and the photographs," he said, "it just flew out of my mind." His anger from the morning had clearly dissipated and had been replaced by something else. Worry? Concern? His face was hard to read.

"What is it?" Gina interrupted, looking around to see if Gooch or Little Johnny was watching their interaction. Or worse, if the Signora herself had noticed.

He looked around as well. "I'd prefer to talk privately." He touched her arm. "When's your break? Can we meet upstairs? In the gangway?"

"Sure," she replied, warming a little at the thought of a private conversation. What did he want to tell her? He seemed so intense. She checked her wristwatch. "I'm free in about an hour. I've also got the prints for you in my purse. I'll meet you there."

"I'll go wait." He started toward the back room, where there was usually a card game going on.

"Oh, Roark!" she said, remembering Harriet. He turned back around.

"A woman was looking for you earlier. She's over there." She pointed toward where Harriet had been sitting, but her face was obstructed by some fast-dancing couples, enthusiastically showing off the latest trend.

Roark looked startled. "She's here?" He looked at Gina closely. "Did she introduce herself?"

"Not exactly," Gina said, remembering how unpleasant the woman had been earlier. "She did make quite an entrance, though, right in the middle of Jade's act. Jade was *not* pleased, as you can imagine. I know her name is Harriet, but that's about it. She's here with a—"

Just as Gina was about to complete her sentence, Harriet half-turned in her chair and looked toward them. Giving a little scream, she pushed herself off the chair and launched herself toward Roark.

"Darling!" she squealed, throwing her arms around him. "I've missed you!"

Roark did not embrace her back but stood ramrod straight. "What are you doing here, Harriet?"

"Oh, Roark," Harriet replied, giving him a playful swat. "Does a wife need a reason to see her husband?"

Wife? Husband? Gina stepped back, trying to make sense of the scene unfolding before her. Then Harriet stepped forward and wrapped her hands around Roark's cheeks. While

Gina was still looking on, she brought his face to hers for a full-lipped kiss.

Stunned, Gina stared as Roark appeared to respond to the woman—*his wife!*—before firmly setting her aside.

"I know it's been a while," Harriet said, smirking. "We have some catching up to do."

"Excuse me," Roark said, scowling. He avoided Gina's gaze. "I need some air."

Both women watched him stalk off. "Pooh, what's got him so hot and bothered?" Harriet asked, giving Gina a sidelong glance. When she arched an eyebrow, Gina realized she was still staring after Roark in shock.

Harriet seemed amused. "I guess Roark hasn't mentioned me."

"Have you mentioned Roark to your *date?*" Gina asked, trying desperately to keep the sense of shock and betrayal in check. She strove for a more casual tone. "Vern, wasn't it? He might want to know about your *husband*."

"My date? Oh, that's a good one," Harriet said, giving a small chuckle. "Nah, Vern's just a *business acquaintance*. I wouldn't dream of stepping out on my darling husband." She gave Gina a hard stare. "And I'm back now. For good."

"I see," Gina replied, still in shock. "Well, I need to continue my rounds."

"Ta-ta," Harriet called. Then she smiled, her crooked teeth fully bared.

CHAPTER 7

"Hello, boys!" Gina called out, pushing past the purple and green art deco curtain and into the den of card playing and gambling. Fighting back a wave of nausea over the kiss she'd just witnessed between Roark and Harriet, Gina forced a smile onto her face. The men in the back room deserved a bit of cheer, not the darkness that suddenly threatened to smother her.

This room was a bit darker, with just a few lights strung from the ceiling; no grand chandeliers or sparkly, tinkling glass here. No women here, either—this was very much a room for men. Usually the drinks were tough and tight, mostly straight whiskeys, ales, bourbons, and beer whenever the Signora had procured it. Even when they drank the rot-gut, they didn't usually mask it in sugar, fruits, and syrups, but just cut it with some water or ice.

Many of the back room inhabitants were ex-servicemen, men seeking to avoid the public's harsh and judging gaze. To-night was no exception. A handful of men were sitting around the felt-covered round table in the middle of the room, while others leaned against the wall to the side, watching the action. A few were propped up at high tables, crutches and canes all around. These men had all survived the Great War, returning from their time in the wasteland with missing limbs, scarred faces, and other injuries. Many preferred to stay out of sight. She knew some had managed to get jobs, although not all of them could hold steady employment. Some injuries could not be seen, living deep below the surface, in dark spaces of their minds that could never again be brought to light. The Signora, she knew, let them run up outrageous tabs, and they'd pay up when they could, especially when they'd won a few rounds of cards.

These men offered her a means to remember her own brother, Aidan, who'd been recorded as killed in the final weeks of the war, just before the Armistice of 1918. His body had never been returned, but she and her papa had held a small memorial for him. That was the only time Gina had been glad that her mother had succumbed to consumption years before—the agony of losing a son would have broken her. The horror of what the ex-servicemen had experienced could still be seen on the men's bodies and in their eyes, although their smiles were usually genuine and warm when they saw her.

Tonight, though, the men seemed oddly subdued. Usually they hooted a bit and called her name when she walked in. Roark, she noticed straightaway, was not there. *Has he left? Guess there's no point in meeting him in the gangway.* She felt so foolish. He'd told her his wife had left him, but it had never occurred to Gina to ask him what would happen if she came back. Knowing he was still married really bothered her. She knew lots of girls who wouldn't care about that, but she did. She sighed, looking around at the room, looking at the men's faces, trying to figure out what was wrong. "Smokes, boys?" she asked. "Lulu is about to perform. Lemme know what drinks I can bring, too."

"Sure thing, Miss Ricci," a tall black man named Ralph Jenkins replied. He was leaning against the wall, smoking his Lucky Strike. Like several of the others, he moved too stiffly for a man in his early thirties—another ill effect of the Great War.

Although everyone else always called her Gina, Ralph always called her Miss Ricci. *My mama taught me to respect women,* he had told her once, when she'd teased him, *and that's what we do in the South, where I'm from. So if it's all the same to you, Miss Ricci, that's what I'm gonna call you.* He was the same with the other women as well: Lulu was Miss Evans and Jade was Miss Butler, even though there was more awe in his voice when he addressed Jade.

"We just got a big game going on right now," Ralph added in a low voice, gesturing to the table. "Give it a minute."

Looking around, Gina realized that, while a few of the other men were sitting with their cards facedown in front of them and obviously out of the game, two men were facing each other. One of them was Donny, looking flushed and frankly a bit scared. The other player was Mr. Morrish. Like yesterday, he looked swell, dressed in a gray pin-striped vest and pants. His matching suit coat had been hung neatly from the back of his chair. He'd undone his bow tie so that it hung slightly askew from his neck. The only unruly thing about him was his thick black hair, which clearly had not been combed. His features were impassive, the perfect hard lines of a top-notch player.

There was a huge pile of chips between them. A massive haul.

"I'll see your ten and raise you another ten," the man said easily, not taking his eyes off Donny's face.

Donny began to toy with the expensive watch that he liked to keep in a vest or jacket pocket. Gina had noticed it before, thinking it was the only costly thing that the ex-serviceman owned. He appeared to be deep in thought as he touched the glass face.

Oh, no, Gina groaned, suddenly realizing what he was planning to do. *Don't do it, Donny! Don't risk it!*

Sure enough, Donny set his cards down and placed the watch on the table. "Mr. Morrish," he said, "this is a genuine Swiss watch. My father gave it to me when I returned from the Great War. His father had owned it before him. It's run perfectly for over forty years. I'll see your ten, and I call."

Morrish gave an imperceptible nod, acknowledging the value.

Donny triumphantly played his hand. Four aces, king high. A very good hand. Gina's heart beat faster. This would be a good win for Donny. Like everyone else she leaned forward, waiting for Morrish to turn over his cards.

"Nice hand," he said, before flipping over his own cards, revealing a straight flush. "Thank you, gentlemen. I'll cash out now." He nodded at Gina.

Everyone looked dumbfounded as they watched the man scoop his winnings into his black fedora and slip Donny's watch into his vest pocket. "Yes, indeed. High time for me to head out." He smirked at Gina. "Fetch Gooch, would you, sweetheart? And bring Donny boy here a stiff drink. On me. He looks like he could use it." He peeled a dollar off a wad of cash and placed it on her tray. "Better make it a double."

Donny was still looking stunned, his face and neck fully flushed red as he realized the devastation that had just befallen him. "Futz!" he said, slamming his hand on the table.

The other men began to mutter and swear under their breath as well. "Take a man's money and run, what a piker!"

"For crying out loud! You can't just leave a man down like that," one of the other servicemen called to Morrish as he moved out of the gambling den. "Take his father's watch? Don't give him a chance to earn it back? That's real low!"

"Sorry, lads, that's the way of it sometimes." With that, Morrish strolled out of the room, giving Gina an infuriating wink as he walked by.

"Whiskey, straight. A double," Gina said to Billy a few moments later. She lowered her voice. "For poor Donny. I think he just lost a fortune. What was he thinking to gamble away his father's watch!" She slapped Mr. Morrish's bills on the bar, pushing them toward Billy, not wanting to touch the money tainted by Donny's loss.

Billy just grunted as he tossed his towel over his right shoulder. "That boy got in over his head. Happens sometimes."

"It's not right," Gina protested. "The hand was one and done. I thought they'd get a chance to win their money back. Play a few rounds! It's only fair."

"You still looking for fair?" Billy asked, stifling a yawn. "I thought you'd been here long enough to know better."

"I know. I do," Gina said. That knowledge didn't make her feel any better. "Oh, Donny!"

She turned her attention back to the tables, looking over the patrons, trying to get the image of the wounded ex-servicemen's downtrodden face out of her mind.

To her dismay, Mr. Morrish had seated himself on one of the high tables by the dance floor. She marched over. "Do you want another drink, *sir?*"

"Gin and tonic sounds good right now," he said. "Later, when I'm done here, I may be ready for a Hanky-Panky." He winked at her, but she didn't respond.

"I'll be back with your drink in a moment," she said, turning to go.

He reached out to touch her hand but drew back when she flinched. "Say, Gina, you seem a little heated. What's the problem, honey? The tip wasn't big enough for you?"

"How could you have taken his watch?" she asked, smiling tightly through clenched teeth. "Donny's already lost so much! How could you?"

Morrish's jaw tightened, the smile dropping from his face. "I won it on the up-and-up."

"Give him the chance to win it back," she pleaded. "It's only right."

"Nah, I promised myself that I'd only play a hand. That's how I keep the game fun. I never want to be controlled by the cards." He looked her up and down. "I'll play another hand—with you. You can win it back for him."

She shrugged. "I don't play cards."

"Well, that's too bad," he said.

Who does this guy think he is? Gina thought, feeling a flash of irritation course over her. As Donny's downcast face hovered in her thoughts, she knew she couldn't give in. "How about we trade for it? I've got a nice watch of my own you might like."

His eyes traveled to her shiny art deco wristwatch. "Pretty. Not my style."

"Not this one," she said, impatient. "A different one. Equally valuable. More, I'd bet you."

She'd remembered that she'd found an expensive watch among the items bequeathed to her by Marty. Her papa hadn't wanted to wear it, and she'd been pondering taking it to the pawnshop. She pushed aside a quick sense of guilt about giving Marty's watch to this scoundrel. *It's for a good cause,* she reassured herself.

He paused, studying her. "Is Donny your boyfriend or something? Why would you do that?"

Her lip curled. Trust a man like him to make that assumption. "No. He's just a friend. A friend who's already lost so much."

"I see." He looked toward the curtain. "I'll think about it. Right now, I think the show's about to start."

On cue, Lulu and Jade came out, prancing in unison to the instrumental that opened "Hard-Hearted Hannah." No matter how intricate the routine or how high their heels, Gina had never seen either of them lose their balance. If it were her, she'd have broken her ankle on the first high kick.

For this second set, the women were doing one of their

more comedic routines, singing in baby-girl voices with silly doll-like expressions that made everyone laugh and clap their hands. The audience stayed jacked up, growing even more excited as they moved into the next part of their act, called "Singing in the Bath." Though the commentary from the sidelines was getting fairly lewd, the Signora looked on with approval, from her position just outside the corridor entrance that led to her private salon.

To Gina's irritation, Harriet was still seated in a corner, where she was watching the pair's antics intently, even mouthing along with the lyrics.

She noticed, though, that before Lulu pranced off the floor, toward her dressing room, Mr. Morrish caught her hand and leaned down to murmur something in the redhead's ear. She giggled as she pressed her hand to his chest in a suggestive way, and giggled even more as he lifted her hand to his lips and kissed it. Then she glanced at Gina and gave her a little wave. Mr. Morrish grinned at her, too, and Gina looked away.

Just then, Ned began to play a quick piece on the piano. Hearing the tune, patrons who'd been tapping their toes hopped out on the dance floor, excited to try out the Lindy—the new dance craze from New York that had just reached Chicago.

Her cigarette tray back around her neck, Gina gave Mr. Morrish the side-eye as he sat, idly examining his recently won watch.

During a momentary lull in the evening, Gina, Lulu, and Jade stood together at the piano, their backs to the bar, keeping an eye on the crowd.

"Say, Gina," Lulu said, fluffing her hair, "you wanna go on a double date with me tomorrow afternoon? You're not busy, are you? Just for a few hours. It'll be fun to get all dolled up and have someone else take care of you for a change!"

Ned looked up from the piano. "Get that girl out on a date! It will be good for her!"

"I don't know, Ned—Gina's probably already got two dates lined up already," Jade said, her snide tone conveying the opposite. "A real social butterfly, this one is."

"I've noticed," Ned replied, giving Gina a little wink.

"I do date, sometimes," Gina said vaguely. Since she'd broken off her engagement with David a few years ago, she hadn't had the heart to date much. She'd never been one to balance a bunch of guys at once like Lulu anyway, but it was even harder because she needed to spend so much time taking care of her papa. When she'd met Roark earlier that year, she'd begun to thaw, but then he'd held back. Now she knew why.

Gina's eyes flicked over to where Harriet was speaking animatedly to Vern. The image of Harriet wrapping her arms around Roark's neck rose in her thoughts. She remembered how Roark had accepted Harriet's embrace. *I'm not going to pine over Roark,* she thought. *He's not available and that's that.*

When Gina stayed silent, Lulu poked her side playfully. "C'mon, say yes for once!"

Gina groaned. That's what she got for putting off these double dates. "Who's the guy?"

"Your most ardent admirer," Lulu said. "He's *very* handsome."

"Ooh la la," Jade said, looking at her fingernails.

Lulu swatted at Jade. "Enough of that," she said.

"Tell us more," Ned said, his hands still running easily over the keys.

"You've met him," Lulu said. "A swell fella. Wavy black hair. Real darb. He said he wanted to get to know *you* better."

"I bet he does," Ned said. "Too bad Gina's not interested in dating anyone."

"You stay out of it," Lulu said to Ned. To Gina she continued, "He said he'd set me up with one of his friends if *you* agree to come." Lulu's words came out in a rush. "I won't deny that I tried to get him for myself, but he seemed hellbent on *you*, Gina. His friend owns an automobile. He said he'll take me for a ride."

"You don't say?" Jade smirked. "Sounds like he's taking you for a ride already."

"I'm not going anywhere in just anyone's automobile," Gina said. She'd read the news enough to know that was never a good idea. "Certainly not someone I've never met."

"Smart girl," Ned said, moving over so Jade could sit on the bench beside him.

"'Course not, silly," Lulu said. "He said they'd take us for ice cream. At Maisie's parlor, over on Loomis. At three o'clock. Come on, Gina. Say yes! I want to have some fun, and I don't think he'll like it if I show up without you." Here she crossed her arms and put on a playfully pouty expression.

"So I've met this guy?" Gina said. "Who is he?"

"Yeah, he was playing cards with the men in back when I got here. His name is William Morrish. Said he had some unfinished business with you, whatever *that* means."

"Oh, *that* guy!" Gina exclaimed. "No way!"

"What, why not?" Jade asked, looking interested again. "Did he try to pull something already?"

"Did he tell you how he makes his money?" Gina demanded. "Bilks men of their bucks!"

"Well, not exactly," Lulu said, quailing a bit under Gina's vehemence. "He plays cards, I know that."

"Did he tell you he took all of Donny's dough earlier?" Gina pressed. "As well as his father's watch? Which was also his *grandfather's* watch? Come on! He's a cad!"

Lulu looked chagrined. "I'm sure he didn't mean to."

"I'm sure he did," Jade said, before sashaying off to see to a customer.

"So you don't want to go?" Lulu said, her mouth turning down a bit at the corners. This time her pouting expression seemed real. "That's okay. I get it."

"On the other hand . . . ," Gina mused, thinking about Donny. "He told you that he and I had unfinished business? I think I know what he means."

"Yeah?" Lulu asked, brightening a bit. "So you'll come?"

Gina's eyes flicked to Harriet again. *What do I owe Roark anyway?* She straightened her headdress in the bar mirror. "All right, I'll do it."

"Yoo-hoo, Gina!" Harriet called soon after, waving a half-full ruby-colored drink. "I need you! Can you come here?"

Gritting her teeth, Gina walked over to Harriet's table. Her companion, Vern, was nearby, talking loudly to some gentlemen at another table. "What do you need?" She couldn't bring herself to address Harriet as Mrs. Roark.

"That piano player," Harriet asked, swishing her glass in the direction of Ned. Seeing them turn toward him, Ned gave a little wave.

"What about him?" Gina asked.

"You and him a thing?" she asked. "He's a handsome enough fellow."

"He knows it, too," Gina replied, waving back to Ned. He was a real playboy. A nice one at least, she couldn't deny. She ignored Harriet's question. "What do you want? Need another Marlboro?"

Harriet looked up at Gina, her smile much warmer than it had been earlier that evening. "Say, doll, I think you and I got off on a bad foot earlier. I can tell you're fond of my husband, and any friend of his, I want as a friend of mine. How about we start and introduce ourselves, proper-like. Okee-dokee?" Without waiting for Gina to answer, she jumped in. "I'll start. My name is Harriet Roark." The wide crack between her front teeth was really prominent when she smiled.

Her heart feeling a pang at the woman's name, Gina reluctantly identified herself. Then, as pleasantly as she could, she said, "I heard you left Roark. Ended the marriage."

Harriet gave a dismissive wave of her hand. "Nah, it wasn't like that. Maybe he got his nose in a twist after I left, but we'll get that straightened out soon enough."

Gina couldn't resist digging in a bit more. "What about the man you came here with? Vern? You certainly appear to be *close* pals."

"Nah, me and Vern, that's just business." Harriet grimaced. "Meh, men. Let's talk about something more interesting. How about you? Like working here? Good tips?"

"Not bad," Gina said, giving the table a final wipe. "If you'll excuse me—"

"They have any openings?" Harriet asked.

Startled, Gina looked back at her. "Why, do you sing? Or dance?"

"Both. Been a hoofer for a few years now. 'Course, this place isn't really big enough for me, but it'll do for a while. While me and Roark figure out what's what. Vern—he's a promoter, you know. Got me some auditions on some stages in *New York City.*" She said the name of the city as if it were ensconced in bright lights.

"Broadway?" Gina asked, feeling skeptical.

"Off-Broadway. For now. Vern wants me to audition here. I mean, it's nothing like what I'm used to, but now that I'm moving back to Chicago." She gave Gina a bright smile, her crooked front teeth on full display. "Say, can you put in a good word for me with the Signora?"

"Maybe the place isn't big enough for you."

"Oh, poo! It's good enough," Harriet said. Her eyes narrowed, though her tone remained cloyingly sweet. "You'll do it, right? If not for me, then for your *pal* Roark. You want him to be happy, right?"

"Of course," Gina replied. *Just not with you.*

Still fuming over her conversation with Harriet, Gina went to the ladies' room to splash some water on her cheeks. Her throat felt raw from a great knot that had formed there, and there was a bitter taste of unshed tears in her mouth. *I'm not going to cry over Roark,* she thought, splashing her cheeks again. They still felt so warm.

She'd often wondered—more often than she cared to admit—what kind of woman Roark had married. He'd been close-lipped about his wife, but a few things had slipped out from time to time. They'd married young, a few years after the Great War, when he was just starting his career as a police officer. She had accommodated his war wounds, but something had changed after he was injured again while still on the police force early last year. A gun battle gone wrong, he'd mentioned once, with the injury so severe that he'd had to use a cane for over a year. It was then that Harriet took off, unable to attend to him as he needed.

Gina frowned. When Roark had mentioned his marriage, he always made it sound like it was over. He'd even made it sound like Harriet had run off with another man. Certainly a wife who left her husband after he'd been gravely wounded could not be viewed as very attached to either the man or the marriage. *Did I misread something?* she asked herself again.

She was about to leave when she heard the sound of a woman crying in one of the stalls.

"Uh, miss?" Gina called through the door. "Everything hunky-dory?"

There was silence and then the sound of a flushing toilet. Gina began to fluff her brown hair. She pulled out the tube of lipstick she had grabbed from the salon and applied it in the mirror.

The woman stepped out and gave her a quick frightened glance. It was Alma, who'd been there the other night.

She was still carrying her elegant red bag, although it clashed slightly with her orange dress. Some women had a bag to match every getup; Alma was evidently not one of those women.

"Are you all right?" Gina asked. She handed Alma a rolled-up white towel so she could wash her face. "Should I get a friend? Did someone bother you? Should I get Gooch?"

Alma dried her eyes and mustered a smile. "Oh, it's nothing like that," she said. "I'm such a ninny. I came out tonight, but I'm not ready. My father died a few weeks ago, and I-I just heard about F-Fruma." She broke off and began to weep softly into her hands.

Gina felt a pang. "I'm so sorry," she said. "I didn't mean to pry."

"No, I don't mean to be a bother," Alma replied. "It's just that . . ." Tears filled her eyes again. "I'm sorry."

"No need to be sorry," Gina said firmly. She remembered the loss of her mother keenly. Not to mention when her brother, Aidan, died. Then, of course, Marty, just this year. "Never be sorry for the grief you've suffered."

"Thank you," Alma replied. "You're very kind."

"Not at all." More briskly, Gina added, "How about I go fetch one of your pals?"

"No, no, don't bother them," Alma said. "I'll just stay here a while and then I'll go home. I'll let them know when I leave."

Gina could hear a record being played. Annette Hanshaw. "You Wouldn't Fool Me, Would You?" That meant Ned was on break and she would need to be on hand to switch out the records. "I've got to get back out on the floor," she said. "Will you be all right?"

Alma sniffed. "I'll be fine."

"Gotta run. Have a pal walk you home, would you?"

"I will. Thanks again."

The conversation with Alma in the ladies' room reminded Gina that she couldn't put off telling the Signora about Fruma any longer. Standing before the door to the Signora's private salon, Gina took a deep breath and knocked.

The Signora opened the door, giving Gina the once-over. "Straighten your headpiece." As Gina reached up to fix the offending accessory, she asked, "What is it?"

"May I speak to you? Privately?" Gina asked, her heart beating quickly.

The Signora stepped aside, letting her enter. "Please sit, Gina," she said, gesturing toward the elegant art deco sofas in the middle of the room.

Gina had only been in the room a handful of times over the past ten months, and it was hard not to look around in awe before she seated herself. *How had the Signora developed such grace and sophistication?* she wondered, not for the first time. After all, the Signora had grown up on the rough streets of Chicago's West Side, just like Gina, but now could be mistaken for a Gold Coast heiress.

Gina decided to start with the easier of the two matters. "There's a woman here who asked to audition for you," she said. "Says she's Mr. Roark's wife."

The Signora seated herself opposite to Gina. "Harriet."

"You know her?"

"I do." The Signora tapped her red polished nails on the sofa's wooden arm. "She's here right now?"

"Yes." Gina hesitated, hoping her next words would not sound catty. "She sounded like it would be a step down to work here."

"So Harriet is complaining, but still wants a job here." The Signora's cool gray eyes were like shards of dark ice, incisive and knowing, as she studied Gina's face. "You are worried about her loyalty? Or just about her working here?" As Gina began to stammer out a response, the Signora held up her hand. "I do not need to know. I expect my employees to get along. Thank you. I will speak with her."

As she started to rise, Gina interrupted her, her words coming out in a rush. "Signora, one other thing. I think that the Third Door may have sold some bad hooch last night. Poisonous hooch. Someone even died!"

"What are you talking about?" the Signora said, sounding slightly perturbed. "Slow down. Tell me what happened."

Gina explained, as carefully as she could, everything she knew about Fruma and Stan, and the coroner's preliminary thought that Fruma had died from a bout of alcohol poisoning.

"Tell me, Gina, " the Signora replied, her customary mask slipping. "How do you know all this?"

Not wanting to explain Nancy's involvement, Gina opted for the simplest explanation. "Mr. Roark told me."

The Signora tapped one long nail on the sofa arm. "I see. Anything else?"

"No, Signora."

The mask slipped back into place, but Gina could see contemplation in the Signora's eyes when she spoke again. "I thank you, Gina, for your loyalty in sharing this information with me. I expect you to keep this to yourself. Now, back to work."

CHAPTER 8

Gina opened the large envelope she'd been carrying, pulled out the ten prints she'd made, and spread them across the lace tablecloth covering Nancy's kitchen table.

Well done, Gina, she thought to herself, a satisfied smile crossing her lips. Each print represented her different attempts at light and shadow, a skill she'd first learned from Roark when he taught her the basics of photography earlier that year but had improved upon for herself.

"See anything interesting?" Nancy asked, setting a steaming teacup in front of her.

Gina pulled one of Marty's magnifying glasses from her handbag and passed it to Nancy. "See for yourself."

As Nancy perused the photographs, Gina wrapped her hands around the teacup, trying to ward off the pervasive chill in the room. The flat where her cousin lived was a bit on the shabby side, nothing like the one down the street shared by Fruma and Adelaide. Originally she'd lived in a North Side mansion with her parents, but in summer had moved out. *It's closer to the Harrison Street police station*, Nancy had said at the time. *Besides, my parents are driving me batty.*

Despite its run-down appearance, the kitchen was surprisingly bright and cheery, a stark contrast to Nancy's dour personality. The place reminded her of Mrs. Metzger's teashop, with delicate bone china teacups, hand-crafted curtains made of Irish lace, and crocheted doilies everywhere.

"Pretty," Gina said, fingering the lace. "Did someone make this for you?"

"Did it all myself," Nancy replied, looking up. Her tone was matter-of-fact, conveying neither pride nor embarrassment. "Learned to crochet and tat when I was a girl. I've got several chests upstairs. My mother probably hoped I was creating a dowry." Here she snorted. "Helps me think when I've got a problem."

Gina nodded. Nancy's lacemaking probably helped settle her mind the way fixing lamps and toasters did for Gina. The feel of tools in her hands, figuring out the problem, and then righting what was wrong were all very satisfying, and perhaps it was the same for Nancy. For a moment, she felt a surprising closeness to her cousin, a sensation she'd never before experienced.

"Are you hungry? I think I've got some cookies from the bakery around here somewhere," Nancy asked, hopping up from the table. Before waiting for Gina to reply, she began to open and shut her cabinets. As she poked about, Gina glimpsed neat rows of Van Camp's pork and beans, Libby's corned beef hash, Underwood's deviled ham, and, of course, Campbell's soups. Little evidence of any cooking or baking supplies. "Must be out. Sorry."

"That's okay," Gina said, sneezing. As she reached for a tissue, she said, "I heard something interesting last night."

"Yeah? What's that?" Nancy sat back down, picking up the magnifying glass again.

"Well, someone else got very sick on Friday night, after tippling down at the Third Door. Same night that Fruma was there." Gina tapped her fingers on the table. "Apparently even the neighbors commented on how ill he was."

"I see," Nancy replied. "What do you make of that? Do you think that both of them suffered from alcohol poisoning?"

"I'm not sure. Something still seems off to me. I can't explain it. That's why I want to talk to Adelaide again. I just think she's hiding something."

"Hmmm. The coppers call it listening to their gut," Nancy said. "You know, I've been thinking the same thing. We should talk to Adelaide again." She glanced at the kitchen clock. "Let's go over now."

"She could still be at church," Gina commented, glancing down at her watch. It was close to ten thirty on a Sunday morning, after all.

"Nah. Not Adelaide," Nancy replied. "Frankly, I'm surprised she wasn't back at the Third Door last night, boozing it up. She and Fruma were quite the party gals."

"You think she'd go out on the town after her roommate just died?" Gina asked, pouring some more hot water into her cup. *Could Adelaide really be so cold?* "How long were they roommates?"

"Not so long," Nancy replied. "Since July or August, I think. Fruma wasn't living there when I moved here at the very beginning of summer, I do know that. Adelaide took her in after her other roommate left. I don't think she was too happy when Fruma went and got engaged."

"Adelaide certainly seemed jealous of Fruma when I spoke to her," Gina mused, as images of Adelaide came back. Adelaide, kissing the ladies' room mirror, leaving the lipstick stain. Her beautiful necklace swinging into view.

Her necklace. Gina stopped short. "Wait a minute!" she exclaimed, seizing the magnifying glass. She began to re-examine the photographs of Fruma's dead body, one after the other. "It can't be."

"What is it?" Nancy asked, banging her cup against the saucer. "What are you looking at?"

Gina pointed to Fruma's neck where it was visible in one of the photographs. "Put your peepers on this necklace. Jade and amethyst. It's a unique piece."

Nancy cocked her eyebrow. "You're right about that. *Very* unique. It was full of cocaine, too."

"What? Really?"

Nancy looked pleased at Gina's reaction. "Yup. The necklace Fruma Landry was wearing was specially designed for addicts. Chock-full of cocaine. What's more, our chemist confirmed it was definitely the same cocaine that was found around Fruma's nose." She looked back at the photograph. "What of it?"

"I saw Adelaide wearing that same necklace at the Third Door when they were there that night."

Nancy didn't look impressed. "So what? Maybe they each had one in the same style."

"Fruma wasn't wearing that piece when she was at the

Third Door." Gina squinted, trying to remember how the woman had looked when she was alive. "She had on a black opal necklace."

"So Fruma borrowed the necklace from Adelaide. Or Fruma owned it and Adelaide returned it to her."

"Maybe. Fruma didn't change the rest of her clothes... why would she take off her black opal necklace and put this one on instead? Why switch necklaces?" Gina said, picking up the photograph of Adelaide that she'd taken on a whim yesterday morning. The woman's eyes were bleary, and her hair was a mess. She looked sad, regretful. Gina pushed her cup away and stood up. "Something about this isn't right. Let's go."

As Gina raised her hand to rap on the window of Adelaide and Fruma's flat, the front door swung open. Adelaide was there, the same wrap she'd worn the day before tied loosely around her nightgown. Her eyes were red and puffy from crying. "You're back," she said. "What do you want?"

"We just have a few more questions," Nancy said, pushing her body into the doorframe to keep Adelaide from closing the door.

"I already answered all the questions that the *police* asked me. I don't know what Fruma took, I don't know how she died!" Adelaide said, growing agitated. "I certainly didn't know she was dying—it was just as I said. I still have to talk to her p-parents! They're coming by today, and I don't know what to say! Please go!" She tried to shut the door, but Nancy was still standing stubbornly in the doorframe.

"You were angry at her that night, weren't you?" Gina asked. "I know you were."

Adelaide whipped her head around to stare at Gina, her eyes widening as recognition kicked in. "Y-you! You work at the Third Door. I remember you!"

"Yeah, that's right," Gina said, putting a cold stiletto tone into her voice. "I also remember your conversation in the ladies' room. You were upset with Fruma. She stole your guy, you said."

"Well, yes, I was mad about that. George was charming! I guess that's how it goes sometimes." Adelaide's eyes narrowed. "Say, what's a cocktail waitress doing taking photographs in my home anyway? Work for the Feds, maybe? The Drys? Bet that's entrapment. My uncle's a lawyer."

"No, I'm not a Fed. Or a Dry," Gina said. "You're right, I work at the Third Door, but my cousin Officer Doyle here does work for the police. Which is why you called her, right?"

"I-I . . . ," Adelaide began, at a loss for words.

"Were you hoping she might help you clean up your mess?" Feeling Nancy stiffen beside her, Gina added, "Which of course she'd never do."

"I don't have to answer your questions," Adelaide whined.

"Well, maybe you do, and maybe you don't," Nancy replied, edging forward. She could look quite tall and menacing when she wished. "You're the one who called *me* that morning. Of course, I'm happy to ask some of my cop friends to stop by. Or you can just answer our questions." She pressed on the door. "Inside would be preferable."

Looking resentful, Adelaide stepped back so they could enter the flat. She led them to the screened front porch, which was really more of a sunroom.

"What do you want to know?" she asked, slumping down into one of the bright green upholstered chairs and slurping on a pale yellow drink in a porcelain teacup. Gina caught the whiff of apple brandy. A Corpse Reviver, perhaps. Guaranteed to chase the spirits away, or at least that's what she'd heard Billy Bottles claim as the Third Door was finally closing during the wee hours of the morning.

Nancy nudged Gina as they sat down. *You start*, she could almost hear her cousin say.

"Okay," Gina said. "Adelaide—if I may?" At the woman's terse nod, she continued. "How well did you know Miss Landry?"

Adelaide relaxed slightly. "Fairly well, I suppose. We were roommates since summer, after she answered my advertisement. We'd exchanged a few letters. She paid half the rent and utilities. Don't know how I'm gonna get another roommate now," she added, thrusting out her lower lip like a child.

"Tell us about Fruma's fiancé," Gina said. "Neither of you seemed too happy to see him at the Third Door."

"Ex-fiancé. Vidal Bartucci." Adelaide spoke his name with contempt. "He couldn't accept it was over between them. He'd been calling our flat for weeks. Neither of us expected he'd turn up at the speakeasy, though."

"You don't say?" Nancy said, her expression not giving anything away. "Why'd they break up, do you know?"

"Oh, this and that," Adelaide said. "Fruma liked to toy with people."

Something in her tone made Gina look at her with suspicion. "I remember you mentioning that George was not the first guy Fruma had stolen from you. Was Mr. Bartucci *your* guy first?"

Adelaide crossed and uncrossed her legs. "Vidal and I went on a date or two, nothing serious. When I introduced him to Fruma in July, he fell head over heels for her. The ninny proposed only six weeks after they met."

Gina and Nancy exchanged a quick glance. "You continued to let her room with you even after he dumped you for her?" Not many women would be capable of such a thing.

Adelaide snorted. "Vidal was a sucker. I knew she'd toss him when she was done with him. He was charming, that's true. Not worth fighting over, though." A shadow passed over her face. "Not like her family would have let her marry him anyway. Just like mine wouldn't have. She'd have been living paycheck to paycheck with him—anyone could see that."

The venom in her voice was stark, but Gina couldn't say whether it was directed at Fruma, Vidal's lowly status, or the poor opinions both their families would have had if either of them had actually married Vidal.

"Those men you were with the other night," Gina said, switching up the conversation. "You said you'd just met them."

"Thought they were the cat's pajamas. At least Fruma thought so." Adelaide gave another mirthless laugh.

"It seemed like you thought so, too," Gina commented. "You'd called dibs on the one man. George, wasn't it?"

Adelaide opened and shut her mouth, a dull caricature of a fish. She crossed her arms. "Listen," she said. "I was a bit zozzled that night—didn't know my ups from downs. George was handsome, dreamy, you know. Reminded me of a film star. I saw him first, that's all I meant. All the men are charmed by Fruma. That other guy, Daniel, was, too. Why? Why were they so enamored with her? Was she really prettier than me?" Her tone was resentful until she heard herself. "Oh, God. I am awful." She looked like she was about to break down in tears again.

We're not getting anywhere, Gina thought. She decided to change tactics. "There was a moment, when I served you drinks, that Fruma seemed upset about something. Something about jumping out of an airplane?"

"Oh, that." Adelaide shrugged, resuming her passive state. "Fruma was trying to impress them. Maybe I was a little impatient with her. Better if she just kept her danged mouth shut about that stunt. She'd been peddling that story since August! It's not like anyone believed her. They might have pretended to, but come on! She *had* to have made up the whole thing."

Something clicked in Gina's memory, a distant recollection from the summer. "What stunt was that?"

Adelaide paused to gather her thoughts. "Fruma had been living with me . . . I guess about a month at this point. Back in August. She came home one day and said she'd jumped out of an airplane at over twenty thousand feet. Didn't use an oxygen tank, either."

Adelaide went to the window, drawing back the curtain to stare aimlessly out the window. At Nancy's cough, she plopped back down on the sofa and leaned back, as if the effort had exerted her. "No other aviatrix had done such a thing, or so she claimed. She was found wandering out in Joliet. She claimed that's where she ended up after she'd jumped from the plane."

"What?" Gina asked, exchanging a glance with Nancy. "Did she imagine herself a Leta?"

Everyone remembered Leta Wichart, the stuntwoman who'd been killed jumping out of a plane in Los Angeles back in January for an adventure film. Everything had gone horribly wrong when the twenty-two-year-old Chicago native had plunged to her death after her parachute had failed to open. Inexplicably, there had been an odd rush of copycats around the country, with women claiming to have done what Leta had died doing.

"Did she do it?" Gina asked. "Do the stunt?"

Getting up abruptly, Adelaide headed over to a small writing desk in the corner of the room, yanked the top drawer open, and pulled out several newspaper clippings. She slapped them down on the patterned ottoman between their chairs and slumped back into the seat she had just vacated. "Judge for yourself," she said, resting her head in her arm.

As Nancy and Gina glanced at the headlines from different newspapers, Gina began to recall some details from the story. WOMAN BREAKS RECORD FOR HIGHEST JUMP FROM AN AIRPLANE, one headline read. WOMAN FOUND WANDERING AND CONFUSED; CLAIMS TO HAVE JUMPED FROM AIRPLANE, read another. Someone had written the name of the paper at the top of each clipping. *The Indianapolis Star. The New York Times. The Washington Post.*

Gina looked at Adelaide, who had begun to sob softly into her elbow. The sound was ugly, raw, and completely understandable.

"Some people said she didn't actually jump out of the

plane," Nancy pointed out. "I remember hearing that she had the pilot just land in a nearby field and she took the train back to Chicago."

"Everyone was laughing at her. You know what my parents said when they heard about it? That I should give her the boot," Adelaide said. "I didn't want to do that. Fruma was fun, good for some laughs. Better for her to just shut up about that stunt, you know?"

"Still, those men at the Third Door were paying *her* lots of attention," Gina reminded her. "Especially that guy George. Daniel, too. They gave you a ride home, didn't they?"

Adelaide's smile brightened slightly. "Yeah. George had a Duesenberg Model J."

"So they dropped you off. Then what happened?" Nancy asked. "We know she was already sick when she left the Third Door."

"She was still in her evening clothes, in full makeup, when she died," Gina said aloud, remembering the crime scene. She began to pepper Adelaide with questions. "Why hadn't she changed her clothes? Washed her face? Rolled her hair? Did she stay up for a while? Why didn't she want to go to bed?"

"I don't know." Adelaide's tone became flat, and a faint flush arose in her cheeks. "She was busy, I suppose."

"What do you mean?" Nancy asked.

"You invited the men in, is that it?" Gina asked, piecing together the scene. *That's why Fruma was still wearing her evening clothes.* "Was one of the men with Fruma when she died?"

"George. I never learned his last name. Anyway, they didn't stay very long." Adelaide put her hand to her forehead.

"Look, I've got a raging headache. I don't know what happened to her, and I'm sorry she died. Even though I got mad at her sometimes, she was a real lark. A pal."

As she moved, a little gold spoon threaded on a long gold chain swung away from her neck. "Nice necklace," Gina commented.

Paling slightly, Adelaide tucked the miniature spoon back inside her dress. "Thanks," she said.

Nancy glanced at Gina, her lips giving a funny little twitch. "Does that spoon come in handy?" she asked Adelaide, who put her hand to her neck.

"What do you mean?" Gina asked, at the same time Adelaide said, "What are you talking about?"

"May I?" Nancy asked, leaning forward. Before Adelaide could protest, the policewoman had grasped the spoon in her right hand. "This spoon is for cocaine, am I right?"

Interesting, Gina thought as she studied Adelaide, who was looking increasingly disturbed by the turn in the conversation. "You were wearing a different necklace the other night," Gina commented.

"Well, of course, I don't wear the same jewelry every day—" Adelaide began before Gina cut her off.

"I remember that you were wearing a beautiful jade and amethyst necklace," she said. "I also remember that Fruma was wearing a chain with a black opal."

Adelaide blanched and looked startled. "Wha—? No—" She seemed to be trying desperately to think.

Gina continued, "What's interesting is that in the photographs I took, Fruma was no longer wearing the black opal but rather the jade and amethyst. *Your* necklace. Can you explain that? Why would she have switched necklaces?"

"She d-didn't," Adelaide said, looking frightened. "N-no, that necklace wasn't mine. It was Fruma's. I never wore it. You're mistaken." Adelaide touched her forehead again. "Look, I've answered all your questions. I'm sorry Fruma died, but I had nothing to do with it. My head is pounding, and I need to rest. I'll ask you to leave me alone."

"All right, then. Have it your way," Nancy said, pulling a small case from her pocket and withdrawing a card. She held the card out to Adelaide, and the woman accepted it before she could stop herself. "Here's my new card, with some new numbers on it. Let me know if you see George or Daniel—I'd like to speak with them. Or if you can remember anything else."

Adelaide gave a tense nod and shut the door behind them.

CHAPTER 9

"What's that card you gave her?" Gina asked her cousin as they stepped back into the bright October sunshine.

Nancy handed her another card from the small leather case. NANCY DOYLE, it read. POLICE INVESTIGATIONS. Below her name were two telephone numbers. The first was Nancy's, TA5-0236. The other was very familiar. "Hey!" Gina exclaimed. "Harrison seven, one nine three seven!"

She poked Nancy in the arm. "Why'd you put Marty's old number on your card? My number?"

Nancy rubbed her upper arm where Gina had jabbed it. "There may be times when people want to give me information and might not be able to reach me."

"So, what, I'm your secretary now? Fielding your clients?" Gina asked. "Is this even an official card?"

Nancy changed the subject. "Did you believe her?" she asked as they walked down the street. "That Adelaide didn't know anything about how Fruma died?"

Spying a tin can on the sidewalk, Gina kicked it a few

steps ahead of her, watching it skitter into the curb. The label on the can was a dull and faded blue, looking like it had once contained Planters salted peanuts. She'd kick it all the way home if she could, the way she and Aidan used to do when she was little. "I don't know. She was hiding something. I'm sure she was lying about Fruma's necklace." She kicked the can again. "Why would she do that?"

Nancy shrugged. "Who knows? What did you make of the story she told—about Fruma jumping out of the airplane?"

Gina thought about how Fruma had looked the night before she died. Energized, animated, playful. "I'm not sure," she said, considering Nancy's question. "I'm sure she *was* telling them about it. I heard bits and pieces when I was serving. I do think, though, that Fruma's the kind of woman who might pull a stunt like that. Or at least, the kind who'd lie about doing it. If only we could talk to George. Or Daniel, for that matter. They might be able to tell us about what happened after the four of them left the Third Door."

"Yeah. I don't know how we can go about finding them without their last names."

"I can poke around, talk to some of the regulars," Gina said, although she didn't remember ever having seen them at the speakeasy before that evening. "They might turn up at the Third Door again. I'll keep an eye out."

The two women fell silent as they walked. "What are you going to do?" Gina asked, giving the can an extra-hard kick so that it skittered down the street. "Are you going to tell the cops investigating Fruma's death that she'd been at the Third Door earlier that evening?"

"They probably already know about that. Adelaide must have told them."

"She might not have told them about George and Daniel—she seemed embarrassed about having brought them back to their flat."

"That's true," Nancy said. "They also don't know that we have an eyewitness who knows what they look like."

Sticking out her foot, Nancy intercepted the can before Gina could kick it again. "I'll tell those bozos on the force when I'm good and ready," she said, kicking the can hard into the sewer.

"Hey," Gina said, a bit miffed.

"Sorry," Nancy replied, not sounding contrite. Then she spoke in a rush, as if she finally had the chance to say something she'd been waiting on. "Say, Gina, my parents want to know if you'll come over for luncheon next Sunday."

Gina sighed. *What did Aunt Charlotte and Uncle John want now?* Each of the few times she'd interacted with Marty and Nancy Doyle's parents—her great-aunt and great-uncle—she'd felt that they wanted something from her. Their relationship, such as it was, was awkward, contrived, and new. "Why do they want to see me?"

"To be honest, I don't know." Nancy looked like she was going to say something else but then stopped herself. "I told them I'd invite you. I also told them I didn't know if you'd come."

"I assume Papa is still not invited."

Nancy's silence said it all. The decades-long tension between the Doyles and her father had not been smoothed over, nor was it likely to be anytime soon. When her mother had agreed to marry her father so many years ago, a rift had begun that neither side seemed bent on bridging.

"I guess I'll see what they want," Gina said, wishing she had something else to kick.

After she and Nancy had parted ways, Gina continued on home. When she mounted the front steps, she could see that some neighbors had left a few broken items on the porch for her papa to fix, their names tucked on cards under the objects. For the last few years, her father had been fixing household appliances at low cost to her neighbors, sometimes taking very little payment for his services. Toasters, lamps, irons, sewing machines—most things just needed a little tightening although some objects, like radios, were not so easy to fix.

The cards were all addressed to her papa, making it clear that no one knew she'd been taking on most of the harder jobs herself for the better part of a year. With his tremor, Papa just couldn't handle the more delicate tools or manage the intricate manipulations required to fix certain pieces. The work had brought in some needed extra income, and she found that fixing things helped her think.

Today, though, she wanted to focus on other things. She set the lamp and toaster on the long table in the living room that they used as a workspace.

"Papa!" she whispered from the doorway of her father's bedroom. The curtains were drawn, so that only a single shaft of afternoon light had filtered into the room. Not that

there was ever much light anyway, given how little space
there was between their flat and their neighbors' home next
door. Only a narrow walkway separated the two buildings.

Not hearing any response, she tiptoed into the room.
Her father lay under the covers, lightly snoring. He must
have gone back to bed after breakfast.

Gina sighed. He would only have needed to take a nap
like this, so early in the afternoon, if he had taken another
heavy dose of his pain medication. He seemed to be taking
more and more these days. Even though he tried to hide it,
she could tell that the pain just would not go away.

In the corner she spied what she had come in to
retrieve—the stacks of *Daily Tribunes*, courtesy of Mrs. Hayford, who dropped the paper off each morning when she was
done reading it. He used to read the papers at the kitchen
table, but for the last few months he'd taken to reading them
in bed, looking them over till he fell asleep. He never wanted
to throw them away, either, because he was fond of rereading
the comics and sports sections. She used to scold him for this
packrat thinking, but as it was getting harder for him to go
to the barbershop, she knew it was the only way he'd get his
news. Now she was glad that she hadn't thrown the papers
away.

Being careful not to disturb her father, Gina carried a
stack to the kitchen table and began to sort through them,
trying to locate any papers from August that might give
news about Fruma's stunt with the airplane.

"Bingo!" she whispered a few moments later, tapping
the paper delightedly. "I found it!"

WOMAN JUMPS FROM AIRPLANE; SETS RECORD FOR JUMP

BY AMERICAN FEMALE. The newspaper was dated August 14, two days after the stunt occurred, and now she remembered glancing at it before. This time she studied the photo of Fruma posed in front of the airplane, dressed in baggy jodhpurs and a buttoned-up jacket. Her hands were on her hips, a saucy smile on her face. With her leather aviation helmet pressing her hair down, she looked very similar to the famed female aviator Amelia Earhart. The caption on the photo said the image had been taken at a private airport near Joliet, a city over fifty miles southwest of Chicago.

Gina settled in to read the story, which gave a lengthier version of what Adelaide had related earlier. Fruma Landry, age twenty-four, had taken it upon herself to jump from an airplane at 20,000 feet, in order to set the world's record for women. Something that even Amelia Earhart had never done. A daring young socialite, the newspaper had called her.

According to the story, after Fruma had jumped out of the plane and her parachute opened, she passed out. Then, in an incapacitated state, she'd drifted through the open air, for miles and miles, until she had finally landed in a farmer's field outside Joliet.

Gina shook her head. *Hard to imagine*, she thought, continuing to peruse the article.

Upon reviving herself, Fruma had hitched a ride with the farmer to the local train station, where she caught a train back to Chicago's Union Station. At that point she seemed to have promptly called the press to relate the affair, still dressed in her aviator's outfit. She pulled a roll of film from her pocket, which contained the preflight photograph, and gave it to one of the reporters gathered there.

When pressed by the reporters, Fruma was a bit vague on the details. *How long were you in the air?* Fruma didn't know. *What was the name of the farmer who found you and drove you to the Joliet train station?* Fruma couldn't remember. She also couldn't pinpoint the exact place she'd landed, other than that it was "a 25-minute truck ride to the station." Last, she couldn't explain what had happened to the parachute, guessing that it was "with the farmer, I assume." She also couldn't explain what had happened to the pilot, or where he might have landed the plane.

The reporters didn't seem to mind the holes in her story, or at least, not at first. They seemed to have taken it all in stride, seeing it as a lighter-hearted piece in the midst of an outbreak of violence that had occurred during the heat of summer.

The very last line of the story was particularly interesting, and Gina read it twice. The reporters had evidently tracked down Fruma's fiancé to get his thoughts on the remarkable tale. "What a foolish stunt!" Vidal Bartucci had replied. "I'm quite stunned by it all! That's my Fruma. Always dreaming up wacky stuff. These sorts of antics will stop, of course, after we marry."

Gina set the page aside and began to look through other newspapers from later in August. By the end of the following week, Fruma's heroic tale had begun to turn on its head. MIRACLE OF WOMAN'S LEAP FROM AIRPLANE UNDER SCRUTINY, one headline read, with a subheadline underneath: FAMED AIRPLANE JUMPER CLAIMS IMPROBABLE "TWIN."

What in the world? Gina read through the piece quickly,

then reread it, trying to make sense of the changes in the story. A cabdriver, it seemed, had seen Fruma Landry's photograph in the paper and read about her claims. As he told the reporter, on the day of her supposed flight, he had picked up a fare who looked exactly like Fruma Landry outside a private airport in Joliet, who had requested a ride to the train station. At the time he had thought nothing of it, assuming that the woman must have taken a private flight to the airport.

Only when the cabdriver read about Fruma's claim and saw her photograph did he begin to probe her story. As he explained, when he picked up the woman, she'd been wearing a "smart-looking green dress and matching hat" and carrying a small suitcase and handbag. She was not dressed in her aviator's garb, as she was in the photograph and when she spoke to reporters. Nor was she carrying a parachute.

"So odd," Gina said out loud. The cabdriver's account definitely made it seem like she had faked the whole stunt.

Fruma, it seemed, had insisted she was telling the truth. "Everyone has a twin," she'd said when presented with the cabdriver's story. Gina could almost hear the smile in the quote. "He probably picked up mine. What can I tell you? I jumped out of the plane like I said, and I certainly wasn't wearing a green dress and matching hat."

Dutifully, the newspaperman went so far as to look up Fruma's birth record from Evanston Hospital, confirming that she was not in fact a twin.

After that, the story completely pivoted. A headline from the next day screamed, LOCAL WOMAN'S "FANTASTIC" AIRPLANE

STUNT CONFIRMED A HOAX. An interview with an unnamed maintenance worker at the airport revealed that the pilot had confided before the flight that he didn't believe that Fruma would really take the leap, and he considered it all a stunt to grab attention. This information, coupled with the truck driver's story, was enough to destroy Fruma's credibility.

What kind of woman would tell a story like this? Gina wondered.

Apparently the newspaper reporter had wondered the same thing and had spoken to her fiancé again, posing this very question. "Aw, my fiancée's always going on about something," Bartucci had said. "That's just her thing. She likes to stretch the truth. Of course, a real woman would not do such a thing. Certainly no woman could have accomplished such a feat anyway! She got you all, didn't she? A real riot, that one!"

Gina looked through the other newspapers, but there didn't seem to have been anything more about the story. Thoughtfully, she set aside the three newspapers with stories that mentioned Fruma. She returned the rest to her father's room, setting them in the corner where she'd found them.

Before she left the room, she gazed down at her father's sleeping face. For once, the pained expression etched into his face had smoothed over with the peace of sleep. Did he dream about her mother? Or maybe his long-dead son? Finally, she tiptoed out of the room, so as not to disturb what looked to be the best sleep he'd had in a long time.

"Ready?" Gina asked when Lulu opened to the door to her flat around two thirty. Lulu lived just around the corner from Gina, and they had agreed to meet there first, before walking to Mr. Morrish and his friend at Maisie's ice cream parlor. Judging from Lulu's appearance, she still needed a few minutes more to preen in front of a mirror. Fortunately, Lulu worked fast, adding a last coat of lipstick before slipping on her coat and shoes.

"You look swell," Lulu said, giving her a wolfish whistle.

Gina poked her arm. "Enough of that."

As they tripped along the pavement, Lulu elbowed her. "I don't know why they couldn't just pick us up from my house."

"Because we don't know them," Gina replied, poking her back.

"Don't know them *yet*, you mean," Lulu replied, giving a little shimmy with her shoulders. "I hope William brings me a cute guy. If he's only half as swell as *your* guy, I'll be satisfied."

"*Mr. Morrish* is not my guy," Gina said, shifting her handbag back and forth in her hands. After she had made lunch for her father earlier, she'd gone over to her other flat above the Third Door and rooted among Marty's belongings. In her handbag she'd put Marty's watch, some cufflinks, and a gold collar pin. She hoped that they would be enough to compensate for Donny's watch. She'd left a small box of other jewelry, mostly rings, hidden under the floorboards where she'd first discovered it.

As they neared Maisie's, Gina glanced at her watch. "Ten minutes early," she said.

"Great, time enough for a smoke," Lulu replied. She began

to rummage through her far larger handbag. "Say, Gina," she said, imitating one of the older regulars at the club. "I'm looking to try a new brand tonight. How about you let me try out a few, on the house, and I'll make it worth your while."

"Oh, sure thing, Mr. Ding-a-ling," Gina replied sweetly, staying in character. "So long as you let my friend Mr. Gucciani here try out a few new moves, on your face. On the house. I promise, it will be worth your while."

Both women laughed. "Ah, never mind, I knew I rolled a few earlier. Here they are," Lulu said, as she opened up her holder to place a cigarette inside. She lit the end and took a puff, leaning against the store. Gina popped a stick of peppermint Wrigley's into her mouth, enjoying the minty burst of flavor.

As she did so an elderly couple strolled by and regarded them with extreme contempt.

"Hussies," the man said with a pronounced sniff.

"Tarts," the woman said, adding in a very haughty tone, "Smoking in public! Such a sight would never have been seen, back in *our* day."

"Back in *your* day, women couldn't vote, either," Gina called back before she could stop herself.

"Or have fun," Lulu added with a wicked smile. "We're just waiting for our dates. I don't even know mine."

The pair looked completely scandalized. "What do you expect from women dawdling in front of the *ice cream parlor*?" the woman said to her husband before rushing him along.

"Ah, the *ice cream parlor*," Gina said, when the couple was out of earshot. "A den of iniquity if there ever was one. Far worse than any speakeasy."

"Well, surely you heard *the tales*," Lulu replied with a smirk. "Remember when Maisie's first opened?"

The women giggled. When the ice cream parlor had first opened its doors, just before the Great War, she remembered being warned against going there. Stories kept going around of young girls enticed to Maisie's, and other parlors like it, lured by the promise of the delicious new treat, only to be taken advantage of by nefarious men with bad intentions.

"I do! I was twenty before I set foot inside!" Gina replied. "My papa didn't think it was respectable."

"Well, it's respectable now," Lulu said.

"I'm not so sure. We are meeting Mr. Morrish there, after all."

"Delighted to hear you speak my name, Miss Ricci," William Morrish said to them from behind, causing them both to jump. He nodded at Lulu. "Miss Evans."

Gina clapped her hand to her mouth, wondering if he had caught her little joke at his expense. Lulu extended her hand immediately. "Mr. Morrish," she said, giving him the same familiar once-over she had at the Third Door.

"Please, call me William," he said, turning to Gina. He was more handsome than she remembered, and she caught her breath a bit when he smiled at her. *What would Roark think about that?* she wondered, then forced herself to dismiss the errant thought. *Who cares?*

They were both introduced to Mr. Morrish's companion, who was clean-cut, well-dressed, and friendly. "Lucas Yanofsky," the man said, watching Lulu flick her cigarette to the ground and delicately stamp it out with her purple boot. "Call me Luke."

Lulu immediately slipped her arm into Luke's and led the way into the ice cream parlor.

"Shall we?" William asked Gina. He did not offer her his arm, nor did she take his.

They seated themselves in the corner, at one of the fifteen or so elegant gold-painted tables scattered through the parlor. William and Lucas, she noticed, had positioned themselves so that they could see the whole room at once.

What else goes on at this place? Gina wondered. In its innocence, Maisie's reminded her of Mrs. Metzger's tea shop, one of the Signora's storefronts, where respectable women could get a spot of liquor added to their chocolates and teas, without having to brave their way into the speakeasy below.

She noticed four gleaming gambling machines in the back corner of the ice cream parlor. Two were slot machines, and the other two were trade stimulators. Customers could play them for small prizes and payouts. Right now, three boys were howling over their wins and losses.

"We should get some of those machines at the Third Door," Lulu said idly.

William shook his head. "Nah, that'll attract the attention of the Feds. Drinking's one thing, gambling's another—combining them will bring them right to your doorstep."

Gina nodded. The Signora would never go for such a thing, she was sure of it. Besides, the presence of slot machines at the Third Door would probably detract from the speakeasy's sophisticated feel, even if they were in the back room where card games were played.

A waitress dressed all in pink handed them each a menu. Although Gina really wanted coffee and one of the cannoli she'd spied among the confections when she walked in, she looked over the ice cream offerings. Each had an imaginative title and enticing description. The Bull Moose. The Buster Brown. The Mutt and Jeff.

"So hard to choose! They all seem dreamy," Lulu said. "I'll take a Gibson Girl. What about you, Luke?"

"A Dunce Cap," he replied. "Suits me, don't you think?"

After ordering a Tango, Gina waited to see what William would order. It only took him a second, as if he were used to reviewing the ice cream selections. "Peg o' My Heart," he told the waitress. He didn't look at all embarrassed by the romantic nature of his choice, which was named for a popular song from before the war. "The flavors are swell."

"So you were at the game today?" Lulu asked the men after the waitress left. "Who'd the Cubs play? The Pirates?"

"Yeah, it was the last game of the regular season," William replied, his eyes on Gina. He seemed to be sizing her up. She had to force herself not to squirm under his gaze. "Cubs lost, eight to three. Hope it's not a bad omen for the World Series."

"You believe in omens?" Gina asked, arching one brow. "I guess I never met a gambler who didn't."

"Nah, not omens so much. I just read people." His smile was teasing. "Do you want to know what I can read about you right now?"

"I'm not sure I do," Gina said, sitting back in her chair. Seeing Lulu and Luke in conversation, their heads close together, Gina spoke to William in a low tone. "So, I never saw you at the Third Door before Friday night. Was that your first time there?"

"Yeah," he replied, his expression growing guarded. "I had some business to attend to."

With the Signora. She wondered what they'd discussed.

Before she could ask anything else, he grinned at her again. "I'm pleased you knew that was my first time there. That means you noticed me." He took a sip of water. "You're why I came back on Saturday night. I wanted to see you again."

He's just trying to charm me, she thought. "I noticed that you were watching the customers, especially some of the women." She thought about how his eyes had lingered on Fruma and Adelaide in particular. *Why had he been watching them so closely?*

He misread her silence. "Jealous?"

Gina grunted. "Hardly." She hesitated. "You know, one of those women you were looking at died that night."

Not a muscle in his face twitched. A perfect poker face. "I heard about that," he said. "Sad."

When he didn't say anything more about Fruma's death, she sighed. "Let's talk about our unfinished business."

"In due time," he replied, setting aside his water glass. The waitress had returned with a tray full of sundaes. "Let's enjoy our ice cream first."

"Jeepers!" Gina exclaimed as she took in the elegant display. Each sundae was artfully displayed in a different-colored glass. William's Peg o' My Heart was in a light green footed bowl, with two scoops of vanilla ice cream delicately covered by marshmallow whip and chocolate syrup. Banana slices had been carefully laid around the rim, and the whole thing was topped with whipped cream, nuts, and a green cherry. Gina's Tango was in a tall phosphate glass, designed to show the layers—first a scoop of chocolate ice cream covered by butterscotch sauce and ground nuts, next a scoop of vanilla ice cream covered by marshmallow sauce and more nuts, all topped by a peach slice and a delicate cloverleaf wafer. Both were a work of art.

"Right now, let's enjoy," William said, picking up his spoon. *"Slainte!"*

After savoring the first bite, Gina set her spoon back in the dish. She wanted to get back to business. "I'm prepared to make an exchange for Donny's watch. Did you bring it with you?" *What if he didn't? What will I do?* She squirmed a little in her green-cushioned chair.

"Stop looking so nervous. I brought it." He laid Donny's watch on the table. "What did you bring me?"

She pulled out the watch she had retrieved from among Marty's belongings.

"Your boyfriend's?"

"No, I don't have a boyfriend—" She broke off when she saw the satisfied expression on his face.

"Just checking," William said, licking his spoon. "You're persistent, aren't you? I like that quality."

"I'm sure the watch is worth a lot." *At least I hope it is,* Gina thought, feeling a wave of despair. "It's a good trade."

He didn't pick up Marty's watch. "Maybe, maybe not. I'm a bit disappointed you wouldn't play me for it, though."

She glanced over at the gleaming slot machines in the corner. "How about a different kind of wager?"

"Bah. Those machines are all chance," he said, scowling when he followed the direction of her gaze. "Or they're rigged. No skill to them."

"Then make the trade," she said, pushing Marty's watch toward him.

He tapped his fingers on the table as he studied her. "What did you have in mind?"

"How about we each try our hand at one of the machines? Whoever pulls a better hand wins. If I win, you accept my trade. Donny's watch for this one."

"That's it? What happens if I win?"

Now it was her turn to frown. "You keep the watch."

He laughed, seeming genuinely amused. "So I win by being allowed to keep what is already mine? Something I won fair and square?

"Did you?" Gina asked, remembering what the other ex-servicemen had muttered in the back room. "Win it fair and square, I mean?"

His eyes hardened, and Gina felt a chill run over her. "I was j-just teasing," she floundered, suddenly feeling afraid.

William's angry look disappeared as quickly as it had come. "Never call a man a cheat," he said lightly. "Least, not if you want to live to tell the tale. If I win, then you come out with me on another date." He held out his hand. "Deal?"

Reluctantly she shook it. "Deal."

He held it a little longer than necessary. When she pulled her hand away, he handed her a quarter from his pocket. "Ladies first."

They walked over to the slot machine, and William spoke to the boys. "Excuse me, kids. Can you give the lady some room?"

Surprised, they stepped away from the machine. "You're

gonna play the quarter slots?" one of them asked. Playing for nickels was risky enough.

"Seems like a waste of money, but here goes." She put the quarter in, and they all watched the three images of fruit float by. After a few seconds the first stopped. Cherry. Then the second stopped. Another cherry. Everyone cheered. Then the third pulled in. Apple. To her surprise, there was still a payout of three quarters.

Lulu clapped her hands delightedly from the table. "Yay, Gina!"

William smiled indulgently and placed his quarter in. A moment later, two lemons and a cherry came up. Nothing came out.

"I won," Gina declared. "You'll accept my trade?" She slid Marty's watch from her bag and held it out to him.

William lifted his eyebrow, but he handed her Donny's watch without comment. He examined Marty's watch and slipped it onto his wrist. "You really don't gamble much, do you?"

Lulu and Lucas exchanged a glance but didn't say anything. Inwardly Gina groaned. *Marty's watch was probably worth more than I realized.* Then she fought the pang, thinking about Donny and how thrilled he would be to get his watch back. "No," she said shortly.

"Well, maybe you'll come out with me again sometime. I'll take you somewhere that really swings."

"I spend every night in a place that swings."

He looked slightly disappointed by her pointed rebuff. "I see. Well, I can't say I don't appreciate a dame who knows what she wants and gets it."

Standing up, she held out her hand. "Thank you for the ice cream."

His hand closed around hers, and he leaned down and kissed her cheek. "I'll be around. Whether I win another date with you or not."

CHAPTER 10

The teapot was just starting to sing when there was an impatient *rat-a-tat-tat* at the door of Marty's flat. She didn't have time to guess it was Nancy before her cousin called out, "It's me, Gina. Open up."

She set down the pencil she'd been using to solve a puzzle in the newspaper and let Nancy in. "How'd you know I was here?"

"Mrs. Lesky. I told her to give me a ring if she saw you."

Of course. Mrs. Lesky, Little Johnny's mother, could easily be bought off. *Makes me think I'm gonna need to start paying her off myself, just to keep my whereabouts private.*

Gina walked into the kitchen and took the teapot off the range. "Tea?" she asked, holding out a second cup.

"Sure," Nancy replied. "Add some brandy to it, will you? I'm off duty."

"What brings you here, Nancy?" Gina asked, pulling a small unmarked bottle from behind the icebox and setting it on the table. Even though individuals could possess liquor, she never wanted to be in the awkward situation of being asked where she had procured it.

"I want to talk through our case."

"It's *our* case now, is it?" Gina asked. "Seems like Fruma's death was all due to an accidental overdose of cocaine. Maybe mixed with some bad alcohol."

"Except that can't be all it is," Nancy said, taking a sip. "I can feel it in my bones. I've been doing this long enough to know that something isn't right. Let's talk it over again." She pulled out the envelope full of prints that Gina had given her the day before.

"It *is* strange," Gina agreed, blowing on her tea to cool it down. "I agree, there are some questions here." She picked up her pen and a piece of paper, sketching out ideas and pictures as she talked. "So, the main question I have is about the necklace. For some reason, Adelaide's necklace ended up around Fruma's neck. I guess I can't prove it, but I'm certain that she lied about it. Why lie about something like that?"

"Mmmm, good question," Nancy murmured, pulling out a much dog-eared brown leather-bound book and a pen. She began to jot something down. "Go on. What else?"

"What's that you've got there?" Gina asked, momentarily distracted.

Nancy turned it toward her so she could see the words embossed on the cover.

"Whoo-hoo!" Gina crowed, before reading the title out loud. *"You Can Be a Detective."* Without asking for permission, she took the book from Nancy and began to rifle through it. There was a pocket in the back with some handwritten notes in it. "What is this?" she asked. "A home study course?"

"Yeah. What of it?" Nancy said, flicking a crumb from the table. "I wanna show the captain that I've got what it takes." Taking the book back from Gina, she flipped to a few handwritten pages in the back of the book. "See, here's my first assignment. I got a C-plus. 'How to trail a suspect.' The next one I need to do is 'How to interview the suspect's acquaintances.'" She set the book on the table between them.

Gina pursed her lips. "Do we *have* a suspect? How can we even do an interview with no suspect? How can we interview the suspect's friends? In fact, do we even know a crime has occurred?"

Nancy just grunted dismissively. "I'm sure Fruma was murdered. My gut is telling me so. So I'm looking at Adelaide as a suspect. She had opportunity, access, means."

"Fruma wasn't the only one who took sick after drinking at the Third Door that night. For cripes sake, we don't even know what killed her," Gina reminded her, reaching for the book again, looking at it with real interest. "What about motive?" she asked, pointing to the table of contents that divided the book into Motive, Means, and Opportunity. "Why would Adelaide kill Fruma? Jealousy?"

"Yes," Nancy replied. "You said yourself that Adelaide was upset with her, jealous even, because one of the gentlemen preferred Fruma to her."

"Well, in that case, what about Fruma's ex-fiancé?" Gina asked. "He seemed jealous enough at the Third Door the other night. Tried to get her attention, but she wouldn't give him the time of day."

Nancy frowned. "I suppose that's true. Maybe he was in cahoots with Adelaide."

That didn't seem so likely to Gina, but she didn't feel like challenging Nancy's theory. Instead, she pulled out the three folded papers from her bag and opened them on top of the prints. "Look, I found these accounts of Fruma's stunt in the newspaper. See how the story played out?"

Looking impressed, Nancy turned the papers so she could peruse the stories for herself.

"See what her fiancé said about her?" Gina said, pointing to the different passages which she'd starred earlier with her pen. "He just dismissed everything she said. He didn't believe in her at all."

Nancy read the fiancé's name out loud. "Mr. Vidal Bartucci. I'd like to talk to *him*. Hmmm. I can get his address from the city clerk's office. One of the secretaries owes me a favor."

She picked up the phone and dialed a number while Gina kept looking through the book on detecting.

"Got it," Nancy said a few minutes later. She hung up the phone. "He doesn't live too far from here. Let's go talk to him."

"What, now?"

"Got something better to do?"

Gina glanced at her watch. One p.m. Her father wouldn't need her until later that afternoon. "Sure, why not?"

As they walked over a few streets, Gina said. "Maybe we should think about what we're going to say to Mr. Bartucci."

"Nah. Let's play it by ear, see if he tells us the truth," Nancy said. "I can tell when a man's lying."

"Learn that skill from your home study course?" Gina

couldn't help but tease. She glanced at the address of the graystone on their right. "Should be a few doors down."

Sure enough, as they neared a rococo graystone in the middle of the block, a man stepped out, pulling the front door shut behind him. He was wearing a dark gray pin-striped suit, and a gray fedora complete with feather was pulled down low over his brow. Gina recognized the man who had harassed Adelaide and Fruma at the Third Door on Friday night. "That's him," she whispered, nudging Nancy.

"Mr. Bartucci?" Nancy called, hurrying toward him. "Can we have a word?"

He dismissed Nancy's drab clothes with a single glance. His eyes lingered a little longer on Gina, though she didn't get the feeling that he recognized her from the speakeasy. "What do you want? I'm busy."

"We just wanted to talk to you," Nancy said. "About Fruma Landry."

His eyes narrowed. "What about her? I've already talked to the cops. I don't know anything about my fiancée's death. I have nothing else to say to the press, either."

"We're not with the press," Gina said adroitly, giving Nancy a sidelong glance. "But we do have some questions."

"I was just leaving . . . her parents need my help." He shuffled his feet. "The medical examiner still hasn't released her body, and I'm about to head down there to demand that they do. I said I would do it. Her parents have suffered enough."

"You weren't still her fiancé, though, were you? I heard that she'd broken it off with you a while back," Gina said, not bothering to mince her words. "In fact, she hadn't been returning your calls for several weeks, isn't that right?"

"Who told you that?" When Gina didn't answer, he continued, sounding agitated. "Look, I haven't talked to her in some time. We've both been busy."

"You talked to her at the Third Door," Gina asserted. "I saw you myself."

The color drained from his face. "Oh yeah, I ran into her there. I'd popped over for a nightcap. Didn't expect to see her." He blinked back a tear. "I never thought that would be the last time I'd see her."

Gina gave Nancy a meaningful look. *Your turn.*

Nancy picked up the conversation, switching to a new topic. "What did you think of Fruma's airplane trick? The one she did back in August."

He frowned. "The stunt she *says* she did, you mean. What a lark! That was Fruma, always fooling around. She was a high-spirited gal, that was for certain." A shadow passed over his face. "I wasn't at all happy when she told me about it."

"Didn't you believe her?" Gina asked. "So thrilling!"

"Well, at the time, sure. She was so delighted and happy with herself. Told me she had done something majestic and brave. Of course, I thought it was very stupid. I told her so. What man wouldn't think the same? Who wants their fiancée jumping out of an airplane? Why would she have done such a thing anyway?"

"*A real woman would not do such a thing,*" Gina said, quoting what he had said in one of the newspapers.

"Exactly," he said, not realizing that he was just agreeing

with himself. "I wasn't at all surprised when the whole thing turned out to be a hoax."

"Right," Gina replied, pulling out the news story she had clipped from the newspaper yesterday. "I think you told the press specifically that it couldn't have been true. That *no woman could have accomplished such a feat.* You said that your fiancée had been foolish, and that's *just how women are.*"

"What?" Mr. Bartucci exclaimed, snatched the clipping from Gina's hand. "I never said such a thing!" Then his face crumpled as he read it for himself. "So this explains it!"

"Explains what?" Nancy asked.

"Why Fruma was so cold to me. Why she broke off the engagement. She never told me why. I know it happened right at the end of August." He crumpled up the newspaper clipping and threw it on the ground. "That jackass reporter. I didn't realize he'd printed what I'd said." He looked at them suspiciously. "Are you sure *you're* not with the press?"

"No, we're not." Gina half expected the man to push for more, get them to explain why they were asking questions. "Wait, before you go. What was Fruma and Adelaide's relationship like? Hadn't you dated Adelaide first?"

"Aw, that was a long time ago. Kid stuff. We just had a few dates. Went to a few petting parties. Nothing special. That's how women are these days. It's not like I was courting her. I thought she understood that. What I had with Fruma was real." He looked sad. "Until I blew it." He walked away then, resembling a dog that had been kicked in the ribs.

Gina stared after him before bending to pick up the newspaper clipping he had cast to the ground. "What a buffoon," she commented, smoothing out the piece before carefully folding it up and placing in her purple embroidered handbag. "Not particularly discreet."

"Sounds like he and Fruma deserved each other," Nancy replied. "He probably just wanted his name in the paper, like her."

"Maybe," Gina replied. "Maybe with a fiancé like that she wanted to prove something. Prove she could do more with herself." She thought again about the woman she'd seen at the Third Door. Laughing, expressive—Gina felt an odd pang then that such a lively personality, even one who might well have been a liar, had been extinguished. "I wonder what this reporter's angle was, why he dug deeper into Fruma's story. Not just that exposing the hoax but interviewing the fiancé as well. It seemed like his intention was to humiliate Fruma even more."

Nancy glanced at the man's name in the byline. "Russell Kowalski. I don't know him, but I know some other people at the *Daily Tribune*. They can fix up a meeting. I'm not sure what would be the point in talking to him, though."

Gina shook her head. "I don't know either, really. I do know that Fruma was still telling that story like it had really happened. She wanted George and Daniel to believe her. Maybe she was funny in the head, but who would keep telling a lie after the story had been exposed as a hoax? I can't explain it, but I feel like we should understand this better."

"It's worth looking into," Nancy agreed. "I have to work all tonight, and I'll need to sleep tomorrow during the day. How about I arrange through my contact at the *Tribune* to have Mr. Kowalski come to the Third Door tomorrow evening? Maybe around eight o'clock? That way you can talk to him, too."

Gina hesitated. She wasn't sure what the Signora would say about her speaking with the reporter at the Third Door, or with Nancy, for that matter. Still, she wanted to be there for the conversation, and that seemed like the first opportunity to do so.

"Okay, I can plan to talk a bit on my break, if possible." Slightly awkwardly Gina added, "You'll have to get your glad rags on, or Gooch won't let you in." She hesitated, running her eyes over the woman's matronly clothes. "Do you need to, um, borrow something?"

Nancy heaved a tortured sigh. "I think I can manage to get gussied up for one night. See you tomorrow night."

CHAPTER 11

As Gina neared the tearoom the next evening, she saw a small figure slumped out in front, pedestrians picking their way around him as if he were a sack of discarded refuse to be avoided. It was Jakob, his arms wrapped around his half-filled sack of papers, looking dirtier and more tired than usual.

"I'll take a paper, Jakob," she said, holding out a penny.

He handed her the paper, but his face looked drawn and sullen. Every movement seemed to be an effort.

"Hey, how's your papa?" she asked.

He shrugged and dug his toe into the dirt. "Still not right. Laying in bed all day. He's not sick. He's just laying there, looking at the ceiling. We can't afford a doctor." He gulped. "I'm gonna see if I can get a job at the yards, where he worked, while he's off. Maybe the boss will hire me in his place. Selling news isn't bringing in enough."

Gina frowned, not knowing what to say. There wasn't any way this child could do his papa's job. *Maybe I can talk to the Signora about it,* she thought, although she had no idea how the proprietress would respond.

"Come with me, Jakob," she said, reaching down to pull him to his feet. She began to drag him toward the pharmacy.

"What? Where——?" He jerked away when her intent became clear. "Not going in there! Mother says I mustn't."

"Not the speakeasy, silly!" she whispered. "Medicine. I was just thinking that Mr. Rosenstein might be able to mix something up for your papa——"

"Don't have no money!" the boy shouted, his voice catching on his tears. He ran away then, his cap in his hand so he wouldn't lose it. Gina stared after him.

"Gina? What was that about?" It was Mr. Rosenstein, with his shop hand, Benny, standing behind them, a dark brown textbook in his arms. The pharmacist stared down at her through his spectacles. "Who was that boy?"

"His name is Jakob. He's a newsboy," Gina replied, still staring in the direction Jakob had fled. "His father is awful sick, and they can't afford a doctor. I thought maybe——" Here she stopped, and swallowed. "I don't know, that he could get some medicine."

Mr. Rosenstein looked sorrowful. "Without a prescription from a doctor, I can't make him any medicine. However, if he were to come back and tell me his father's symptoms, there might be something basic on the shelves that will soothe his ailments."

"I'll tell him so, the next time I see him," Gina replied, her worry not allayed. Hearing the church bells distantly toll the half hour, she said a small prayer for Stan and his family, hoping the man would be all right.

After she slipped on her cocktail dress, Gina still had a few minutes to spare, so she paged through the paper she'd bought from Jakob, stopping when a small item caught her eye. The headline was buried under an advertisement related to a sale on women's winter cloche hats.

ANOTHER "MODERN" SOCIALITE DIES FROM OVERDOSE.

She smoothed the paper so she could read the three inches of text. "Modernity claims another unwilling victim," the short piece heralded. "On Saturday morning, October 5, 1929, Fruma Landry, age 25, was found dead in the flat she rented with a roommate. Still clad in her evening party clothes, Miss Landry died either from alcohol poisoning or a cocaine overdose after a night out with friends. Autopsy results still pending. She is survived by her parents, Norma and Richard Landry, from Wilmette, Illinois. Services to be held at the Johnson Funeral Home in Wilmette on Saturday."

She looked at the byline. Not Russell Kowalski but another reporter.

Probably not worth talking to Mr. Kowalski, then, she thought, wiping some drops off a table.

About an hour into her shift, Gina slid into the back room, where seven or eight of the ex-servicemen had gathered. Five were at the table, half-heartedly playing cards; the others were sitting on high stools, like Ralph, or leaning against the tables around the room. Donny was nowhere to be seen. *Roark's not here, either,* Gina found herself embarrassed to note. The World Series was on everyone's mind.

"Can't believe the Athletics beat us three to one!" the dealer muttered, dealing out cards to the other players with his left hand. His right hand hung at his side, useless. "I really thought we had a chance!"

A general rumbling of agreement followed. "Yeah," one of the men at the table said, picking up his cards. Under the dim lights, his bald head gleamed, revealing a long scar that ran down the length of his scalp and neck. Gina swallowed, wondering what kind of injury he'd sustained that would leave a scar like that. "I thought ol' Charlie would h-h-hold him and we'd reclaim the l-l-lead."

"Nah, Sal. Our bats were cold," a third man at the table replied. He frowned at his cards. "Hornsby was cold all day."

"Well, he'd better heat up!" the dealer complained. "Run 'em back to Philly."

After she made her rounds, she pulled Ralph aside. "Hey, can I talk to you a sec?"

"Sure thing, Miss Ricci," he said, and they moved to a corner of the room. "You're mad about Roark's wife being back in town?" he asked, grinning to show he was teasing. "Don't worry, doll. He's giving her the one-two-three once and for all. At least, we told him he should."

Her face flushed. "What? Oh, no! Nothing like that." She swallowed, trying to regain her composure. "This isn't about Roark." She pulled Donny's watch out of her bodice and held it out to him. "I, er, got this back for Donny. Can you make sure he gets it, please?"

Ralph stared at the watch, then reached out to close her own fingers around it, hiding it from view. His earlier teasing tone was gone. "Where'd you get that, Miss Ricci?" he asked, looking afraid of her response.

"I got it back from Mr. Morrish," she replied, speaking quickly, unnerved by the look of horror on his face. "I was hoping that you would know where Donny was. That you could get it back to him. He's already lost so much, I couldn't bear that he might lose this, too." She blinked away the tears that had welled up unexpectedly. "I think my brother—Aidan—would have wanted me to do this for a brother in arms. " She held it out to him again. "Please, Ralph. Take it. Give it back to Donny."

This time, Ralph took it from her. "Miss Ricci, how'd you get this back from Mr. Morrish? That man—do you know who he is? What people say about him?"

"Yeah. I know."

"People don't steal or double-cross a man like that and—" He didn't finish the thought, but it was clear. *People don't double-cross a man like that and live.*

"Don't worry about me. He gave it to me, fair and square."

Ralph narrowed his eyes. "Forgive me, Miss Ricci. You gotta understand! That man plays for keeps."

Gina smoothed out her dress, thinking about her exchange with Mr. Morrish. "Everything's hunky-dory. Don't worry. Just give it to Donny. Don't say anything about me." She smiled. "After all, we don't want him thinking a woman's fighting his battles for him."

"What should I tell him, then?"

"Just say that Mr. Morrish had a change of heart. Or anything. Just leave me out of it."

Ralph smiled, but his eyes were troubled. "You're aces, Miss Ricci. That Mrs. Roark ain't got nothing on you. Roark, he'll see that. Everyone knows he's not happy."

Gina flushed slightly. *What would Roark think if he knew she'd been out with Mr. Morrish?* she wondered. Then she fluffed her hair impatiently. *Well, he's married. He can do what he wants. As can I.*

Gooch was standing in one of the darker corners of the speakeasy floor, his watchful presence subsumed by the shadows. She wondered about him sometimes. She'd learned earlier that year that he'd known her papa when they were both young men, and that he was fiercely loyal to the Signora. He was silent, less likely to crack a smile than Little Johnny, though both men could inspire fear and obedience in others. She knew little else about him. She didn't even know if he was married or had children, though she suspected that his life was fairly solitary, if not outright lonely. Sometimes Gina thought he had a certain fondness for her, as the daughter of Frankie the Cat. She tried to wheedle information from him from time to time, even though he tended to be tight-lipped.

Since the joint wasn't so busy yet, she sidled over to take a chance.

"Say, Gooch, you remember Stan? A regular? He was here for a while last Friday night. Then he took sick."

"Oh yeah?" Gooch asked, keeping his eyes straight ahead, in the direction of a couple who had started to argue at their table. "What about him?"

"He's still not better. His son just told me."

"Not our problem. Stan can't handle his hooch," Gooch said, still looking in the direction of the couple. "She's going to dump her glass on his head. Just wait and see."

Gina glanced over at the heated pair. "I think she's going to toss it in his face."

They both chuckled. Then Gina continued with their earlier conversation. "Maybe something is really wrong with Stan."

This time Gooch did look down at her. "Just stay focused on drinks and smokes. Don't ask for trouble."

Gina sighed. That was the kind of thing people were always warning her about.

As she walked by, the woman reached up and turned the cocktail over the man's bald head, so that ice and fruits and sticky stuff cascaded down his face and onto his shoulders. Heading to the back for a mop, she glanced at Gooch. He winked at her before starting the process of hustling the man out of the speakeasy.

"Two Gin Blossoms," Gina said, placing the sweet honeyed cocktails in front of a pair of giggling coeds. They were trying to muster up the courage to start dancing out on the floor.

Out of the corner of her eye, she noticed Nancy descending the stairs, looking like a nervous Nelly. She'd tried really hard to fit in, wearing an ugly mauve dress that was shapeless even for flapper standards. It looked straight out of a charity bin. Still, she'd tried. She wore some cosmetic jewelry and sparkly rhinestone combs in her hair, making her matronly bun look a bit more festive.

"Sit here," Gina said, waving to her cousin. "I'll get you a drink. Be right back."

Nancy frowned. "Be quick about it."

"Gin and tonic," Gina called to Billy, nodding in Nancy's direction. "Put it on my tab."

"Isn't that the *policewoman?*" he asked, a note of derision entering his voice. "What's she doing here? Hoping to catch some ladies of the evening? She'd be better off on Maxwell Street, rather than trying to catch 'em here. The Signora won't like it."

"Well, tonight she's just Marty's sister. My cousin," Gina replied. "I asked her to come out for a drink."

Hearing his late friend's name, the bartender sighed. "That's Marty's sister? I forgot about that. You can save your money. Tonight her drinks are on the house."

He handed her the gin and tonic, which she brought over to Nancy. Billy had even added a lime wedge to the rim of the glass. Usually he only did this for the big spenders who expected a fancy garnish to adorn their drinks.

He needn't have bothered. Nancy eyed the lime suspiciously, but did squeeze a few drops into her drink before setting the remainder aside.

"Did you see the paper this morning?" Gina asked her. "There was a piece in there, about Fruma. Said she'd died of a cocaine overdose *or* alcohol poisoning."

Nancy shrugged. "That's just what the coroner's office told that reporter. They haven't completed the autopsy, as far as I know." She sipped her drink. "Mr. Kowalski will be here at nine o'clock."

"How'd you get him to meet you?"

"I told him I wanted to share some news about Kitty Malm."

Gina gave her an approving glance. Kitty Malm, also known as the "Tiger Girl," was one of the city's most famous murderesses, having killed a night watchman on a botched robbery a few years back. "Good cover story," Gina murmured, then moved away to tend to some nearby patrons eagerly calling for their drinks.

As she passed by Ned, he waved her over. "I see your cousin's here. Shall I sing her song?" he asked, playing the first few notes of "The Laughing Policeman."

"Oh, Ned," she said, swatting at him. "Please don't."

"Fine, I'll sing one for you instead . . . even though it's really a duet," he said, beginning to play "Kiss Me Sweet."

That Ned. Always a playboy. What are we gonna do with you? Still, she couldn't keep from bouncing along to the lively tempo as she walked away.

Gina continued to serve drinks over the next forty minutes or so. Around nine o'clock, she noticed a slightly portly, middle-aged man coming to stand at the balcony rail above and survey the room. He descended the stairs, moving with energy and purpose. When he reached the bottom step, she was there to greet him with her cigarette tray. "Smokes?" she asked.

"Not right now, toots. Catch me later." He looked past her then, settling his eyes on Nancy. Her cousin was looking impatient and grumpy, though she was on her second gin and tonic in less than an hour. Would the woman ever relax?

"Excuse me," he said, walking over to Nancy. "Nancy Doyle?" Gina heard him ask as she started over to the bar. "I'm Russ Kowalski."

"Yeah, that's me," Nancy replied. "How'd you figure that out?"

"Let's just say I make it my business to know people."

Before Gina was out of earshot, he spoke to Nancy in a low tone. "You said you wanted to tell me something about Kitty Malm?" he asked.

Nancy launched into a story about the Tiger Girl's doings and was still talking when Gina returned with the drinks soon after. Turned out one of the wardens was an old pal of Nancy's and she really did have an inside scoop. "I have it on good authority she's only pretending to be reformed so that she can file an appeal, but she's got some tricks up her sleeve."

"You don't say," Mr. Kowalski murmured, pulling out a small notebook to jot a few things down.

Gina hovered as long as she could, waiting for conversation to turn to Fruma and Vidal and the airplane stunt.

A flutter at the side of the room caught her attention. Jade and Lulu were standing there, in their slinky low-cut dresses, waving at her. *What are they doing? Why are they just standing there?*

Then, with a start she realized that Ned had already taken off for his cigarette break and the girls were waiting for their number to start. She hurried over to the record player and slipped the first record onto the turntable. It was Bix Beiderbecke and His Gang's "Somebody Stole My Gal."

As the music began to play, the two women pranced out, shimmying their shoulders and extending their long legs in high kicks, the crowd clearing around them.

"Get hot! Get hot!" the patrons shouted.

The Signora came out briefly to watch them, checking on their performance and her customers' activities. The excited whistles and catcalls must have been at about the right level, because she soon disappeared back into her salon. Kowalski, Gina noticed, was watching the girls with an approving smile, although Nancy just looked impatient.

When the first number ended, Lulu continued on her own with a quick, spirited high-stepping routine to "My Blue Heaven" to more shouts and hoots. Jade had moved to the bar to sip soda water.

Gina found herself snapping and tapping her foot along with the music. She'd never wanted to perform in front of people, but she loved watching Lulu work the room. As soon as the last notes faded away, and before the crowd could surge back onto the floor, Jade moved confidently to the center of the performing area. At a bigger place she would have had a spotlight highlighting her statuesque form. Here she stood silently, displaying a barely contained energy as she waited, the slightest of smiles on her bright crimson lips.

The room silenced as Gina deftly switched the records. She put on the orchestral version of "Me and My Gin," and as always Jade commanded the room with her first sultry words. *"Hey—Wait for me . . ."*

The entire speakeasy remained hushed until the last note of the popular song. Then, at once, everyone burst out into wild applause. "Jade! Jade!" they shouted, demanding an encore. The Signora had reappeared, and when Jade looked in her direction, she gave the slightest shake of her head. Jade threw up her hands. "All done for now, ladies and gents," she called before walking triumphantly off the floor. Leave them hanging and begging for more, as the old stage show saying went.

The energized crowd gladly took to the dance floor when Gina slipped "Broadway Rag," a quick-footed dance piece, onto the gramophone. That would have to do until Ned returned to the piano.

Catching Gina's eye, Mr. Kowalski held up his empty glass, then pointed to Nancy's drained glass as well. When Gina brought them their gin and tonics a few minute later, she lingered at the table, hoping to be on hand when Nancy finally asked Mr. Kowalski about Fruma. Slowly she made a great show of wiping the moisture off the table, then placing two white napkins down, then laying the drinks. She even elbowed Nancy a bit. *What are you waiting for?*

To her surprise then, Mr. Kowalski laughed and patted the stool beside him. "Park it, toots. I know I'm handsome and all." Here he patted his protruding stomach with a comical air. "I'm going to assume there's something else you want from me. I know it's not to tell me more about Kitty Malm. So let's cut the malarkey. Why did you two bring me here tonight?"

The reporter really was very observant. Gina didn't sit down on the stool he'd indicated, but she thrust out her hip and pulled the newspaper clipping from her bodice. "All right, then. We have a question about this." She laid the clipping on the table in front of him.

"Oh, this case," he said, looking interested.

"Can you tell us about it?" Gina asked. She tapped on the headline: LOCAL WOMAN'S "FANTASTIC" AIRPLANE STUNT CONFIRMED A HOAX,

He took a sip of his drink. "Story's all there. Woman plans elaborate hoax. Woman takes us all for fools. What's there to ask?"

"Why'd you go after her like that?" Gina asked. "Why'd you have to prove her wrong? As far as I can tell, you were the only one who did."

The reporter leaned closer. "Simple. I hate liars. Especially pretty dames who take men for a ride."

Gina raised her eyebrow.

"No, I'm serious," he said. "I could tell there was something off about Fruma's story. Just didn't hang right," the reporter said. "When that trucker came forward saying he had picked her up at a private airport in Joliet, I knew she was conning us. Tried to say that it was just another woman that looked like her. Poppycock, that's what that was. I aimed to find out why."

"What about what her fiancé said about it? What did you think about that?" Gina pointed to the passage in which Fruma's fiancé was quoted as saying, *My fiancée's always lying about something. That's just her thing.*

He shrugged. "Just that he knows her, I guess." His eyes narrowed. "How about you tell me why you're interested. What's your angle?"

Gina drew in her breath. Mr. Kowalski was good. He'd deftly turned the tables on her, and she didn't like it. "I don't

have much time. We'll answer your questions if you answer
ours."

"Shoot, doll."

"Her fiancé. What did you think of him?" Gina asked.

The newspaperman looked up at the ceiling. "That guy.
Vidal, wasn't it? You know, there was something off about
him, too. Quick to mock her. I had to hand it to her, she
stuck to her story even after it was clear the details were all
getting messed up in her head. She just loved the limelight.
He was embarrassed by her but then laughed at her, too.
Not a real nice trait in a future husband."

"Typical, though," Gina said. Nancy nodded in agreement.

"Yeah, maybe so, but I don't like that either. She's probably better off without him."

Gina noted that he spoke of Fruma as if she were still
alive.

"He seemed real broken up about her death," Nancy
said. Gina kicked her ankle. She hadn't intended to give the
reporter any information.

The reporter did a double take. "Her death? This
woman—Fruma Landry—is dead? When did that happen?
How?"

"What, you don't read your own newspapers?" Gina
asked, raising her eyebrow.

Mr. Kowalski frowned. "I was away on a short holiday.
Usually do read them. Must have been recent. Last weekend,
I'm guessing?"

With a quick surreptitious glance around, Gina pulled
out the short news account detailing the woman's death.

Mr. Kowalski read it over quickly. "Suspected overdose. Partying too much." He set it aside. "A shame."

"Yes," Gina replied cautiously, unsure how to proceed.

"Not an overdose, though, is that it?"

When neither woman replied, his voice grew hard. "Don't try to con me. I got a nose for news. Not an overdose, I take it? Are you thinking the fiancé had something to do with it? That why you're asking questions about him?" He looked from one to the other. "Come on, tell me. Off the record. We can help each other."

Gina and Nancy exchanged a glance. "We spoke to him yesterday," Nancy admitted.

"Interesting." Kowalski leaned forward. "In an official police capacity?"

"No," Nancy said hurriedly. "I mean, it could have been just an overdose. The coroner will know soon enough. I just want to be on hand if there's something else." Her eyes gleamed with ambition.

"What's your deal?" Kowalski asked, looking up at Gina. "What's it to you?"

"Just curious, I suppose," Gina said, not wanting to say anything about seeing Fruma just a few hours before her death. There was something odd about it all, but she couldn't put her finger on it. Right now she wanted to keep that information to herself, and she hoped that Nancy wouldn't bring it up.

"How's about you let me poke around a bit, see what I come up with?" He was practically panting now, like a bloodhound hot on the scent. "Sometimes things shake up after someone dies."

Nancy handed him her card. "Call us if you find anything out."

Kowalski took the card and, after taking his wallet from his vest pocket, tucked it carefully inside. He handed them each one of his cards as well. "I expect the same favor from you." He smirked at Gina. "You can call me anytime, with any news you like."

Taking her towel, Gina turned away without saying another word and began to vigorously wipe a nearby table. *Why am I getting involved here?* she asked herself. *Fruma probably just took too much cocaine and did herself in by accident.*

She sighed. *Everybody has an angle,* she thought. When she turned back to the table, both Kowalski and Nancy were gone.

CHAPTER 12

"*Prices slosh around in another pepless day. Tape followers flabbergasted,*" Mr. Rosenstein said, reading the front-page headline in the *Daily Tribune* out loud. "*Oy vey!* The stock market! I think I've been losing money for days."

"It'll bounce back, though, right?" Gina asked, only half paying attention to the pharmacist. Some nights, Gina helped out in the pharmacy until it closed at around eight thirty or nine p.m., before heading down to the Third Door. The speakeasy was a bit slower midweek, and the Signora hated idleness in any form.

"Who's to say?" Mr. Rosenstein asked, clearly agitated. He continued to read, periodically muttering strangled statements out loud. "The market keeps slipping and slopping around! Price currents are crisscrossing each other! Yesterday's volume was the smallest in weeks!" Finally, he set the paper aside with a huff. "This is bad, I'm telling you."

"Is it?" Gina asked. She didn't really understand the market, although her father had spoken recently about putting their small savings into stocks. Everyone she knew seemed to have been getting in on the action. Even the shoeshine guy who worked with a crate outside the barbershop had bragged about buying some stocks, but she didn't know how it worked.

"No stocks for me. I've just got all my money saved in a pickle jar at home," Benny chimed in, echoing her thoughts. Ever since she'd first met Benny back in early January, she'd known he'd been putting aside money from his paycheck to help pay for more education. He had his sights on Howard University, a college for black students, and wanted to stay on for medical school. His plan was to be one of the first black doctors in Chicago when he finished up in a few years. For a while now, Mr. Rosenstein had been helping him apply for a scholarship. "Under my bed," he added.

"Benny!" Mr. Rosenstein exclaimed, wagging his finger at his assistant. "For Pete's sake, no need to tell anyone where you hide your money. It's probably a good thing you didn't get into stocks—they've been fairly volatile."

"Probably worse to bet on the Cubs," Benny said. "They're still not looking so hot."

"*Ja*, don't do that either," the pharmacist agreed, diverted from the troubling stock market news. He'd grown keen on the American pastime after he emigrated from Germany before the Great War, and he and Benny had been glued to the radio for weeks, listening to the daytime games. "Down two! In our own town," Mr. Rosenstein grumbled.

"I thought we'd blow those A's away," Benny said, ready to recap the game, play by play, inning by inning. "After that home run by Jimmie Foxx in the third—hoo boy! A different game."

"Hornsby still hasn't returned to his MVP form," Mr. Rosenstein said.

"Well, the Cubs will get one back on Friday in Philadelphia. I just know it," Benny declared.

"They'd better!" Mr. Rosenstein replied. He glanced at his watch. "I'm going to run home, have some dinner with the missus, and then I'll be back to lock up. Gina, you're here another hour, right?"

"Yes, sir." Gina shook off a slight daze to answer him. She enjoyed spending time with Benny and Mr. Rosenstein, even when they were overly preoccupied with baseball standings and box scores, but she couldn't help tuning them out when they had been on the subject for a while.

She began to empty a crate of shampoos by lining each bottle on one of the lower shelves. She could tell from the disarray that whatever illicit bottles had been hidden in the crate's false bottom had already been removed. Still, that didn't keep her from sliding out one of the slats to reveal one of the empty hiding spaces. She shook her head, marveling at the cunning required to hide liquor in such ingenious ways.

Soon after Mr. Rosenstein left the drugstore, a very young woman, probably in her midteens, strolled in, casually surveying the shelves. Her clothes were current but cheap, as if she cared about being spiffy and stylish but didn't have the money, or perhaps the taste, to purchase better-quality outfits. Her jet-black hair was unusually long, not bobbed as most girls' hair was but pulled back in a loose bun at her neck. The careless effect somehow suited her. She didn't seem to be seeking anything in particular as she roamed the aisles.

Something about her surreptitious manner caught Gina's attention. She followed the girl over to the cosmetics section, stopping a few steps away at the end of the aisle. She watched the girl trail her fingers along the edge of one of the shelves, fingering the tubes of lipstick and jars of rouges, face creams and eye shadows. Her purse was open at her hip, as if she'd forgotten to snap it shut.

Gina watched the girl pick up a jar of wrinkle cream and read the label while her left hand closed over a tube of cherry lipstick. So quickly that Gina almost missed it, the girl dropped the tube straight into her open bag, with a flick of her wrist. Setting the jar back on the shelf, the girl shut her bag and continued down the aisle.

"You're a little young for wrinkle cream," Gina said pleasantly.

The girl looked startled. "Yeah, sure. You're right. I thought it was something else." She continued to wander down the aisle. "I put it back."

"What about that item in your purse? Are you going to put that back, too?" Gina asked. As the girl feigned a look of surprise, Gina shook her head. "Don't bother. I know you just nicked the lipstick."

"I don't know what you're talking about," the girl replied.

"Oh, that's the way you're going to play it?" Gina asked, her manner still pleasant.

The girl stiffened and looked like she was about to run, but shrugged. "Just wanted to look at it in better light." They both glanced through the window at the dark street beyond. The absurdity of her statement hung in the air. She put the tube back on the shelf. "Not my color anyway. Too pink for me."

Gina expected the girl to flee the store in embarrassment, but instead she remained where she was, looking miffed, as if she were the one who'd been wronged.

"I think you'd better leave," Gina warned the girl. "Or I'll have to have someone escort you out."

The girl glanced at Benny, who threw up his hands. "Not me," he said.

"Someone else," Gina said. Either Little Johnny or Gooch was just a shout away, at their customary perch that overlooked the alley, on the other side of the pharmacy's back door.

"Okay, settle down, would ya?" The girl's manner was downright infuriating now. "I just wanted to see who called the shots around here. Appears to be you."

"What do you mean?" Gina asked.

The girl took a step closer. They were nearly eye to eye, but Gina was a hair taller. "You happy with your hooch?" the girl whispered, sounding conspiratorial.

At her words, Benny stepped back behind the soda counter and began to wipe down the fountain. *This is your world, not mine*, she could almost hear him saying. Working for the owner of a speakeasy was just a temporary means to a very different end. Like Mr. Rosenstein, he didn't want to get involved with the goings-on below the shop. For this, Gina didn't blame him.

"No hooch here," Gina said, gesturing to the door. "Since you're not buying anything, it's time for you leave."

The girl put her hands on her hips. "You know what I heard? I heard you got a bum deal on a recent batch." When she smiled, she revealed sharp canine teeth, giving her a slightly feral appearance.

"Who told you that?" Gina asked, taking the girl by her elbow and dragging her to a corner, despite Benny's disapproving eye.

"The news is . . . around. Which brings me to my point. I'm here to extend you an offer."

"What? How old are you, anyway?" Gina asked, trying to hide her surprise. "Thirteen?"

"Fifteen." The girl's tone grew conspiratorial. "I got connections. I can bring you some good stuff, soon. Tonight even, if you want a sample."

"What's your name? Your *real* name."

"Stella." Of course no last name.

"I think it's time for you to go, Stella," Gina said. Though she'd only been employed at a speakeasy for ten months, she knew enough to know that this was not how deals were usually made.

Stella looked down at her polished fingernails in a bored way. "Heard someone died from stuff they drank here. Some others got real sick."

"Nah," Gina said. "The coroner's report is not in yet. That woman might have died of an overdose. Or killed herself. No one can say."

Stella's eyes widened, and her mischievous smirk widened. "Didn't know about a woman. I heard tell the person who died was a man. He'd been drinking here, all night I heard, and a few hours later he keeled over dead. Alcohol poisoning, doll. Something we know about in my line of work. Don't need no coroner to tell us so, either."

"Oh yeah? Some guy?" Gina said, trying to sound casual, even though her heart had started to pound. Her thoughts went immediately to Stan. "Who? What's his name? I didn't hear about any guy dying."

Stella leaned over. "Never caught his name. Not really my problem."

"Yeah, well, what happened to him?"

"He was found out on the street. Just a few blocks from here."

It couldn't be Stan, then, Gina thought with an immense sense of relief, glad that the newsboy's father had not succumbed to his illness. Still, news of another death was alarming. She tried to sound unconcerned. "Yeah? Well, maybe he was knocked off. Or died of natural causes or something."

"Maybe so," Stella said, clearly skeptical. "I'm just telling you what I've heard. I got a buddy who knows the guy who knows the other guy who found him. Found dead on the street, in a real nice suit. Young guy, too."

Stella's smile was sly as her hands stayed planted on her hips. "Everyone knows you're selling bad hooch out of this place. Caused people to get sick. Now you're saying that there were actually *two* deaths! In one week alone! Such a shame, really."

"What's it to you?" Gina asked.

"We supply Rinaldi's candy store with real good gin.

No one there's ever took sick." She paused, appearing to reconsider. "Not real sick, anyway."

"Good for you," Gina said, unable to hide her sarcasm.

Stella shrugged. "Healthy customers come back. Sick customers, well, they don't return, do they?"

When Gina didn't reply, Stella's tone grew conspiratorial. "Listen, I know you don't really call the shots down there. I was just teasing you before. I'm just asking that you deliver my message to the Signora, can you do that for me? I'll make it worth your while, too. Stop by Rinaldi's if you want to know more. They can tell you where to find me."

Without waiting for Gina to reply, Stella flounced off, letting the door bang behind her. Slowly, Gina righted several bottles that Stella had displaced on her way out, thinking about what the girl had just said. Could it be true? Had someone else, in addition to Fruma, died after drinking something bad at the Third Door? One death could be glossed over, perhaps, talked away as an unfortunate accident, but could two?

Gina could feel the sweat soaking her dress. *If news of a second death linked to the Third Door got out, what would happen to the speakeasy?*

Sitting down at the soda counter, Gina picked up the newspaper that Mr. Rosenstein had set aside earlier and flipped through the pages. Sure enough, when she looked at the newspaper carefully, she found a notice about a man who'd been found dead over on Polk Street. 28-YEAR-OLD STOCK TRADER FOUND DEAD. FOUL PLAY SUSPECTED.

Resting her head on her hand, Gina pored over the story.

A man's body had been discovered late Saturday afternoon
in a back alley. A cursory review by the medical examiner
suggested alcohol poisoning, although they were planning a
more thorough examination. Because he was not carrying a
wallet or any other identification, the police suspected he'd
been robbed, either when he was incapacitated or after he
was already dead. He was identified as Daniel Roth.

Gina studied the accompanying photograph. It depicted
a young man clad in a dark suit, with an arrogant jaw and
perfectly groomed hair that curled gently across his forehead. Had this man been at the Third Door? He certainly
looked familiar.

Daniel Roth. Daniel. Gina grew uneasy as recollections of
last Friday evening flooded back. He was, almost certainly,
one of the men whom Fruma and Adelaide had been been
cavorting with. Not the louder, more charming one they'd
been fighting over, but the one who had tipped with the ease
and arrogance of a man born to money.

Apparently Mr. Roth had not shown up to join his
family for dinner last Sunday night. Concerns only began
to emerge the next day, when his mother had telephoned the
bank and found that her son had not shown up at work on
Monday. At her insistence, the police had checked his posh
Gold Coast residence, where his servants informed them they
hadn't seen him since he'd left for work on Friday morning.
After checking area hospitals, the police discovered him at
the morgue, assigning an identity to Roth's corpse.

Gina rested her face in her hands as she thought back to
Friday evening. Daniel had seemed irritable, annoyed, jealous
maybe. Perhaps he'd already been feeling sick by that point.

It couldn't be a coincidence, could it? Fruma and Daniel getting deadly sick at the same time. The police and the newspaperman hadn't connected the two deaths. Yet Gina had, and now Stella had, too. It seemed only a matter of time before the news got out.

"Did we get many customers while I was eating supper?" the pharmacist asked, satisfied and revived by his wife's matzoh ball soup.

Benny shot her a warning glance. *Don't mention the conversation with Stella.*

Gina nodded. She wouldn't burden Mr. Rosenstein with knowledge he wanted nothing to do with. Like Benny, the pharmacist acknowledged that the Signora used his store to help cover her below-ground operations, but he had no wish to be more involved than necessary.

"It's been slow, so I've finished tidying up," she said. "In fact, would you mind if I left a few minutes early? I need to make a phone call before I head downstairs."

"*Ja*, sure thing," the pharmacist replied, rubbing his stout belly. "Maybe I'll have time to have another bowl before bedtime."

Gina hurried to the phone booth on the corner, dialing Nancy's number as soon as she had dug a nickel out of her purse. "Nancy," she said when the policewoman picked up on the other end, "did you hear the news about that financial guy who died? I think he was at the Third Door that night, too, along with Fruma and Adelaide. His picture looked familiar. I think he's one of the men that they left with. His name was Daniel Roth."

She paused. When Nancy didn't say anything, Gina continued in a burst. "Word on the street is that he got some bad hooch. From the Third Door." The silence on the other end of the phone was getting annoying. "Nancy, are you there?"

"I'm here. I'm just thinking," her cousin's voice came back, crackling now in irritation. "So this was all a case of bad spirits after all," she muttered, sounding angry and disappointed. "All right, well, a case is a case, and I'll take care of it."

An unpleasant sensation crossed over Gina. "Wait, Nancy," she said, a bit desperately. "What are you going to do?"

A harsh click on the other end indicated that Nancy had already ended the call.

Gina stared at the phone in her hand and slowly placed it back in its cradle, regret washing over her. *What did I just do?*

Then, more urgently, *What is Nancy going to do?* The unpleasant feeling persisted. *Do I need to tell the Signora? Did I just rat out the Third Door, and Billy Bottles?* That thought produced an actual sense of dread, and she went down to the Third Door, bracing for the worst.

CHAPTER 13

"Ned," Gina whispered to the piano player. "Can I get a swig?"

Although he raised a blond eyebrow, Ned slipped her his hip flask. After a couple of swallows of something that burned her throat, Gina began to settle into the rhythms and pacing of an ordinary evening at the speakeasy.

A whole night and day had passed since she'd made the phone call to Nancy, telling her cousin about Daniel Roth's death. Her shift last night had passed uneventfully, and her interactions with everyone had seemed typical, at least on their end. The whole time she had felt strained and wary, assuming at every moment that Nancy would come stomping into the Third Door, a legion of baton-waving policemen and Feds following behind her.

This morning she'd rung Nancy multiple times, even stopping by her house before work, wondering what her cousin had meant when she said she'd "handle" it.

Now, back at the Third Door, Gina was doing her best

to stop fidgeting. Maybe she'd misread Nancy's intentions. Maybe she wasn't going to do anything after all.

Tonight, only Lulu was working. Jade had gotten herself a gig over at the Sunset Café, which she'd been pretty excited about. Whatever arrangement the singer had worked out with the Signora seemed to suit them both, and Lulu never minded being the sole performer. Ned was on his break, leaving "Flag That Train" to play in the background. While a few patrons were tapping their toes to the lively beat or swaying a bit, no one had gotten up to dance. More people were smoking, causing a heavier haze to hang over the air.

Gina slipped into the back room to check on the men there. Roark was not there. She hadn't seen him for several days now. *Was he with Harriet?* she wondered.

Stop stewing over Roark, she told herself. She didn't know what she'd say when she saw him, anyway.

She turned her attention back to the customer she'd been serving. "Just one sec, doll," Gina said, expertly cutting the tip off the end of a White Owl cigar—Babe Ruth's brand. She handed the cigar to the portly gentleman, who flicked a quarter onto her tray.

When the music stopped, Gina threw on another jazzy piece, causing some patrons to sway and move with abandon. Sometimes she enjoyed it when the room got like this— there was more seduction and a different kind of wildness.

Through the smoky haze, Gina noticed Gooch escorting several people down the stairs. Her heart skipped when she recognized Nancy along with two policemen, though none of them were in uniform. One of them was Captain O'Neill, Nancy's supervisor, a decent enough cop who, as

Gina had learned earlier that year, was willing to weigh evidence before making a decision. Although she'd also seen him take a bribe, so she couldn't be sure where his loyalties were. She thought the other man might be Officer Dawson, whom she'd seen around.

Why are they here? Gina wondered, feeling sweat bead on her forehead.

Seeing them, Little Johnny sidled over. Gooch spoke with the bouncer before returning to his perch at the speakeasy door. Little Johnny slipped out, presumably to summon the Signora.

"Your cousin's back again, I see," Billy muttered. "What's she want now?"

"I don't know," Gina hedged, though her heart was starting to pound. *What is Nancy doing here? What is she going to say?*

Nancy looked over then, but her eyes were cool when their eyes met.

The Signora emerged and beckoned to Nancy and the two cops to follow her back to her private salon. Little Johnny followed them out of the room. The Signora's expression was smooth and reserved—she was not one to expose what she was thinking to others. Only a single strand of hair out of place suggested a sense of irritation. The patrons continued their private conversations and flirtations, oblivious to anything being amiss, which was just the way the Signora wanted it.

A short while later, Little Johnny emerged and stood beside the bar. Gina was near enough to hear what he said to Billy Bottles. "Take your break," he commanded the bartender. "The Signora wants to see you."

If he was surprised or worried, Billy didn't show it. He tossed his towel onto a shelf at the back of the bar. "Be right back." He glared at Lulu and Gina. "You can handle a few martinis between the two of you, right?"

Lulu gave a little squeal and immediately went behind the bar. Billy Bottles scowled. "Don't muck it up," he said to her.

"We won't," she said, a bit saucily. "Me and Gina, we make the best drinks."

"There'd better still be some booze here when I get back," the bartender grumbled.

As they passed by, Gooch gave Gina a long measured glance. There was a question there, and Gina felt herself flushing. She knew what that look meant. *How loyal are you?*

Gina could only guess what Nancy had told the Signora, including who had connected the dots. Maybe Adelaide. Maybe they knew it was her. What must they think of her? Why *hadn't* she given the Signora a heads-up about the two deaths and their possible link to the Third Door? She sighed. There wasn't anything she could to about it now.

A woman came staggering up to the bar then, her silvery evening gown a stark contrast to the pasty pallor of her face. "I'll have a Gin Blossom and a Bee's Knees," she said, enunciating each word carefully in an obvious effort to appear sober.

"Oooh!" Lulu exclaimed, practically clapping her hands. "Nifty! Let's do it!"

"I haven't made a Gin Blossom yet," Gina said, glad for the distraction of what was going on in the Signora's private salon. Over the last few months, she and Gina had been learning how to make a few of the most common cocktails, mostly from watching Billy's deft moves as they waited at the bar.

"You'll need gin, some elderflower liqueur, a bit of lime juice and some club soda," Lulu instructed, pointing to the bottles on the shelf. "Mix the first three ingredients before you shake the drink, but wait to add the club soda—! Oh no, Gina!"

Not heeding her warning in time, Gina had shaken the drink with the club soda already added, causing it to spray all over the front of her dress.

"—or it will fizz over," Lulu said, belatedly, trying not to laugh.

"Ugh, I'd better get changed," Gina said, looking down at her soiled dress. "This won't do."

"I'll clean this mess up," Lulu said, throwing a towel on top of the spreading puddle. "You go change."

As Gina hurried back to the women's salon to don her other dress, she could hear Billy shouting from behind the door of the Signora's private quarters. "Who says we're selling bad liquor!"

Gina stopped to listen. The Signora said something that Gina couldn't hear, but it sounded like she was trying to calm the bartender down. She pressed her ear to the door.

Then she heard Nancy, sounding more authoritative than Gina had ever heard her be before. "Two deaths were discovered Saturday. Both confirmed poisonings. Both individuals were confirmed by witnesses to have been drinking here, together, several hours prior to their deaths on Friday evening. There are accounts of other individuals who took violently ill as well." Nancy paused. "Seems fairly conclusive that it was due to the alcohol that was served here."

"I've heard enough of this!" Billy replied, and before Gina could jump out of the way, he'd burst out of the salon, striding past.

"Billy?" Gina asked, faltering at the fury of his movements. "Are you okay?"

Ignoring her, he grumbled the rest of the way down the short corridor. "Not my fault," he said. "Can't believe they're blaming me!"

Oh, dear, Gina thought, watching him kick the wall. *That's gonna hurt.*

She expected that he would turn down the long tunnel intended for rolling in barrels of beer and providing a quick exit for patrons in case of a raid. Instead he stalked back onto the speakeasy floor. Gina followed him.

"Keep serving, would ya?" he growled at Lulu, who happily agreed. "I'll be back in twenty. There's something I gotta do."

Gina glanced around the speakeasy. No one seemed to have noticed anything amiss, and their drinks all seemed well attended to. She sidled after the bartender, mindful of the fact that the front of her dress was still sporting a noticeable stain from the dousing from the Gin Blossom.

Moving off the main floor, Billy slipped into the secret stockroom behind the bar, where most spirits were kept. Gina followed him, fearful he might do something more to hurt himself. His foot had to be hurting from the wall he'd just kicked.

Gina pressed lightly on the stockroom door, half expecting that Billy would have locked it behind him. Yet it opened easily, and she slipped inside, surveying the space. Unlike the rest of the speakeasy, this place was dark and quiet, with just a few bare electric lights hanging from an untiled ceiling. There were rows of bottles, all resting horizontally. One section had wine; the other sections seemed to have bourbons, whiskeys, and gin. Probably the finer stuff was laid out neatly on the shelves. She'd rarely been in here, and she wasn't sure that she was welcome now.

Billy had his back to her, his arms crossed. He was staring at several crates that had been stacked in the corner. She coughed to alert him to her presence. "Billy," she said, "what gives?"

"That *cousin* of yours claims we put out a bad batch of alcohol. A few people died after drinking here last Friday night." He crossed himself, and out of a long-remembered habit, Gina did the same. "God rest their souls."

"*Did* you put out a bad batch?" she asked.

He growled an expletive at her, and she took a step back in shock. For an elderly man with a slight build, he had a fearful presence.

"Naturally not on purpose!" she added hastily, trying to soothe him. "Do you know which crate the bad alcohol was from? Maybe that would help you figure out if there's any of the bad batch left, and where you got it from."

He sighed, his fierce demeanor crumpling a bit. "I don't know. How can I know? I'll have to have the chemist come down and check everything. And that would mean we need to stop serving tonight."

Gina tried to remember what Fruma and Daniel had been drinking. "I think a few of the people who died had been drinking mainly sidecars. One of the other men who got sick—Stan—was drinking gin and tonics."

"So gin, sugar, simple syrup, mint . . ." He threw up his hands in an angry gesture. "I did get a few cases of gin that Friday morning. Local, not *imported*. Maybe that was the bad batch. That's the last case over here."

Local meant someone nearby had made the gin. Imported would mean brought in out of Canada through a port on Lake Michigan. There was a difference in quality, to be sure.

"Could be," Gina said. "How much gin do you go through every day?"

"Friday, Saturday were busy. Tuesday, Wednesday were slow. We had the Rum Runner special this week, so more rum than gin, I remember."

"Only a few people were sick . . . maybe just a single bad bottle, then, that you used in a single evening?" Gina asked, trying to work it all out.

Billy wasn't completely listening, though, intent on looking at the bottles in the case. She watched as he began to hold them up one at a time to the single light that gleamed dimly from the ceiling.

She watched Billy pull out a case and began to pull at the bottles. Kinsey's was the name on the label. "Not very neat, are they?" Gina said, looking at the slapdash way the label had been applied.

"Whaddya mean?" he asked, reaching for the bottle.

She showed it to him. "See?"

He slapped his head. "Oh, no! That punk!"

"What is it?" Gina asked. "Who are you talking about?"

Billy uncorked the bottle and smelled it, and then, before she could stop him, he poured a little onto his index finger and stuck it in his mouth.

"Oh, Billy!" Gina cried. "For heaven's sake, spit it out! What if you get poisoned?"

Billy grimaced. "That's some real rotgut. He must have mixed in some bad batch with the good stuff. May even have soaked off a label and slapped it on this bottle. Who's to say?" He made a punching motion with his fists. "What I do know is that I'm gonna take him down. Give him the old one-two punch."

"No, wait!" Gina exclaimed, her alarm growing. "Tell Gooch. Have him come with you."

"Not bringing him or any of the Signora's goons into this. Sometimes a man has to fight his own battles."

The bartender walked out the door and went down the tunnel toward the ladder that led to the gangway. As Gina hurried after him, she saw Roark enter the speakeasy.

"Gina, I was hoping to talk to you—" Roark began.

"No time now." She indicated the front of her dress. "I gotta go change before the Signora sees this mess."

"Oh, yeah, okay." He studied her. "I'll see you later, then."

"Sure," she said, pretending to move off to the ladies' dressing room. When Roark moved out of sight, Gina turned around and scurried after Billy, who was walking toward the ladder that led from the tunnel up to the gangway outside the speakeasy.

She didn't know why she didn't tell Roark what was going on, but it just seemed easier that way.

Billy moved quickly. *What can he be planning?* she wondered. The murderous look on his face might get him into trouble he couldn't handle. Although she wasn't sure she could handle it either, truth be told.

"Billy, wait!" she called.

"Go away," the bartender said over his shoulder, still striding down the gangway. "This doesn't concern you."

"What's going on, bearcat?" Roark asked, appearing suddenly at her side. He was panting slightly.

She turned toward him, squaring her shoulders. "What are you doing here?" she asked, not sure if she felt more irritated or glad that he had followed her out of the speakeasy.

"You looked worried. I knew you were up to something, not just changing your dress. Tell me, Gina. What's going on?"

"I'm afraid he's going to get himself killed," she said, watching Billy move swiftly toward the end of the street.

Roark followed her gaze, "Who, Billy? Come on, Gina. You gotta level with me here."

"I'll explain as we go."

As they followed the bartender, Gina quickly filled Roark in on how Nancy had arrived to inform the Signora and Billy about the two deaths, and their apparent connection to the Third Door. "His name was Daniel Roth, and he'd been drinking with Fruma. Both died a few hours later. Billy was fired up. Said he was gonna go have words with some guy, and I don't know what he's planning to do."

Roark whistled. "Well, that's his reputation on the line, to be sure."

"You think they'll close the Third Door? The police came in civvies, not uniforms," she said, panting at the effort it took for her to walk in her red high heels. When she stumbled a bit, Roark grabbed her arm, and she shook him off impatiently.

"Huh. Well, that says something," he said. "The Drys would've just busted up the joint. Sounds like they're willing to work with the Signora here. Still, two deaths from bad alcohol. No easy way out of that one." He paused. "So, two known dead, and some others who were violently sick?"

"Yeah. I know of one for sure. Stan Galinsky. His son is the newsboy who sells outside the drugstore. The boy told me his papa hadn't gotten up for days."

"That's too bad," Roark replied, but his mind seemed to be on something else. "Gina, I've been wanting to talk to you about something. Even before all this happened. I'd heard Harriet—"

"Your wife," Gina interrupted, looking away.

"Harriet's *not* my wife. Not really. She left me, as you may remember me telling you," he said, sounding irritated. "We've been separated for over a year. I had heard she was back in town and looking for me—"

"You didn't seem so separated the other night," Gina interrupted again. "When she kissed you."

"I know. I'm sorry." He sounded regretful. "That's Harriet for you."

Gina stayed silent. She wanted to say she didn't care,

that it was okay. The fact was, she did care. More than she wanted to.

"I heard you had a date," he said, looking straight ahead. "Sorry, word gets around."

When she didn't say anything, he sounded a little annoyed. "That guy Morrish—that bum's no good for you."

"And you are? Wait—shhh!"

They had reached Taylor Street, where it intersected with a small cross street that Gina did not usually frequent. As she looked around, she felt out of place, especially given the suggestive quality of her red dress. Wearing it in the speakeasy was one thing; out on the street was completely another. Roark, perhaps realizing the same thing, took off the jacket he'd been wearing and handed it to her. She wrapped it around herself, the light scent from his soap and aftershave wafting from the cloth.

Billy had come back into view as he passed under a streetlight. He was still swinging one of the bottles in a purposeful way. She touched Roark's arm and pointed. "Look, he's there. What's he doing?"

"I don't know," Roark said, edging himself in front of her. "Wait here."

"Not a chance." Pushing past Roark, Gina called out to the barkeep. "Billy!"

The bartender turned impatiently. "What are you doing here?" he barked. "Scram!"

"Please come back to the Third Door with us," she pleaded. "I don't want you to do anything stupid."

"They'll wish *they* hadn't done something so stupid," he said. He held the bottle by its neck and tapped it into his other hand, as a batter might do with his bat while waiting to swing.

"Billy," Roark said, "how about I come with you?"

"No," Billy said, his voice grim. "This I gotta handle myself. Wait here. I see him now."

Gina and Roark stood in the shadow of the building, watching Billy approach the two men lounging on the corner. Both men were close to a foot taller than the barkeep.

"Hoo boy," Gina murmured, her heart beginning to pound. "Maybe we should do something?"

The question hung in the air. She wasn't sure what they should do, anyway. Beside her, she could feel Roark's body tense as they both watched the scene unfold, unsure of what was going to happen.

All of a sudden, Billy swung the bottle at one of the men, cracking him hard over the head. The man staggered from the blow and then dropped to the ground.

"What the——?" Gina started to say, about to move forward, but Roark held her back.

Billy smashed the bottle on the wall, so that it cracked in half, leaving a dripping, jagged mass in his hand. He brought the jagged edges up to the second man's neck while the man cringed against the brick wall. "Where'd you get this stuff, Nate? I'm warning you, don't lie to me. You already crossed me once, you'd best not cross me again."

Behind them the man on the ground had begun to stir. Before Roark could stop her, Gina ran over and stepped on his arm, with just enough weight to keep him pinned to the ground. He sagged back, putting his free hand to his forehead with a groan.

Nate continued to look belligerent, despite the broken bottle that Billy was waving near his face. At the sight of Roark though, the defiant look in the man's eyes disappeared. *He's gonna squeal*, Gina thought, and sure enough Nate began to spill what he knew. "Yeah, I got some of the bottles from another guy. Half the cost. Mixed them in. Figured you'd never notice."

"I paid you ten dollars for the lot," Billy growled, bringing the jagged edge back to the man's throat again.

Cautiously, Nate put his hand in his pocket and pulled out a money clip. "Here you go," he said, peeling off a few fives. "Something for the inconvenience."

Billy pocketed the cash with a grunt, keeping the bottle at the man's throat.

Gina was still puzzled. "Did you put the labels on yourself, then?"

"Yeah, easy enough to soak the labels off and paste them back on."

"Sloppy," Gina said.

Nate shrugged. "Gotta make a living."

"Who'd you get the hooch from?" Billy pressed. "The Stanleys? Heard they took over the alky cookers around here, back when the Genna brothers got knocked out of the business."

Oh the Genna brothers. Gina remembered how they'd come to a less than glamorous end. Clearly there'd been some other crime boss who'd jumped in to take up the slack. In this case, the Stanleys must have a few henchmen who would make the rounds, first providing one-gallon copper pots to needy home brewers in the area, delivering the corn sugar

and yeast to them, and returning a week or so later to collect
the bottles of newly fermented liquor. A nice profit could be
turned in this illegal liquor trade, although probably only
a pittance would be seen by the gin-making families themselves.

At first Nate didn't want to reveal his source, but as Billy
pressed the bottle ever so slightly into the man's throat, he
sighed. "That batch I sold you was made by my granny, all
right?"

Billy pulled back the bottle. "Granny Brown?"

"Yeah," the man replied, looking sheepish. "I just
wanted to get her a little more money."

"That's a risky venture," Billy said. "Cutting out the
Stanleys like that. You could get her killed!"

"We gotta talk to Granny Brown," Roark said. He
glanced curiously at Gina. "You want me to walk you back
first?"

Gina glanced at her watch. They'd been gone far longer than her break allowed. Might as well go all in, at this
point. She shook her head in answer to his unspoken question. "I'm coming, too."

Roark and Gina followed Nate to a nearby flat. The man
Gina had been keeping pinned down with her high heel had
gotten up and walked hurriedly in the opposite direction,
not wanting to take part in the forthcoming altercation.
Billy and Nate walked ahead.

"Don't try to warn her," Roark said to Nate.

They followed him up to a second-floor flat. The pun-
gent smell of corn sugar and yeast, mixed in with the regular

stench of daily living, overwhelmed them as they moved down the corridor to the last door at the end. Gina pressed her hand to her mouth and nose to keep from gagging.

Nate unlocked the door and beckoned them into a small living room that was completely covered in lace doilies. All three men removed their caps as they entered. An old woman was sitting on a sofa knitting, a small brown dog at her feet. A baby tied into a bouncing chair was rocking happily, sucking on the metal bell of her rattle. The radio was on, and a man's baritone was singing an aria from an Italian opera.

The woman switched off the radio abruptly, staring at them all suspiciously. Her gaze lingered on Gina's red cocktail dress, which could be seen under Roark's jacket. "What's this, Nate?"

"Mrs. Brown," Billy said, taking off his cap. "Seems like Nate here sold me a bad batch of gin the other day. Made some of my patrons sick. Says he got it from you."

"Oh, that you, Billy? My eyes aren't so good anymore." Her eyes flicked toward Roark. "He a Dry? What about *her*?" Her eyes returned to Gina's skimpy silk dress. "We don't need your sort of business here."

Your sort of business? Gina almost pulled the coat around her to cover up, then stopped. Suddenly she didn't care one bit about what the people in this room thought about her.

Roark said, "Can we try the batch you've just finished up? I can get a chemist to test it. See if it's making people sick."

"You should be talking to the Stanley brothers. Their hooch is bad."

"Well, I don't order from them," Billy replied. "At least I didn't. May have to now. Just gotta try what you've been making."

"Gonna cost you for a sample," she said.

"Oh, for heaven's sake," Gina began, but Billy handed the woman a dollar.

Granny Brown plucked the baby out of the bouncing chair and led the way into the kitchen, the brown dog at her heels. The kitchen table was completely covered by the still, a one-gallon copper alky cooker. The counter was covered with beet slices and potato peels, and something was simmering in the still. Some dark jars labeled JUNIPER OIL and BOOT'S GLYCERIN were lined up along the counter as well. Gina stepped a little closer to the still, interested in how the parts fit together.

A blanket covered part of the table. Nate pulled the blanket off, revealing a number of bottles, some filled, some empty. Pulling out three small glasses, he popped open one of the bottles and was about to pour out.

"No," Roark said. "We'll just take a bottle with us. Can't risk being sick."

Billy had already slung back his shot. With a grimace he wiped his mouth on his sleeve. "Some real rotgut there." He gave Nate a warning look. *Don't ever try to sell this to me again.*

Nate nodded, getting the silent message.

They left, just as the baby started to cry. To soothe him, the woman dipped a small towel into the hooch and then into some sugar and gave it to the baby to gnaw on. "Teething," she said, her gruff expression growing more tender as she looked down at the child. "Gin and a bit of sugar helps every time."

When they returned to the Third Door alley entrance, Billy Bottles went back inside without a word. Gina slipped off Roark's jacket and handed it back to him. "Thanks."

"Hang on a second, would you?"

"I really need to go—"

"Gina, please let me talk to you. About Harriet."

"Roark, I don't really have anything to say about that." She rapped on the door, three knocks in quick succession. Little Johnny opened it.

"Coming?" she asked Roark.

"Not if you're too busy to talk to me." He held up the bottle he'd taken from Nate's granny. "Besides, I'm going to take this to the forensics lab. The chemists there can check it right away."

"What, you're going now?"

"Yeah, I'd like to help Billy clear his name as soon as possible. I'll let you know what the scientists at the lab say."

"Okay, well . . ." Her voice trailed off. "I'll be going now," she said.

He grabbed her arm. "Don't go out with Morrish again."

"What? Hey, you can't tell me what to do." She shook off his hand. When Little Johnny coughed in a parental way, she added, "Let me know what you find out."

She stalked back inside, leaving Roark by the speakeasy entrance. Little Johnny looked slightly amused but didn't say anything. If he was curious about what Billy, Gina, and Roark had been doing in the middle of a shift, he hid it well.

CHAPTER 14

"The Cubs got one back!"

"We'll take those A's yet!"

"Hornsby better keep that bat swinging!"

The mood in the back room was raucous, as the ex-servicemen hooped and hollered about the third game of the World Series that had been played that afternoon at Philadelphia's Shibe Park.

Out on the speakeasy floor, there were more whispers than shouts, as news about last night's raid on Capone's gaming joint spread. It had happened on South Michigan Avenue and had taken nearly the full detective force from the state attorney's office.

Maybe that was why the police hadn't been in uniform when they spoke to the Signora, Gina thought. *Maybe they didn't want to spook the other operation by the Drys.*

No one brought up the police visit to the Third Door the night before. She'd felt a wariness from the other staff—after all, this was not the first time she'd brought the police to their doorstep. The cops had probably been paid off, as they usually were. Still, even they wouldn't keep looking the other way if the two deaths were proven to be connected to the Third Door.

"I heard the men barricaded themselves inside," Ned said, still talking about the raid. "Took the Feds their all to smash down the doors."

"Fifty-four men arrested in one go!" Lulu whispered. "Can you imagine? Sounds like the Feds confiscated everything. Tables, racehorse sheets, roulette wheels, you name it."

Gina nudged Lulu. "Was Luke there or something? You seem to know a lot about it!"

"Yeah, and William, too. They both got out right before the detectives came."

"Lucky there wasn't a shootout," Jade commented, admiring her new bracelet. She hadn't wasted any time spending the extra cash she'd picked up from performing at the Sunset Café. "They all could have been killed. Another bloodbath."

Gina shivered at her words, remembering how shocked they'd been back in February when members of the Moran gang had been shot down by rival gang members disguised as policemen. The St. Valentine's Day Massacre had turned the whole city upside down.

"That's for sure," Ned replied.

"I wouldn't want to be around Mr. Capone right now. He's gotta be plenty mad," Billy said, pretending to swing an invisible bat. Seeing Gina flinch, he grinned. "Just thinking about the Cubs, doll."

"Smoke, sir?" Gina asked, speaking to an older man sitting alone at a corner table. He was dressed in a fine gray suit, and his hands were clasped together on the table. Despite his loosened tie, he had a genteel old-money quality. He looked less like one of the Loop business crowd who had strayed a bit off the beaten track than a man who should have been out drinking fine rum on a yacht. When he jumped at her words, she put her hand to her mouth. "Oh! So sorry to startle you, sir!"

He swept his eyes over her tray. "Got any Preferencias?"

She knew that was a high-end Cuban cigar, and not one she usually kept stocked on her tray. "I'm not sure, sir. I can check the humidor in the back. It may take me a few minutes."

He gave a weary wave of his hand. "That's fine. I'm not in a hurry. I'm just here for a smoke. Just some club soda, if you would."

Gina put in the order with Billy and got instructions on where to find the Cuban cigars in the walk-in humidor behind the bar, which was connected to the rarely used cigar room. The Signora's husband, Big Mike, used to entertain high spenders in here, but she'd never seen the Signora do so.

She unlocked the cigar room and entered the humidor. As she regarded the beautiful inlaid oak cabinets, she thought about what Billy had told her. Cigars from Cuba in the first cabinet, cigars from Europe in the middle, and those from the United States in the beautiful boxes to the far left. The shelves extended far above her head, so she dragged over the small step stool that Billy kept in the corner. She had just climbed up to peer at the names on the boxes when she heard a voice behind her.

"Very impressive." It was the man who had ordered the Preferencia.

"Oh, sir," she said, realizing that she'd forgotten to lock the cigar room door behind her. "Customers aren't supposed to come back here. Billy's orders."

The man didn't move, but his eyes were still traveling over the cigars. "There they are," he said, pointing to a different area of the humidor.

"Thank you," she said, dragging the step stool over. "How about I bring them out, and you can select—"

"I just wanted to see the place that killed my son."

"Sir—?" Gina asked, starting to feel nervous. The muffled noise from the speakeasy seemed very far away.

"My son, Daniel Roth. I was told that he was here that night. Got himself poisoned by the swill they serve here." His eyes filled with tears. "He should have been home that night. His mother was expecting him for dinner that weekend. Now he'll never be home again." He approached one of the two leather chairs that were on one corner of the cigar room and sank down in one. "I lost my b-boy!"

"I don't know what to say," Gina said, her hands clutching the silk folds of her dress. "I'm so sorry for your loss."

"Uh, Gina—Miss Ricci, are you all right?" A woman appeared in the doorway. It was Alma. She glanced at the man, who had started to weep into his hands. "I saw him follow you in, and I—shall I go fetch Gooch?"

"Yes, please," Gina said gratefully. She went over to the man and sank down beside him, then turned on the small Tiffany lamp on the table beside the chair. She turned back to Alma. "He may need to find the Signora, too."

Instead of leaving, Alma continued to watch them, concern etched on her face. "Will you be all right?"

"I'll be fine. Please, get Gooch."

A few minutes later, Gooch entered with the Signora behind him, guarded looks on both their faces. Alma had trailed after them. "We'll handle this, Gina," the Signora said crisply, taking in the man's still-slumped position. She looked meaningfully at Alma, who darted away with a nervous squeak. Mr. Roth hadn't moved or said anything else. "Later you can tell us exactly how you allowed *this* to happen."

When Gina came back out, she stood at the bar for a moment, trying to collect herself. The encounter with the senior Mr. Roth had frightened and concerned her. Seeing his grief firsthand had been hard to take.

Alma sidled up to her. "Everything okay now?" she asked, touching Gina's arm in concern.

"Yes," Gina replied. "Thanks for getting Gooch. He's handling it. Well, the Signora will, that's for certain."

"That man—I heard what he said," Alma said, lowering her tone. "About that man's son getting poisoned here. What happened?"

Gina frowned. "Maybe some bad alcohol," she replied, turning her head so that Billy wouldn't hear her. "It's hard to say." Knowing that the Signora wouldn't like her to engage in speculation or gossip, she smiled at the woman as she ended the conversation. "I've got to take some drink orders. The girls are getting ready to take the floor. Thanks again."

A while later, Gina was balancing her drink tray when she saw the Signora escort Mr. Roth across the room, her arm linked firmly in his. She could see that Mr. Roth was

clutching an unlit cigar in his hand. Probably a few more of
those fine ones had been tucked away into his vest pocket.

After she had laid down a pair of Negronis, Gina felt
a firm tap on her shoulder. She turned to face Gooch, who
was looking more stern and tough than usual. "Gina," he
said, "Mr. Roth should not have been allowed in the cigar
room or the humidor. That room is off-limits to patrons,
unless specifically invited by the Signora."

"I know, sir. I'm sorry. He wanted a very specific cigar,
and Billy was busy. I must have left the door open behind
me, and he followed me in and then started crying and—"
She gulped.

"Gina." At his tone, Gina shut her mouth abruptly and
waited for him to continue. "You're to let me know immediately if Mr. Roth approaches you or anyone again. We
don't want any trouble. He's just the sort that could cause us
trouble. *Capiche?*"

"I think he was just upset about his son's death . . ." Her
voice trailed off as Gooch continued to regard her impas-
sively. *"Capisco,"* she added lamely. The message, as always,
was clear.

"Heard you were poking around Granny Brown's place the
other day."

Gina glanced at Stella, who was standing in the alley,
her hands perched defiantly on her hips and her jet-black
hair pulled back in a loose chignon. The young bootlegger
was probably just out of the bouncer's sight from his perch
on the other side of the green door.

Stella had clearly been waiting for her before she began her Saturday evening shift.

"Who told you that?" she asked, trying to mask the odd wave of apprehension that had flooded over her. She got the feeling that Stella had been waiting for her.

"Doesn't matter who told me," Stella replied. "I know it's true. Don't even try to deny it."

Gina shrugged and pushed past Stella, toward the Third Door. "I'm not."

Stella grabbed her arm. "Did Granny Brown sell you the bad stuff? I bet it was her."

When Gina didn't answer, Stella continued. "Did you tell Billy and the Signora that we can get them a better deal? Supply you with spirits that won't kill off your customers?"

Gina shook off her arm. "Leave me alone."

"Did you talk to them?"

"No!" Gina said, banging on the door. "Now scram."

"You'll be sorry!" Stella cried as the Third Door swung open and Little Johnny appeared, crossing his arms in front of his chest.

"Good evening, Gina," he said, opening the door for her. He scowled at Stella. "Move along."

For a moment she stared at him, but when he stepped forward, his jacket swung open, displaying his handgun as he towered over her. "I said, move along."

This time, Stella did not need to be told twice. She turned and walked away.

CHAPTER 15

Gina brushed the rain from her bluish gray cocoon coat before handing it to the Doyles' maid. "Here you go," she said, trying to act nonchalant in the midst of the elegant splendor that pervaded her great-aunt and -uncle's posh North Side home. "Will you let my aunt and uncle know that I'm here?"

"The Doyles just sat down for luncheon," the maid said.

Gina glanced at her watch. *Jeepers, I'm five minutes late. Stupid motor coach!*

"They asked me to bring you straight in when you arrived. Although, perhaps"—she gave Gina an anxious smile—"you'd like to freshen up first?"

Without waiting for her consent, the maid led Gina to a nearby powder room to primp for a few minutes. Just as well, too. Her mauve cloche hat, while charming on, had flattened her hair into a bell-shaped helmet, and her mascara had smeared a bit in the rain. She thought about scrubbing it all off, but instead applied the deeper red lipstick she'd been wearing for several months now. *I don't really owe them anything,* she thought. *I don't have anything to prove, either. They cut us out of their lives—Mama, Papa, Aidan, me. If anything, they owe* me.

Smoothing down her blue polka-dotted dress, she remembered the first time she'd visited the majestic house, back in January after the funeral of her cousin Marty Doyle. She'd never met any of them before—her sweet mama had effectively been banished from the family home when she married her papa. Gina had never known why they'd been so angry about her mother's choice—maybe because back then he'd still been Frankie the Cat, a man who got into scrapes working for the Signora's father-in-law and was a boxer to boot. Maybe it was because they'd wanted their dear daughter to marry into the Daleys or any of the other rising Irish political families.

Soon after, she'd learned that Marty had left everything to her, as the surviving issue of her late mother. They'd been so suspicious of her motives at first, especially Nancy. Yet it was Nancy who'd filled in some of the gaps she'd been so desperate to close.

The maid ushered her into the richly paneled mahogany dining room, where she found Charlotte and John Doyle, her great-aunt and great-uncle, already seated at either end of a very long table, with Nancy seated glumly in between.

"Hello, Aunt Charlottle, Uncle John," she said to each in turn. "Nancy," she added more stiffly. *How could you have betrayed me?* She wanted to scream it at her cousin, but naturally she refrained.

"So glad you could join us, Gina dear," John murmured, kissing her cheek.

"Finally," Charlotte added. "Please sit." She nodded at the maid. "You may serve the soup now."

Leek and potato, her favorite. Gina picked up her spoon and plunged it into the bowl, her mouth watering in anticipation. Her aunt gave her a stern look. "John, if you'll say grace."

Reluctantly, Gina set her spoon back down and put her hands in her lap while her uncle said a short prayer of thanks.

"Amen," she said when he was done, and quickly downed a spoonful.

"So the Signora is still holding on alone, even after Big Mike is out? Still running the business on her own? No outside help? No one else pulling the strings?"

"Just her," Gina replied, still working eagerly on the soup. Certainly she couldn't imagine anyone else other than the Signora running the day-to-day operations of the Third Door. Even before her husband, Big Mike, had been sent to the Joliet penitentiary for breaking a variety of laws, the Signora had been the steel and stone that kept the Third Door in place.

Having sopped up the last bit of soup with some brown bread, Gina watched sadly as the maid whisked her bowl away. She had hoped she might have another serving. Happily, though, a moment later, the maid reappeared with roasted lamb and cabbage, and she dug in again.

"Delicious," she said, smiling up at the maid.

The red-cheeked maid smiled brightly. "I'll let Cook know."

Her aunt leaned forward. "Gina," she said when the

maid had left the room again, "we've heard some troubling news about the Third Door. Two patrons died after drinking there! So shocking. Please, tell us all about it."

Gina glanced at Charlotte. Despite her look of concern, there was an excited gleam in her eyes. *I hadn't taken Aunt Charlotte to be so bloodthirsty,* Gina thought. She glared at her cousin. "I would have thought *Nancy* would have given you a full accounting." *Like you told the Signora, even though I asked you not to.*

"We'd like to hear it from you, dear," John added.

Well, that's peachy, Gina thought. *He's bloodthirsty, too.*

Nancy abruptly stood up. "Excuse me," her cousin said. "I have to use the loo."

"Such vulgar language, dear," Charlotte said to her daughter. "You are excused."

When Nancy stalked out of the room, Gina's aunt and uncle turned expectantly back to her. "Nancy never tells us anything," John said with some disgust. "So why don't you tell us all about it."

Unsure how much to disclose, Gina went with what might get reported in the papers. "It's simple, really," she said. "It looks like some customers may have gotten some bad liquor, which ended up poisoning them. Other people got sick, but as far as we know, no one else died."

Both tsk-tsked. "However could that have happened?" Charlotte asked.

"It seems that Billy *might* have bought a case or two of gin from"—she thought about Nate's granny with her kitchen still—"a *less experienced* supplier. That will never happen again."

"We worry about you, dear," Charlotte said. "So many

rough people where you work. Not to mention, their suppli-
ers seem questionable. You seem so unprotected there."

Gina pushed her plate away. "Do you mean you want
me to quit?"

"Oh, no, dear! Quite the opposite," John replied, his
smile tight. "We're very interested in the Third Door."

Gina stared at him. "Why are you interested in the
Third Door?"

At his wife's cough, John fell silent.

"Let's just say that we think we could offer the Signora
some help," Charlotte said easily. "We'd like to see you all
protected a bit more. Perhaps you could help us arrange a
meeting. We haven't been successful in this regard."

"What kind of meeting?" she asked, staring down at the
porcelain bowl. *What was all this protection they were speaking of?*

"Oh, this and that," Charlotte replied.

"The Signora is very busy," Gina started to say, before
sinking under her aunt's stare. "Y-yes, I can let her know
that you'd like to speak with her."

"Good," Charlotte replied, looking satisfied. She looked
over at her husband. "Now tell Gina why we asked her to
come here today."

So there was a different reason? Gina wasn't sure if she should
feel relieved or not.

"Yes indeed." John pulled a small envelope from his vest
pocket and pushed it toward her. "Just to help you pay the
rent on Marty's apartment for another six months. Or other
expenses you might be facing."

Gina peered inside and saw a wad of bills. Had to be at
least two hundred dollars. Not for the first time, she wondered

exactly how the Doyles had made their wealth. "Jeepers! Thank you, but I can't take such a sum—"

"You can and you will," Charlotte said, looking slightly less stiff. "We were out of your life for too long."

"Th-thank you, Aunt Charlotte," Gina said, feeling more warmth than she had in a long time. Then her great-aunt's next words completely dampened all the good feelings she'd been experiencing.

"Just be sure to set up that meeting with the Signora."

"Wait a sec, Gina," Nancy called to her as they left the Doyles' house a painful half hour later. Once they were allowed to leave, Gina had rushed out the door and was halfway down the walk, donning her coat and hat as she walked. Her cousin was pulling on her coat and clomping quickly toward her, holding her stodgy rain boots in one hand.

"I'm a little irked at you, if you can't tell," Gina replied, striding off, wanting to break away from her cousin. The only problem was that she was wearing black patent leather one-strap pumps that she'd worn to impress her aunt and uncle, and they were already starting to rub her heels raw and cause painful blisters.

"Believe it or not, I can tell." Nancy pulled her boots on as she walked, hopping along the way. She glanced at the sky. "At least it stopped raining. Might start again soon, though."

Drat! Gina thought. She'd left her good umbrella at the Doyles'. She had no interest in going back for it, though.

"So what gives? Why the bad mood? I know my parents can be a handful, but—"

"What possessed you to bring the police to the Third Door?" Gina demanded, not slowing her pace. "The Signora and the others may not trust me now."

Nancy drew herself up, no longer goofing around. "What *possessed* me was my belief that some wrongdoing had occurred. I am a police officer, after all, sworn to uphold the law."

Gina sniffed. "Were you upholding the law when you asked me to come and take photographs before calling the police?"

Nancy stood stock-still. "That was different," she muttered, but Gina could tell her retort had hit its mark. Then Nancy's bravado returned. "Besides, it turns out I was right, wasn't I? Wrongdoing *did* occur at the Third Door." She hesitated. "Just not in the way I thought."

"What do you mean?" Gina asked, giving Nancy a sidelong glance.

"I got a call this morning. Some news I really shouldn't share with a *civilian*."

"What's your news?" Gina asked.

Nancy began to wheeze. "Hey, can you stop for a moment? I need to sit down."

"Let's sit here," Gina said, gesturing toward a black iron bench by a small stone fountain. From the looks of it, the fountain hadn't been in use for a long time. She sat down, slipping out of her shoes to examine her stockinged feet. Her blisters felt like they were going to burst.

Nancy sank down beside her. "No one would tell me anything directly, of course. This came to me through the pal of a pal. Had to go outside my own department to get the answers. Those corrupt rats!"

Taking a deep breath, Nancy seemed prepared to draw out the details and fume once again about being left out of important conversations and decisions. "I mean, this is my case!" she said, hopping off the bench and pacing around it. "Captain O'Neill said it was. They don't have to treat me like I'm just a dim-witted child."

"Nancy, you're killing me. What's the news?"

"The coroner's report came back on Fruma Landry," Nancy said.

Gina grabbed Nancy's arm. "Oh yeah? What did it say?"

"She had no cocaine in her system. She died from arsenic poisoning."

"Arsenic!" Gina repeated, startled. That was not what she was expecting. "How did that happen?"

Nancy shrugged. "We don't know. Not yet."

Gina continued to think through the implications of the report. "So not a bad batch of alcohol, which will make Billy Bottles happy, at least. Not an accidental overdose of cocaine, either." Her hand flew to her mouth. "That means that someone poisoned Fruma. People don't commit suicide with arsenic, do they?"

Nancy pursed her lips. "Well, sometimes. Some people will use anything they can find to kill themselves. Still, you're right. That seems less likely. Particularly since it doesn't sound like she was melancholic before she passed."

Gina shut her eyes. "So when did the poisoning happen, do they know?"

"Well, the coroner estimates that she took the poison a few hours before she died," Nancy said. "Apparently the content of Fruma's stomach showed a very large dose of poison, but she'd not yet had a chance to digest it."

Gina sighed. "She arrived at the Third Door around eight or half past. I remember her telling the others she felt sick, a few hours later, right when they were all leaving. Maybe around eleven o'clock?" She shook her head. "The Signora will *not* be happy if a poisoning happened there. It was bad enough to imagine that Billy had bought a bad batch and caused some accidental deaths."

Following her own line of thought, Nancy rapped the metal arm of the bench with her knuckles. "I *knew* all along there was something off about Fruma's death. Seems I was right." She chuckled.

Gina stared at her. "You seem pretty cheerful about this."

"Well, I'm certainly not pleased that my neighbor was killed," Nancy said, exasperated. "That's unpleasant. Still, when I catch her killer—well, that's a promotion!"

"Is that what Captain O'Neill told you?"

Nancy made a rude gesture with her fingers. "Well, the captain will have gotten the coroner's report, too. I'm sure he's going to take over the investigation, unless I can prove to him I can handle it." She banged the arm of the bench again, then pulled a small flask out of her coat pocket. After a quick look around, she took a gulp, sputtering as she swallowed. Seeing Gina's expression, she chuckled grimly. "Helps me get through visits with the parents." She took another swig.

Gina studied her cousin. There had to be more to this sudden nervous drinking. "Something else is bothering you, Nancy. I can tell. Spill it."

Nancy made an impatient sound, and then slumped down in seeming defeat. "I don't know how to sort through all of this. I don't know what's the next step." She groaned. "How will I ever prove myself to them? This is what detectives are supposed to do."

Her unexpected vulnerability was surprising. Gina had only ever seen Nancy pushing blindly along, relying on grit, instinct, and surprise. Maybe the detective correspondence course was helping her be more methodical.

"Let's talk this through," Gina said, pulling on her lower lip. "What about the other victim, Daniel Roth? Did he die of arsenic poisoning, too?"

"The coroner hasn't finished his autopsy yet. Soon, though."

"Could Fruma's drinks have been laced with arsenic? Why? Who would have done that?" Gina continued to think back to that evening, striving to remember what she had noticed. "She and Daniel were both sick, but George and Adelaide were not."

"Could Fruma have been targeted for some reason?" Nancy asked, after digesting Gina's words. "She seemed to have made some enemies. Who would have hated her enough to kill her?" She snapped her fingers. "Her ex-fiancé was there that night. Maybe he was jealous."

"Could be." Gina thought about Vidal. He seemed more forlorn than vindictive. "Why poison Daniel, then, and not George? It was George that Fruma was flirting with, trying to make Vidal jealous. Although the more I think about it, I don't actually think George drank much, either. Fruma kept drinking his drinks as well as her own."

"What about Adelaide? Was she drinking, too?" Nancy asked.

Gina thought about their encounter in the ladies' room at the Third Door. The necklace that swung out of Adelaide's dress. How the woman's nose had bled. "I think Adelaide was high on cocaine," she said slowly. "I don't think she was drinking much at all."

"You said that Adelaide seemed jealous of Fruma," Nancy said, beginning to pace.

"Yes, I suppose so. Enough to murder her? I don't know." Gina remembered how Stan had stumbled down the alley, holding his stomach. "That also doesn't explain Stan Galinsky, since he was violently ill the same evening. That couldn't be a coincidence, could it?"

Nancy waved her hand. "So what are you saying? You think they were all poisoned? Who would do that?"

Gina's heart began to pound as a thought came to her. "Could someone have added arsenic to a whole bottle of gin? And those three—Fruma, Daniel, and Stan—were unlucky enough to have gotten lethal doses?"

Nancy looked startled. "A random attack? Why would someone do that?"

"Why not? There have been close to a hundred bombings in Chicago this year," Gina replied. "The people who do that kind of thing don't care who they hurt. Maybe someone has a personal grievance against the Signora. Maybe they wanted to send her a message by poisoning her patrons."

"That seems a bit far-fetched," Nancy said. Though her words were dismissive, her forehead was puckered in thought.

"At lunch just now, your parents told me that the Third Door needs protection," Gina added, seeing that Nancy still looked skeptical. "More than what Little Johnny and Gooch can provide. While you were powdering your nose, they asked me to set up a meeting with the Signora."

The mocking smile faded from Nancy's face. "Gina, do you have any idea who my parents *are*? What they *do*?"

Gina swallowed. Nancy's tone made the hackles on her neck rise. "No," she whispered.

"Let's just say that their interest in protecting the Third Door is not about protecting *you*." Nancy's voice was hard, furious. "My parents' family has been controlling joints across the North Side, and now they must be eyeing the Third Door. Right now it's in the No Man's Land. Not occupied by Capone, and the Irish have left you alone, too, right? They're vying to get in. Offering protection is the first step."

Gina slumped back on the hard bench as the mysterious pieces of a puzzle began to fit together. How the Doyles wanted her to stay working at the Third Door. About their bodyguards. About their interest in meeting with the Signora. "Your parents were very interested in knowing more about who had died, but they weren't surprised," she said slowly. "I thought you had told them."

"Of course not. I don't tell them anything. They've got their spies."

Another unpleasant thought came to her then, and she

hesitated to put it into words. "The arsenic . . . would your parents have—?" She couldn't finish the thought.

Nancy handed her the flask and waited for her to take a deep swallow. "Gina, my parents are ruthless. I know that. Heck, I've always known it. Marty knew it, too. So did your mother. In fact, I think that's why she was so ready to leave the family when your papa came along." Nancy rubbed her forehead. "Whether they would do what you're suggesting . . . I hope to God not. Truly, I don't know." She grabbed Gina's arm. "Don't breathe a word of this to anyone. For your own good."

Feeling a little shaky, Gina glanced at her watch. Her mind was whirling from the revelations and the vodka from Nancy's flask. "The next motor coach will be coming soon. I'd hate to miss it."

As they walked toward the stop, Nancy said, "For what it's worth. I don't think Adelaide is in the clear, not by a long shot. That whole necklace issue just doesn't sit well with me."

"Me neither," Gina agreed cautiously. It would certainly be less troublesome to hang Fruma's death on Adelaide than to think someone was engaging in a vendetta to bring the Signora into line.

"I'm still going after Adelaide," Nancy declared as the red motor coach came into view. "I just have to convince Captain O'Neill to keep me on the case."

"That doesn't really explain everything—" Gina began, before getting cut impatiently off by Nancy.

"It explains enough!" Nancy said as they mounted the steps. "You'll see."

CHAPTER 16

Gina added a few more cookies to the plate that her papa was sharing with their upstairs neighbor, Mrs. Hayford. Yesterday, she'd shown her father the money the Doyles had given her, and he wasn't impressed. "They had plenty of time to make up for what they did to you and your mother," he'd told her. "Go ahead and take their money if you want, but just remember that their gifts have strings."

Now, he was focused on the fifth game of the World Series, being played in Philadelphia. He and Mrs. Hayford were seated at the kitchen table, their gray heads close to the radio, listening grimly to the announcer's play-by-play.

Like her papa, Mrs. Hayford had been widowed for well over a decade, and over that time the pair had developed a close friendship. *Someone's making an effort*, Gina thought, smiling down at her neighbor. Mrs. Hayford had gotten her hair done and had painted her lips with a pretty shade of pink. Her day dress, which had clearly been turned and dyed, had been meticulously starched and ironed. Whether her papa would notice that effort, or understand what it might mean, was another issue altogether.

Right now, they were completely focused on the game. It was the bottom of the ninth, and Gina was trying not to make any sound at all. The Cubs had been clinging to a two-zero lead.

"That Pat Malone—what a pitcher! Just one more out, baby!" Mrs. Hayford said, rubbing her hands together. "The Cubs are gonna pull it out! They'll bring the series back to Chicago!"

"Don't jinx it!" her papa replied, knocking his knuckles twice against the kitchen table. "Shh . . . Mule Haas is up."

A bat cracked, and the radio crackled with the sound of a roaring crowd.

"Ugh!" her papa groaned.

The announcer confirmed the bad news. "A two-run homer for Mule Haas of the Athletics off a bad pitch from Pat Malone. The game is now tied, folks, at two-two."

"Futz!" Mrs. Hayford shouted, causing the other two to stare at her in surprise. Gina had never heard her neighbor curse before.

The announcer continued, "The Cubs look bewildered by the sudden change in their fortune."

"Malone just needs to get Bing Miller out," her papa said. "Then we'll go to extras."

"Here's the pitch, and—" Another huge roar from the crowd. "Bing Miller just doubled in the winning run to clinch the series. The Athletics have won! The Cubs are out of contention!"

Her Papa switched off the radio with a single violent move. He and Mrs. Hayford just stared at each other in disbelief, stunned that the series had ended in such defeat.

The telephone rang, causing them all to jump. Gina went to the living room to answer it, glad to have a reason to escape her papa's black mood. It was Nancy.

"Gina!" the policewoman shouted. "The boys are ready to move!"

"What?" Gina replied. "What are you talking about?"

"Adelaide! They're bringing her in for questioning! It was a hard battle, but I finally convinced the captain that something was off about her story." She sounded a bit delirious in her glee. "I just had to promise that we'd wait until the game was over. I just wanted the game to end, I didn't care how. When I thought the game was going to go into extra innings I almost screamed—"

Gina put her hand around the receiver to drown out Nancy's words, hoping her papa hadn't heard such treachery against the Cubs. "So you convinced Captain O'Neill, then?"

"Yes. We're going to pick her up now and bring her over to the police station for questioning. The captain said I can sit in on the official interview."

"I see," Gina replied. Everything had moved more quickly than she had expected, and she suddenly felt uneasy. "Will you arrest her?"

"Probably. We'll see what else she has to say." Nancy paused. "I had to practically beg the captain to let me stay on the case. This will pan out, you'll see. I'm going to get a promotion out of this, I know it. Oh, they're ready to go. Wait, boys!"

Once again she abruptly hung up.

Gina slowly replaced the receiver in its cradle. *What's gonna happen now?*

Gina's movements at the Third Door the next evening felt mechanical and rote. Smile here. Bob there. Pass out some ciggies. Lay down a drink. Smile. Laugh. Finally on her break, Gina stared listlessly into the mirror, a hairbrush idle in her hands. She hadn't heard anything else from Nancy since yesterday afternoon. *How had the arrest gone?* she wondered. Something about it didn't feel quite right, but it was hard to put her finger on it.

"Which ones?" Lulu said, appearing beside her.

Gina shook herself from her reverie. "What?"

Instead of answering, Lulu held out both of her slender arms. On each of her upper arms she wore a gorgeous art deco circlet. One was made of turquoise and silver, and the other was ruby and silver filigree. Both were stunning, and looked beautiful with Lulu's new black and aquamarine dress. Then, without waiting for Gina to reply, she giggled. "Who am I kidding? I'll wear both."

"Of course," Gina said, giving her own hair a final fluff in the mirror.

Around nine o'clock, a woman wearing a tight, cheap red dress came weaving up to Gina, a cigarette dangling from her mouth. She was probably in her thirties but had the careworn face of someone who'd lived a lifetime already.

"You Gina?" she asked.

"Yeah, what's it to you?" Gina replied. She began to straighten her tray. The mints had slid into the gum, and the Signora hated a messy tray. She glanced back up at the woman. "I see you already got a smoke ... is there something else you need? You can order a drink from Lulu or at the bar."

"Nah, I don't need anything right now." She lowered her voice. "A gal pal of mine sent me to talk to you. She needs your help."

"*My* help? What's she need?" Gina asked, looking around. "Is she in the ladies' room?"

"Nah, she's not here. My gal's name's Adeline. Wait, I mean *Adelaide*."

"*Adelaide* sent you here?" Gina asked. "Whatever for?"

"She wants your help. She got tossed in the clink yesterday."

"Oh yeah?" Gina replied. "Is *Adelaide* a *close* friend of yours?" she asked. It was hard to see this woman and the socialite running in the same circles.

"Sheesh! So I don't know her. She paid me to come here. She wants to talk to you. Says she's innocent and you know it, too. Name's Maxine." She stuck out her hand, a languid gesture.

Awkwardly, Gina closed her hand around the woman's ice-cold fingers and quickly released it. "I don't know anything."

"Look, doll, she was real insistent," Maxine said. "Real pathetic, too. I've spent my time in the clink, and I know desperation. She's a sorry sap, no doubt about that."

Gina shrugged. "She should call her parents and have them hire a lawyer. I've seen her digs. She comes from money, I can tell."

"Look, just talk to her, would you?"

"Why? Did she promise you more if I came?"

Maxine gave her a cheeky grin. "You're real smart, I can see that. Come on, be a pal. She'll still be there in the morning. If she ends up going to the women's prison—hoo boy!" Her grin faded a bit. "The other prisoners would eat her alive, I can tell you that. She might not make it out."

Gina had heard enough stories about female prisoners to know that Maxine might not be kidding. The idea that Adelaide could be beaten up or killed while imprisoned made her stomach churn, especially when she recalled her own stint in jail earlier that year. Still, Adelaide could well be guilty. "I'm not making any promises."

"Fair enough," Maxine replied, putting out the end of her cigarette in an ashtray. "How about a fresh smoke for my trouble?"

Gina passed her a cigarette she'd rolled earlier for a customer who'd forgotten that he'd already spent his money. "Take this. Now scram."

Gina watched Maxine leave on the arm of a customer, a stout middle-aged fellow who looked a bit bewildered by the pushy friendliness of his companion. Luckily they were leaving or Gooch might have thrown her out.

What does Adelaide want? Gina wondered again, her curiosity wrestling with her reluctance to get further involved. Still, she felt uneasy over the woman's arrest. *What harm would it do to talk to her?*

She was so lost in thought that she jumped when Gooch tapped her on her shoulder. "The Signora wants to see you. Now."

What now? Gina wondered. She automatically checked her headpiece and smoothed down her dress. Maybe the Signora had seen her pass the free cigarette to the woman earlier. *Hopefully they'll just dock my pay rather than give me a tongue-lashing,* she thought. She was too tired to sustain a rebuke. "Yes, I'll be right there," Gina replied, slipping off her tray and passing it over to Billy. "Be right back."

At her quiet knock, the Signora bid her come in and beckoned toward the fabulous green art deco sofas in the middle of her salon. "Have a seat, would you?"

Gina seated herself on the hard sofa, and the Signora sat down as well, facing her across an ornate wooden table. Gooch came in and stood behind the Signora, crossing his arms in a way that made Gina's heart beat a little faster. Even though she thought the Signora's henchmen had softened toward her in recent months, his positioning made it clear where his loyalties lay.

The Signora came right to the point. "Have you been stepping out with a customer?" she asked, sounding tight and controlled. "While I realize I cannot control your actions—or your mistakes—on your own time, you are not to be making dates while you are working."

Gina flushed deeply at the scolding, her thoughts flashing

to Roark. "I'm sorry, Signora," she said, speaking in a rush. "I guess I knew Roark was married, but I thought they were getting a divorce, and it was just the one date—" Then, at the slight twitch of Gooch's face, she realized her mistake. The Signora wasn't referring to Roark. Her flush grew more painful.

"I was referring to your date with Mr. Morrish," the Signora replied, answering her own question.

"*William Morrish,*" Gooch repeated, emphasizing the man's name.

"What were you doing with him?" the Signora asked. Then she held up her hand. "Or should I say, what did he want with you? Beyond the obvious, of course."

"I'm sorry, Signora. I just went on the date after—" Gina broke off, not wanting to get Lulu in trouble for having set up the date. "I just did it because . . ." She trailed off again, not sure how to explain.

The Signora would have none of it. "Because . . . ? Explain, please." The authority in the Signora's voice was not to be ignored.

"I went out with him to get Donny's watch back. You know, one of the back room boys." Gina looked at Gooch, pleading. "You remember what happened that night, Gooch. Mr. Morrish took Donny's watch during the game."

Gooch's jaw twitched slightly. "Mr. Morrish didn't 'take' it from him, and he didn't cheat," he admonished. "No matter what Donny's friends may have claimed. He's a skilled gambler. Donny was foolish enough to have put it up. Mr. Morrish won the watch fair and square."

"So you say. I think he took advantage of Donny!" Gina exclaimed. She swallowed a gulp, an unexpected wash of emotion cascading over her as she thought about the ex-serviceman. "I had to get the watch back from him. He's lost so much already!"

The Signora paled slightly at her outburst. "Tell me, Gina, that you did not steal from William Morrish."

Gooch tensed as well, a worried look crossing his stoic features.

"Oh, no," Gina replied. "We struck a deal. I kept my side, and he kept his. We're all squared up."

The Signora pursed her lips and exchanged a look with Gooch. "What sort of deal?" she demanded, her voice rising slightly. "He's not the sort of man who will wine and dine you after he gets what he wants. He will take what he wants from you and cast you aside. Have you even thought about what this will do to your father?"

Gina flushed again as she realized what they thought she had agreed to do. "No, no!" she struggled to explain. "I just traded Marty's old watch for Donny's. He accepted the trade. We're all done."

Both Gooch and the Signora visibly relaxed at her explanation. Still the Signora wagged a warning finger at her. "No more deals with him."

"Why? Who is he?" Gina asked.

"You don't know who he works for?" The Signora gave a short mirthless laugh.

Gina looked from the Signora to Gooch, trying to figure out what was going on. "Wh-who does he work for?" she faltered. "For Capone? No, Mr. Morrish is Irish. Someone on the North Side?"

"Just stay away from him. No more dates. It's for your

own good," the Signora said, sidestepping the question. She pointed to the door. "Back to work."

Gina was about to leave, her mind full of questions. Then she remembered her conversation with the Doyles that morning. "Oh, Signora. One more thing. My great-aunt Charlotte Doyle and my great-uncle John Doyle, Marty's parents, said they would like to meet with you. They asked me to arrange a meeting."

Again the Signora and Gooch exchanged a look.

"What about?" Gooch asked.

"I'm not sure," Gina said. "They told me they were concerned about the recent deaths associated with this place."

"They're concerned for your safety," the Signora said easily. "Of course. You've come recently into their lives, and they want you to be protected."

"I'm not sure that's it—" Gina began, but when Gooch shook his head at her she stopped speaking.

The Signora opened her arms expansively. "Certainly. Invite them in for a drink, on the house. That's certainly the least I can do, to honor Marty's memory." Her eyes grew hard. "However, I'm not taking a *meeting* with them anytime soon. I know what they want, and it won't fly."

"What do you mean?" Gina asked. "What do they want?"

"I'm sorry Gina, but that's all I will say about that right now," the Signora said, nodding at Gooch who opened the door. "If you'll excuse me, there are some things I need to do."

The next morning, Gina walked over to the Harrison Street jail, feeling a bit blurry from lack of sleep. Off and on all night she'd been thinking about what the Signora had said about Mr. Morrish. *Should I ask Nancy about it?* She was torn, uneasy about disclosing anything that the Signora had said in confidence.

Gina shook her head. "I can't think about that right now," she said out loud, as she arrived at the jail. Right now, she needed to find out what Adelaide wanted from her. She stopped in front of the wide steps, remembering the last time she'd been there, hauled unceremoniously inside under a trumped-up charge. With great effort, she presented herself before the tired police clerk inside. He looked like he'd been seated there all night long. The name on his uniform was Stevens.

"Name?" he asked, stifling a yawn.

"Gina Ricci," she replied, watching him write down her name on a clipboard. When he looked up expectantly, she continued. "Officer Stevens, I'd like to see a woman who was arrested last night. Her name is Adelaide. She asked me to come see her."

He consulted another sheet. "Adelaide Wheeling?"

"Yeah, I suppose."

"Sorry. No visitors." He yawned again.

"Oh," Gina said, casting about for a reason to stay. "Perhaps my cousin Officer Doyle is around. I'd like to see her."

The officer raised an eyebrow. "Nancy Doyle's your cousin?" At her nod, he continued, his tone not quite admiring, but not dismissive either. "She's a tough one, isn't she? Like a bulldog with a bone."

That sounds about right, Gina thought. "I'd like to see her if I can."

"She's out right now, monitoring a ladies' temperance march," he said, chuckling. He gestured to a hard wooden bench against the wall. "Those women can get real unruly. You're welcome to wait, if you like. We're short-staffed. I don't have anyone who can take you down to the cells right now."

Deciding to wait, Gina sat down, crossing and uncrossing her legs nervously. "Busy night?" she asked, hearing him yawn for the fourth time in as many minutes.

Stevens glanced at her. "Yeah, you could say so. A jewelry store was bombed down on Maxwell Street. Thankfully no one was hurt, but we've got a few men on the case. If they can find any witnesses, of course."

"What's that make? The hundredth in the city this year?" Gina asked.

"Something like that."

The bombing situation in the city was truly getting out of hand. "What is it with all these bombings?" she asked idly, laying her head on the hard back of the bench and staring up at the ceiling.

"You know what I think it is?" Stevens asked, unexpectedly perking up. He clearly had thought about this. When she looked over at him, he was waiting expectantly on her answer.

Too little control over gangs? Too few policemen ready to stop criminals? Too many cops on the take? "No idea," she replied.

"The stock market's to blame!" Stevens declared. "I'm sure of it."

Gina blinked. That was not what she was expecting. "How's that?" she asked, sitting back up.

"The stock market is too open these days. Any hoodlum, gangster, or two-bit lamplighter can speculate on the stock market. You know that, right?"

At Gina's nod, Stevens continued, clearly warming to a favorite topic. "That's fine, of course, for democracy and the economy and all that, but those guys, they don't have the temperament."

"What do you mean?" Gina asked, interested despite herself.

"Bankers, traders—they know that markets go up and down. They roll with the punches. The *vagaries* of the business, if you will. Those other guys, they don't know how to handle it when they lose money on their stocks. They feel betrayed. They feel stupid. They feel conned by it all. So they get angry. So they get violent and bomb the bank or whatever place they invested in." He tapped his pen on the desk. "Fools."

Gina rubbed her chin. "You think that's what it is?" The theory didn't sound so far-fetched.

"Some of them—the ones we've caught—have told me so themselves," Stevens said, shrugging. "Gotta be at least part of the problem, I'm sure of it."

Another cop came in then, a shock of red hair tucked into his hat. Clearly she'd earned enough goodwill by listening patiently to Stevens's theories, because he called out to the other cop. "Hey, Ferguson. This woman here—Miss Ricci, was it?—is here to see Adelaide Wheeling. Take her down for a few minutes, would you?"

Officer Ferguson grunted. "That's all she's got. That one's scheduled to be transferred within the hour."

CHAPTER 17

Gina followed Officer Ferguson down a flight of steps and then through a locked door leading to a long corridor, with four cells on each side. She shuddered as they walked that horrid and familiar path, remembering the events that had led her to her being locked up. As before, the room was chilly and bleak, long shadows cast from the dim electric lights above. The first few cells appeared to be unoccupied, but she could hear the sound of sobbing toward the end of the corridor.

"That's her in there," Ferguson said, pointing at the third cell. He glanced at his watch. "I'll give you ten minutes."

Gina walked over to the cell. "Adelaide?" she said, peering in. She could see a huddled shape shaking violently under a thin brown blanket. "Adelaide! It's me, Gina. Your... friend Maxine said you wanted to see me?"

The soft sobbing stopped, and Adelaide's head popped out from under the blanket, her hair uncombed and tousled. She peered toward the bars, and at the sight of Gina, she brightened. "You came!" she exclaimed. Gina could see her lips were blue.

"Could she have another blanket, please?" Gina asked Ferguson. Without saying anything, he took a blanket from an unused cell and slipped it through the bars of Adelaide's.

"Take the blanket, Adelaide," she said. "Wrap it around yourself."

Unfolding it, Adelaide pulled it around herself, on top of the other blanket. Sniffling, she stood by the cell door.

"Step back from the bars," Ferguson warned. He had seated himself on the sole chair by the entrance. Glancing at his watch, he added, "Eight minutes left."

"Why'd you wanna see me?" Gina asked.

"You got me thrown in here," Adelaide said, pouting. "My parents are furious at me. Told me they're going to disown me."

"Will they really?" Gina asked. She would have thought a family like Adelaide's would do anything to keep scandal from the door.

Adelaide's voice became very small. "I *think* my uncle will come and take care of this," she said, her voice catching. "He's a lawyer. I tried to ring him, but he hasn't returned my calls. I think my parents are punishing me. Told me that this is the consequence of my 'wicked modern ways.'" She began to cry outright "I've nearly blown through my trust fund," she whined. "My parents are going to cut me off."

"None of this is my fault," Gina said, frowning. "If that's all you wanted to say to me, I'm leaving."

"No, no! Wait, please!" Adelaide cried, shaking the bars. "I didn't hurt Fruma. You have to believe me."

"I never said you hurt her."

"You ratted me out to Officer Doyle. You told her what I had said about Fruma in the ladies' room that night. You're making me look guilty."

"You're making yourself look guilty. Look, Officer Doyle and I both know that you lied to us about the necklace, and we don't know why. Might as well come clean."

"Oh, that stupid necklace." Adelaide shook her head, her eyes filling with tears again. "I mucked things up, didn't I?"

"Yeah, you did," Gina replied, not finding it necessary to mince words. "However, I don't get what happened. We don't have a lot of time, so why don't you tell me everything, and get to the point. Start with when you left the Third Door."

"Yeah. We invited the men back to our flat and—"

"Both men? George and Daniel?"

"Yeah. George drove me and Fruma, and Daniel drove separately." A shadow passed over her face at the memory. "I think Daniel was angry about that. I think he thought I'd ride with him. But—"

"But you wanted to stick close to Fruma and George? Be a third wheel?" Gina guessed. At Adelaide's terse nod, she continued. "Okay, so you three drove to your flat together and Daniel followed. Then what happened?"

Adelaide's voice got quieter. "Fruma was really out of it, you know? So drunk. She practically dragged George back to her bedroom. A bit awkward for me and Daniel, you know what I mean? I offered him a gin and tonic, but he said he was done drinking for the evening. So I gave him some water, and he left. He barely said a word. I thought he was pretty mad."

"Could he have been sick?" Gina asked.

"Sick?" Fruma looked up at the ceiling. "Hmmm. Could have been, I suppose. I know he drank a lot more than George had. Still, he hadn't seemed sloshed." She looked back at Gina. "Why? *Was* he sick?"

Gina thought about telling Adelaide that Daniel was dead, similarly poisoned, but she didn't want to interrupt Adelaide's flow. "You said George went into Fruma's room. How long was he there?"

"Not too long." She hesitated.

Gina tapped her foot. "What?" she said. "What happened?"

"I heard him yell something at Fruma and then leave the flat. He slammed the door when he left, so I know he was upset. I locked the door behind him and then ran back to my bedroom. It was scary."

"What did he yell?"

"He called her a tease." She shifted uncomfortably, a flash of regret crossing her features.

"Did you go talk to Fruma?" Gina asked.

"I'm not proud of this, but—no, I was still mad at her. I thought she'd gotten what she deserved. She was crying." Adelaide paused, her eyes filling again. "Then I heard her getting sick. A few times, actually."

"Did you help her? Say anything to her? Check in on her at all?"

"No." Guilt was etched across every line of her face.

"So what about the necklace?" Gina watched her closely.

Adelaide put her hands to her face, covering her eyes. "Look, I completely panicked when I found her dead." She began to pace around the cell. "I didn't know what had happened to her, so I thought it would be easier if the police just thought it was an overdose. That happens sometimes, and no one gets blamed. I thought that I could be arrested for not calling a doctor when I saw her so sick. It was stupid." She shook her head. "I don't know what I was thinking."

"You were high, weren't you?" Gina asked. "*You're* the addict, not Fruma."

Adelaide slumped her shoulders. "That's true. I'd taken some cocaine earlier at the Third Door—you saw me just after. Then I took some more after Daniel left. I was really still out of it the next morning."

"That's why you switched necklaces."

Adelaide sighed. "Yes. It made perfect sense at the time. I took off her black opal necklace and put my special necklace around her neck, so they would think she was an addict." A shadow passed over her face. "I didn't know they'd find out the truth with an autopsy."

"Surely you can see why your behavior is suspicious," Gina said. "You say you thought you'd be blamed for not calling a doctor. It's just as easy to believe that you poisoned her at the speakeasy, so everyone would blame the rotgut." She thought about Billy then. *And it almost worked.* "Then in your addled state you forgot your own plan."

"Please!" Adelaide cried, reaching through the bars. Gina stepped back before she could grab her. "I admit I was a terrible friend. I also admit to meddling with the necklace, but at the time it all made sense to switch them. Please! I don't want to drag my family through a trial!"

Officer Ferguson came over then and rapped on the bars. "Step back," he told Adelaide, before turning to Gina. "Time to go."

"Please, tell the cops what I told you!" Adelaide wailed. "I'm innocent! I swear!"

"That's an addict for you," Ferguson muttered to her as they mounted the stairs. "They commit a crime when they're high and then expect to go on their merry way, scot-free. You can't trust anything they say or do."

"Mmmm," Gina murmured. The officer's words certainly made sense. At the same time, even if Adelaide had been mad at Fruma or jealous of George's attentions, it didn't make sense that she would have killed her by arsenic, which would have required advance planning. If Fruma had been pushed down the steps or run over by an automobile, Gina would have been more likely to blame Adelaide. *Unless she's the world's best actress, I don't think she had anything to do with either Fruma's or Dan's death*, Gina thought. So that meant that someone else had killed Fruma. But who?

Dressed in a clingy silver and red dress, Gina moved easily about the speakeasy, sidestepping two women dancing together. The pair was clumsily parading around the room, their feathers drooping and their headdresses slipping. For a Wednesday evening, the joint was hopping, which was why Gina had been sent down immediately, instead of helping out at the pharmacy as she usually would.

"Oh, whoops!" One of the women giggled, causing the other one to echo her.

"Whoops!"

"Whoopsie Daisy," the first woman laughed, slouching into the other, causing the other to call out, "Gin Daisy!"

Then they looked at each other, bursting out laughing, before they said in unison, "Gin Blossoms! We'll take two more Gin Blossoms!"

"Say, ladies, how about you sit for a while," Gina said, brushing a strand of her hair back behind her ear. "Take a break?"

"Oooh, Neddy Fingers is back at the piano," one of them cried, ignoring Gina.

"He's the Elephant's Elbows!" the other one effused.

Arm in arm they walked unsteadily on their heels over to drape themselves across the piano, giggling foolishly the whole way. Ned's smile was tight until Gooch removed the women from the instrument.

Something about the women reminded her of Adelaide and Fruma. After she'd left the police station that morning, Gina had tried several times to reach Nancy on the telephone, wanting to talk over her conversation with Adelaide. It was hard to not to think about Adelaide's pitiful appearance at the jail. *I hope she survives the ordeal,* Gina thought for the umpteenth time. *Surely her parents will step in, get her a lawyer.*

Lulu and Jade joined Gina then. "Did you hear that Roark's wife is auditioning for the Signora on Friday?" Lulu said loudly over the growing din. She nudged Jade. "Bet she's terrible."

Jade grimaced. "Bet she's not." For the first time since Gina had met Jade, the woman's aplomb was showing some cracks.

"She won't be better than you," Gina said, feeling gener-
ous.

The next moment she regretted her kind impulse, when
Jade replied with over-honeyed sweetness. "She's more likely
to replace *you*, anyway. The Signora would probably rather
have more performers on the staff, which you'll never be."

Gina frowned at the biting comment. "Well, then it will
be certainly easier for *you*, since you'll have to share your
performance time." Jade looked stricken at the thought.
Gina continued, "She's fresh from New York, you know."

Catching Gooch's stern eye, Gina slipped her cigarette
tray from around her neck and picked up her smaller cocktail tray. "Time to switch out, gals. Ta-ta!"

With Jade and Lulu busy getting ready for their sets in the
back room, Gina had to move quickly.

"Another sidecar, my good man," a man at the bar called
to Billy.

To her surprise, Gina recognized him. It was George,
the one who'd gone home with Fruma and Adelaide that
night.

"Hey, Billy, can you make that one on the house?" she
said to the bartender.

When Billy looked at her, eyebrows raised, she murmured, "On my tab, okay? I'll pick it up."

"Hey, sweetheart, thanks," George said, giving her a
once-over. "You're real sweet, you know that? What time do
you get off work?"

"Can it, bub," she said. "I'm not going home with you. I
just wanna talk to you for a sec."

"Oh yeah?" He smiled, the same lazy smile that had worked so well on both Fruma and Adelaide the week before. He patted the bar stool beside him. "Take a seat. What about?"

Gina remained standing by his side, not wanting to bring any undue attention to their conversation. "Your friend Daniel," she said in a low voice. "I heard he passed away a week or so ago. You guys seemed like you had been real good friends."

"Yeah." George swallowed, and a few tears surfaced in his eyes. "That Dan, he was a good man. A real pal."

Seeing that Billy had finished mixing George's sidecar, she brought it over to him. She gave a quick look around before stepping in a little closer. She didn't want Billy to overhear their conversation. "What happened?" Gina asked, trying to sound casual. "Paper didn't say. We know it wasn't bad hooch."

"Yeah, so they say." He swallowed again. "Arsenic, the coroner told us. I can't understand it. Why would he take arsenic?"

"Or maybe someone gave it to him," she said softly.

"You think he was poisoned?" George looked confused. "That can't be right. I mean, the thought crossed my mind that someone might have had it in for him. Then I remembered that this is *Dan Roth* we're talking about. His only enemy is a tennis ball. You should see the way he pounds the racket on the court." Then he realized what he'd just said. "Pounded the racket, I mean." He took a long drink.

"Well, what about later? Did he have more to drink at

the women's flat? I know you all went there after you left this joint."

George cocked one eyebrow. "Say, you know a lot about this, don't you?" He looked around. "What is this, a setup?"

"Relax. I'm just asking some questions," Gina replied. "Here, I'll give you some information. Adelaide was arrested for Fruma's death, did you know that?"

He said his glass down hard. "Fruma . . . d-died?" George looked genuinely stunned, and his eyes began to blink rapidly. "How? When?"

Gina quickly filled him in on the details of Fruma's death, watching him closely. He took another deep swallow. "I can't believe it." He stared at her, drumming his fingers on the tabletop. "You say that Adelaide was arrested for her murder? Why would she have killed Fruma? They were friends! For that matter, why would she have killed Dan?"

"*Did* Daniel come inside the flat with you?" Gina asked, trying to get back on track. She looked around. She'd already spent too much time talking to George.

"Yeah, he came inside."

"Then did you drink some more there?"

"No, we didn't drink anything more." He hesitated, then seemed eager to talk. "I gotta tell you, Gina. They both seemed out of their minds."

"What do you mean?"

He chuckled nervously. "Fruma invited me into her bedroom, and I thought Dan went with Adelaide. I didn't ask. And I don't know if he was still there when I left." He looked sad. "I guess he died on his walk back to his car. He'd parked it on a side street, not too far from here. I heard he was already dead, though, when the thieves took his wallet."

Glancing around the room again, Gina caught Little Johnny's eye. He was looking at them, and he had a warning look on his face. *Get hustling, doll,* she could almost hear him saying. *There are other customers waiting.*

"I'm gonna have to go," she said. "Tell me—did you know Fruma or Adelaide before you met them here?"

"Nope, that was the first time I met either of them."

"What did *you* think of Fruma's story, about her jumping out of the airplane? Setting a world record? I'm just curious."

"You heard about that, too?" George smiled, a sad, taut grin. "Total malarkey. She sure was cute, though. She's a modern girl. She knew what she was up to." His jaw tightened. "Although she'd drunk too much, if you know what I mean. I didn't stay too long, not when I figured out that she couldn't handle her drink so well."

It took all of Gina's self-possession not to reach over and slap the slight smirk that had arisen on George's lips. His next words made her glad she hadn't given in to the impulse.

"Of course, now I know she was sick from the arsenic. I'd never have left if I'd known she was dying. And Dan! How horrible to die like that, out on the street." He sighed. He drained his glass and flicked at Billy to bring him another sidecar. "Who would want to poison a lovely sweet girl like that? I wonder if the cops have spoken to her fiancé? He seemed like a real lowlife from what I heard."

Gina was still thinking about what George had said when she moved into the back room to check on the men playing cards. She was glad to see that Donny had returned, looking lighter than the last time she saw him. When she walked in, she felt even more warmth and friendliness directed her way from the men.

"Hey, doll!" one greeted her.

"Gina!" others called.

Ralph gave her his crooked smile and an approving nod. "I still don't know how you got Donny's watch back, Miss Ricci," he whispered when she set his gin and tonic down in front of him. "I know everyone's happy that you did. He's happy, too."

Roark came in then, walking right over to her, as if he'd been looking for her. "Gina," he said, drawing her away from the table, "the results of Granny Brown's gin are back from the lab. Definitely rotgut, not something anyone should be drinking too much—some wood alcohol mixed in with glycerin and the juniper oil. It doesn't match what was found in the stomachs of either Fruma Landry or Daniel Roth."

"So Billy is completely off the hook? He'll be relieved."

"I already let him know. And the coroner confirmed that Daniel Roth also definitely died of arsenic poisoning, as we assumed."

"They still don't know who poisoned their drinks," Gina added, shifting her weight from one leg to the other. "Nancy thinks it might have been Adelaide, doing it out of jealousy. She had her arrested. I guess you already knew that."

"Yeah, but it doesn't make sense."

"I know. I talked to Adelaide. At the Harrison Street police station."

Roark looked startled. "You did? Why?"

"She asked me to come see her. Pleaded her case to me. And you know what? I believe her. I believe she was dumb enough to do exactly what she said. I think the reason she seemed so guilty was because she had left her friend to die without even trying to get her any help. She didn't call a doctor, she didn't give her an emetic. I mean, to be fair, I don't think she knew what was going on. From her own admission, she was high the night before, and got high again when she found Fruma. That's why she put the cocaine around her nose, why she put the necklace on her."

"I see," Roark replied. "Why?"

"She clearly wasn't thinking straight. In her mind, it made sense to make Fruma look like she'd overdosed or committed suicide. She didn't want people to know how ill Fruma had been or that she had neglected her out of spite. She thought she'd be in trouble for deciding not to call in a physician. Obviously, she never expected that Fruma would be found dead. She also didn't expect that there would be an autopsy." Gina sighed. "Adelaide is going to have to live with that guilt for the rest of her life. Along with the guilt of her jealousy. A prison of her own making. I don't think she should be imprisoned."

"Oh, her parents will never let that happen. They'll buy her way out. Her kind always does."

"There's another thing that's been bothering me. Was Fruma even the target? Or was this a warning to the Signora? That's what I'm starting to think."

"We have to figure out how exactly that arsenic ended up in their drinks."

"Great. How do we do that?" Gina asked.

Roark shook his head. "I have no idea."

CHAPTER 18

"Say, Mr. Rosenstein," Gina called to the pharmacist after the last customer had walked out of the shop. Since her conversation with Roark the night before, she'd been thinking about how exactly Fruma and Daniel had been poisoned. She checked her watch. She had a half hour before her shift downstairs began. "Can I ask you some questions? About arsenic?"

If he was surprised, the pharmacist didn't show it. "What do you want to know?"

Benny had moved closer, curiosity far more evident on his face.

"How long would it take for someone to die after being poisoned by arsenic?" Gina asked.

The pharmacist turned to Benny. "What do you think, Benny? Let's see what all that studying gets you!"

Benny's forehead puckered as he thought about the question. "Well, it depends," he said. "The measure of the dose, how it's administered, the size and weight of the person. There are famous cases of people being poisoned by arsenic for months, but sometimes their symptoms appear to be something else, like cholera or just a general weakness of the body."

Gina nodded. That made sense. "Two people were poisoned by arsenic the same night, and died within a few hours of each other."

The pharmacist nodded. "*Ja*, I heard about those deaths. Given the close time of the individuals' passing, I would say that they were probably dosed at the same time. Probably a few hours before they died."

A few hours before, Gina mused, once again pondering the potential connections between Fruma and Dan. *Who would have wanted to kill the pair?* Perhaps there had been something between them, although Adelaide and George had both claimed that they didn't think they'd known each other before that fateful night at the Third Door. "Fruma and George were the ones who'd been flirting," she said out loud, without thinking.

At her words, the pharmacist made an annoyed sound and Benny turned away. Neither wasted his time on gossip. Gina continued to think. Fruma and George had gone back to Fruma's bedroom for a romantic evening. So, even if someone had been jealous, they would have killed off George instead of Daniel. The pairing just didn't make sense.

"What does arsenic look like?" Gina asked the pharmacist. "What about taste? Is it bitter? Can it be disguised? How could someone be tricked into taking arsenic without their knowing?"

"All good questions," the pharmacist said. He turned to Benny. "What can you tell us about it, son?"

Benny stroked his chin. "Well, arsenic looks like a fine white powder. Hang on, I'll show you." He disappeared into the back room and returned a moment later with a small jar marked clearly with a skull and crossbones, the traditional symbol for poison. He set it on the counter in front of Gina. "Sometimes people purchase this to poison rats and other vermin that they might have in their homes."

Gina thought about that. "So someone would have had to bring the arsenic along with them." She tried to imagine how that would work.

"Possibly," Mr. Rosenstein. "I'd have to check my logbook, but I think I gave some to Mr. Gucciani a month or so ago. A lot of rats coming in from the sewers."

Gina snapped her fingers. "Of course! The arsenic may already have been on the premises."

Benny took out a small piece of paper and metal tweezers, opened the lid, and carefully dropped a few grains of the white powder onto the paper, while Mr. Rosenstein looked on approvingly. "There is more than one type of arsenic," Benny said, "but the most common form is silvery gray and shiny—metallic-looking—and brittle. This is the kind we've provided to the Signora."

"As for taste and smell—arsenic is virtually odorless, tasteless, and essentially colorless," Mr. Rosenstein added. "Easily passed off as flour or sugar, and in fact was often put in those substances to disguise the poison."

"The perfect poison," Gina said. "So it wouldn't be hard to stir some into a drink when someone's not looking. Like a Mickey Finn."

"Sure, just a pinch or two would do the trick," Mr. Rosenstein said.

"Still seems hard to do," Benny said. "Someone would see."

"Let's try it," Gina said, growing excited.

"What?" Both Mr. Rosenstein and Benny exclaimed at once.

Gina grinned. "I didn't mean we'd actually poison anyone. We'll use sugar. Come on."

She walked over to the other end of the drugstore, where the soda fountain was. "Okay, you two sit here," she said, indicating two stools at the counter. Dutifully they both sat down. "Imagine you've got your . . . bubbly drinks."

Gina placed a Coke glass in front of each man. "Now imagine you're talking, having a good time, drinking your bubbly drinks." She regarded the bowl of sugar cubes. "I need to grind those up first."

"Hang on," Mr. Rosenstein said, walking briskly back to the pharmacy counter and returning with a mortar and pestle. "Let's do this right."

In about five seconds he had ground the sugar cubes to a fine powder. Looking at it with a critical eye, the pharmacist said, "This looks about right. Not exactly the same consistency, but . . ."

"It'll do," Gina said, taking the mortar from him. "Okay, so now I want you to pretend that you're just having a friendly drink together—"

"My mama won't let me touch the spirits," Benny interrupted.

"Jeepers, Benny," Gina said, "just imagine you're sitting with Mr. Rosenstein here, and you're talking about, oh, I don't know, the World Series."

"Bah," they both muttered. The sting of the lost World Series still rankled.

"Well, okay, not the World Series. That's obviously a sore subject. Talk about, oh, how about what chemistry class is like at college or something like that."

"*Ja*, that is something we can discuss," Mr. Rosenstein said, "although I think the German institutions are very different from those here in the States."

"Jeepers, we're just play-acting here," Gina said. "So you're not paying attention to me as I lean over and pour some 'arsenic' in your drinks." As she said this, she awkwardly leaned over and tipped an eighth of a teaspoon of sugar into Benny's glass, nearly toppling it over. "Okay, this is not easy at all."

"Someone would have had to be very close to do this properly," Benny commented.

"Without drawing suspicion," Mr. Rosenstein added. Both men contemplated the mortar for a moment, pondering the puzzle.

"Perhaps if the sugar were in a napkin," Benny suggested. "Then maybe someone could walk by, slipping in a dose."

"Like this?" Gina put some of the ground-up sugar in a napkin and shook it over the Coke glasses. Sugar could be seen all over the rim and down the side of the glass, and on the counter.

They all frowned. "No, it needs to be stirred in to dissolve properly," Mr. Rosenstein said. "Otherwise it would be obvious."

"That's right," Gina said, as she wiped away the sugar that had spilled on the counter. "What about if I just gave the glass a quick swirl?" Casually, she reached over and, grasping the glass from the bottom, swirled it gently.

They watched the sugar dissolve easily. "That would do it," Donny said.

"It would take some *chutzpah* to pull that off," Mr. Rosenstein commented. "Someone was very bold to do such a thing, when anyone could see."

"Or someone with nothing to lose," Gina replied. Her mind was racing, as she tried to remember the evening. "Who would be *that* bold, to poison someone's drink essentially in front of them?"

"Maybe the bartender did it?" Donny asked nervously. "Or one of the servers?"

"Billy Bottles? What? No, that's not possible. And I'm positive it wasn't one of us—" Then Gina snapped her fingers as the solution presented itself. "It *didn't* happen at the table. It must have happened just after Billy made the drink, and before one of us picked up the drinks. Someone added the arsenic while the drink was still waiting at the bar. I know it!"

Gina took her apron off and hung it on a hook behind the counter, still racking her brain, trying to remember the evening. Someone had gotten close enough to poison the drinks, that much seemed certain. But who?

"Yes sir, that's my baby," Ned sang from his piano while Lulu pranced across the dance floor. *"No sir, I don't mean maybe. Yes sir, that's my baby now . . ."*

Watching Lulu from her position at the bar, Gina thought back to what she had learned since she'd left the pharmacy an hour before. There were rat traps all over the place, discreetly placed, but visible and accessible to anyone so inclined. In the tunnels, in the bathrooms, and in the dressing rooms, she saw small dishes containing the deadly stuff. What had Nancy's detective book talked about? *Means*. The means was arsenic, and access to it was quite simple.

Gina could see Harriet watching from the shadows of the salon entrance as well, a slight smirk on her face. She was going to be auditioning in about half an hour, after Lulu was done with her set. She'd taken the slot that Jade usually had on Friday nights, causing the singer to sulk for days. It also hadn't helped that Harriet had come in early to get herself gussied up, trying out the cosmetics from the other girls' tubes and vials. At least she'd brought her own costume, which the Signora had approved—a translucent purplish black dress that set off her black hair and pale skin dramatically. Harriet had heightened the effect by applying bright crimson lipstick that belonged to Lulu.

"Gina!" a familiar voice called. It was William Morrish.

"Cocktail for you?" she asked. "Sorry I can't offer you a Peg o' My heart."

"That might be preferable, given that the drinks here have been a bit hit-or-miss." He grinned. "I'll take a whiskey tonic and another date. How about it?"

"I've already got what I needed from you," she replied, smiling. She hoped Gooch wasn't watching her, but she had the feeling he might be. The last thing she needed was another scolding.

"Ouch! I see. How about I go win a few hands at cards? See if I can get some of the men to give up other precious things that you can win back for them?" Though his words were teasing, he was watching her intently.

"I'll fetch your drink," Gina replied, heading over to the bar to put in the order. While she waited for Billy to mix the drink, William's comment came back to her. *The drinks here have been a bit hit-or-miss,* he'd said. She remembered now how she'd brought him the sidecar and he'd sent it back after a single sip.

What had happened next? Gina frowned trying to retrace her steps. She was standing where she'd been that night and then what? She'd placed William's discarded drink on the bar, thinking to tell Billy to dump it in the slush bucket under the counter. Billy had been busy, and then Roark had come. She'd forgotten about the drink. What had happened to it?

She slapped her head as she figured it out. She'd set the drink on the bar by Stan, practically in front of him. Had he drunk it then? He must have, because she didn't remember dumping it in the slop pail. In his inebriated state Stan might have thought she was giving it to him.

Her heart began to pound. "Did I give Stan a poisoned drink?" Hearing her own words out loud, she swiveled her head around, hoping no one had overheard her. An uneasy feeling stole over her as she began to think everything through. William was the one who sent the drink back—had he known it was poisoned? She remembered how he had been watching Fruma that night. Why had he been watching her so closely? And what was it he had said to Gina, when he returned the drink? *Let's just say it would be a real shame if something happened to a girl like you.* She rubbed her arms to ward off a sudden chill.

After Lulu trotted off a few minutes later, Ned continued to sing on his own until it was time to bring Harriet on for her audition.

The Signora had seated herself at one of the small tables, with Gooch standing behind her, arms crossed as usual. Catching the Signora's eye, the proprietess lifted her eyebrow slightly. *Don't you have something to do?* Gina could almost hear her say. Lulu was in the salon getting dressed, and Jade would be changing now. She was the only server on the floor.

Scanning the room, she saw that Roark had seated himself at one of the high tables by the wall. She could see that he was watching her. Against her will, she moved over to him. "Need a drink or smoke?" Gina asked. "Before your *wife* performs?"

"Harriet asked me to come. Figured it was the least I could do." He regarded her intently. "Hoping it will make her sign the divorce papers quicker."

Gina raised an eyebrow but didn't say anything. His presence might signal something different than that to Harriet, but there wasn't much point in saying anything now.

His grin grew wary. "That is, assuming you still want that. I saw you talking to Morrish earlier. Again."

"Oh, that—"

He waved his hand. "I don't need to know."

Just then, Ned gave a final flourish of the keys to great applause from the room. He glanced over at the Signora, who gave a slight nod. Standing up from the piano bench he began to speak loudly. "Ladies and gentlemen," he said. "We have a special treat tonight. We are honored to have Harriet Roark, fresh off the stages of New York, here! Ladies and gents, how about a warm welcome! Miss Harriet!"

Ned sat back down and Harriet trotted out to the strains of a silly song. *"Aba daba daba daba daba daba dab, Said the chimpie to the monk . . . ,"* Harriet sang, in a surprisingly funny and practiced way. After only a few bars she had the whole room laughing at her antics. Gina could see that Jade and Lulu were peering out from the side entrance. They must have rushed to change so they could watch Harriet perform her set. Everyone wanted to see how good she really was.

And she was good. She'd clearly perfected the little-girl voice needed to sing in Helen Kane's boop-oop-a-doop style. As she pranced about the room, singing her silly songs, she'd pause here and there to wrap her boa around one of the gentlemen, bringing huge grins from them and frowns from their dates. Even Gooch looked like he was enjoying the show. *"Button up your overcoat, when the wind is free . . . you'll get a pain and ruin your tum-tum . . . you belong to me . . ."*

She pointed several times at Roark during the set, wagging her finger in a playfully seductive way, each time giving Gina a wicked smile. Harriet continued to sing, the lyrics delightful to the audience.

Beware of frozen funds, ooh, ooh!
Stocks and bonds, ooh, ooh!
Dockside thugs, ooh, ooh!
You'll get a pain and ruin your bankroll!

The crowd laughed good-naturedly along, particularly when she got to the last well-known verse:

Keep away from bootleg hooch
When you're on a spree
Oh, take good care of yourself
You belong to me-e-e!

Jade and Lulu were still looking on from the shadows. Jade was watching with narrowed eyes. When Lulu began to laugh outright, Jade nudged her to stop. Catching their eye, Gina tapped her wristwatch casually, reminding them to be back on the floor by the time Harriet had finished her set. Luckily, the speakeasy patrons had been so delighted by Harriet's performance that they began to call for an encore.

Harriet gave them a teasing smile. "You want more?" she called.

"More," they collectively roared. "Give it to us, sister!" someone called. Jade turned away in disgust.

"I suppose I can do one more," Harriet replied, without checking in with the Signora. "How about 'Dinah,' Neddy?" she called to the piano player.

After getting a nod from the Signora, Ned played the first few notes of the bluesy song. Harriet began to sing, a soulful, throaty sound that was far different from the silly routine she'd started with. When she finished, she gave a few more extravagant curtsies and finally slipped off the dance floor. The Signora followed her out. Jade and Lulu emerged at the very end, and Gina could read their expressions. Harriet was going to be a real rival.

CHAPTER 19

"Hey, cut it out!" Gina snapped, swiping at the drips of soda that trailed across the drugstore counter. Two teenaged boys had been joking loudly and jostling each other for the last fifteen minutes, and they were getting sloppy.

A day had passed since Harriet's audition, and Gina had been on edge the whole time. *What if the Signora does hire Harriet? What would it be like to work with Roark's ex-wife? Or would they even get divorced now?* Harriet had already shown that she was unlikely to give up something she wanted, and that probably included Roark.

Just then one of the teenagers knocked over a half-full glass of cherry soda with a gangly elbow.

"Now see what you've done!" Gina snapped, watching in dismay as the half-filled glass dumped its contents down the counter, leaving a sticky red puddle on the floor. "I have a good mind to make you clean this up yourselves!"

"Sorry, miss," the boy said, looking sheepish. The other drained the rest of his glass rapidly, rightly guessing that she was about to kick them both out.

"Hand me the mop, would you?" Gina called to Benny, who was restocking shelves in the middle of the store. From the other end of the store, she could hear Mr. Rosenstein putting together some medicine for a middle-aged man who'd been complaining loudly about his gout for more than ten minutes. She didn't want him to see this mess, as he was a stickler for cleanliness. "There's a spill that needs attending to. Luckily, these boys here are just leaving."

Roark walked in as the boys exited the drugstore, whistling when he saw her mopping furiously at the spreading puddle. "Your job really is quite glamorous, isn't it?" he asked, seating himself on one of the red stools at the counter.

"Always," she said. "What do you want?"

"I'll take a fizzy drink when you're done," Roark said. He waved away Benny, who had popped his head around the shelves, a stack of soap bars in his arms. "Don't worry, Benny. I'm not in a hurry."

"Sure thing, Mr. Roark," Benny replied, and returned to stocking shelves.

"How you been, Gina?" Roark asked, watching her closely.

"Peachy," she said, drying off her hands. She began to make his fizzy drink, adding the maraschino cherries that he liked. "Harriet performed really well last night. I'm sure she got the job."

"She did. She called me," he replied.

"Oh," Gina said. So Harriet would be a regular fixture at the Third Door from now on. She wasn't sure how she'd feel about that. Actually, she knew. She'd hate it.

"We'll see if she sticks around. I can tell you, I'm not

holding my breath." He seemed about to say something else but Gina interrupted him.

"There's something else I want to talk to you about," she said hurriedly. "I've been thinking about how Stan got sick that night. Like Fruma and Daniel."

"Oh?" Roark said. She wasn't sure if he was relieved or not that she had changed the topic, but he appeared interested. "What about it?"

"Well, I think he had at least one sidecar from Mr. Morrish."

Roark blinked. "Morrish? Are they pals?"

"No, I mean I remember now that Mr. Morrish sent his drink back. Said it tasted funny. It was a sidecar. I'm pretty sure that I left it on the counter, for Billy to dump in the slop bucket."

Gina paused. "He might have thought I'd given it to him. Which, of course, I hadn't. He was too drunk to care."

"So? Morrish sent back a drink. I'm not surprised. He probably fancies himself real knowledgeable," Roark said.

"I'm just wondering . . ." Gina hesitated. "Could the poisoned drinks have been intended for Mr. Morrish?"

"Well, I'm the first to admit that probably a lot of people hate that guy." Roark rubbed the stubble on his cheek. "However, he didn't mention getting sick, right? Obviously, he was well enough for your *date* two days later."

Gina drew herself up, about to respond with a angry retort, when the bell above the store's door jangled.

She looked over expectantly. Instead of someone entering the drug store, something cylindrical was thrown into the store, bouncing twice before rolling to a stop close to where Gina and Roark were standing.

Gina stared at it. "What in the world—?"

Roark glanced down, and his expression changed. *"BOMB!"*

He kicked the object back toward the front door as it closed, then swiveled to push Gina through the back door into the corridor that led to the speakeasy.

A moment later there was a terrible explosion. Gina heard herself scream. The shock of the blast threw them onto the floor of the corridor, Roark falling heavily on top of her. For a moment her ears rang.

Little Johnny came dashing out from around the corner. "What happened?" he shouted. Smoke was already pouring out of the store.

"Bomb!" Roark said, rolling himself off of Gina.

Feeling dazed, Gina struggled to sit up. "Benny," she said hoarsely, pointing to the pharmacy. "Mr. Rosenstein!"

"Stay here!" Little Johnny shouted, disappearing into the smoky haze.

"What's going on?" Gooch shouted from the other end of the hallway, Ned at his heels. They must have raced up the stairs.

"Bomb," Gina said, unable to say much more, watching both men push into the store. "Be careful," she added weakly, still trying to catch her breath.

Now patrons were appearing at the top of the stairs. At the sight of the smoke, they looked alarmed.

"What's going on?"

"What's that smoke? Fire?"

"Bomb!" they began to call to each other. "Time to ske-daddle!"

The handful of patrons who'd come for an early drink stepped over Roark and Gina, still slumped against the wall, and disappeared out the exit that led to the alley. She hadn't seen Lulu and Jade emerge from the speakeasy yet. *They're probably ushering the others out through the tunnel,* she thought. Or at least she hoped they were.

She reached for Roark, finding him sitting with his head on his knees, his arms wrapped around his legs. He was trembling.

Her eyes watering from the smoke, Gina tugged on Roark's arm. "Come on, get up. We gotta go outside. We need some fresh air."

Roark just wrapped himself up more tightly and didn't reply.

"Roark? Can you hear me?" Her own ears were still ringing from the blast.

When he still didn't respond, she put her hands on his shoulders and gave him a good hard shake. As forcefully as she could she said, "Roark! "Get up! Now!"

This time he responded to the command in her voice and let her pull him up to a standing position. She put his arm around her shoulders and then led him out into the al-ley. They both gulped in the clearer air.

Roark was still shaking. Something seemed really wrong. "Are you all right?" she asked, running her fingers over his face. "Roark?"

He half-turned away from her and put his head against

the brick wall of the building. His hand was on his chest, and when she reached to cover it with her own, she could feel his heart beating rapidly. "The bomb," he said with great effort.

The early October evening was just starting to darken, and the other patrons had already fled, to their homes or more likely another speakeasy. Gina and Roark were alone in the alley. He groaned again, still shaking. His eyes had taken on a blank expression, and she got the feeling he was somewhere far away.

"Shhh," she said, putting her arms around him. "Everything is okay."

She didn't know how long they stayed like that. Finally, Roark opened his eyes.

"Are you okay?" he asked, running his hands along her arms and looking anxiously over her body. He was clearly trying to get control of himself.

"Y-yes, I'm okay," she replied. "What was that?"

"Black powder bomb," he said with great effort. "Not a pineapple bomb. The explosion would have been greater, more intense, otherwise."

The Third Door opened, and Mr. Rosenstein and Benny came through with Ned, all of them coughing and gasping for air. They plopped down nearby, their backs to the wall. They looked shaken but unharmed.

Mr. Rosenstein wiped the sweat from his brow and straightened his wire-rimmed glasses. "Who would do such a thing?" he asked, looking frightened. "I remember such a thing happening to my parents, in my town, when I was a child. Back in the motherland. Because we were Jewish. Could something the same have happened here?"

Gina shook her head, still bewildered and dazed from the blast. The pharmacist got back up and began to stagger down the alley, still muttering wildly to himself. "Must see the damage."

Benny followed a pace behind him, and after a moment of hesitation, Gina, Roark, and Ned did the same. They all stared. Gina found it hard to make sense of what she was seeing.

An entire section of the front of the drugstore was blown away. The large front windows were broken, and there was dust and debris everywhere, but overall there didn't seem to have been too much damage.

The Signora, several strands of hair out of place, was talking in low tones with Little Johnny and Gooch. When she noticed the four of them, she nodded and said, "You can go to the tearoom with the others. Lulu, Billy, and Jade are already there. I expect everyone back to work within the hour. The fire trucks are on their way."

Sure enough, they could hear sirens in the distance.

Gina swept her eyes over the rubble, stopping on something out of place. A small brown shoe the toe sticking up out of the debris.

"A shoe—?" she asked. *A shoe!* "Oh my God!" she exclaimed, as her mind made sense of what she was seeing. She leapt toward the rubble and frantically began to pull away the bricks and dirt.

"What—?" she heard Roark say, and then he was at her side, digging furiously at the rubble.

"No! It can't be!" She wasn't sure who spoke next, but

Little Johnny and Benny leapt forward, too, as everyone realized at once that a body lay beneath the rubble. "Hurry!"

Within seconds they had pulled off all the rubble and were staring down at the sallow face and still form of Jakob Galinsky.

"Oh dear God," Gina said, clasping her hands together. *Please let him be all right.*

Grimly, Roark put his head to the boy's chest and listened. For a long moment they all watched, and finally he smiled slightly. "He's alive! Call an ambulance!"

Jakob's pack of papers was still wrapped around his body, and gently Gina eased the bag off, thinking it could serve as a pillow to cushion his head. She removed the last two rolled-up newspapers that he had not yet sold. As she did this, something that looked like a mechanical toy fell out. She picked it up and stared at it, comprehension dawning.

"Gina! That's another bomb!" Roark shouted. Then, as she was about to toss it aside, he shouted again. "No! Wait! Don't throw it!

He crouched down beside her, examining the bomb still in her hand. "It looks intact," he said, relief in his voice. He took it from her hand and laid it carefully in the rubble. "We'll deal with that in a moment."

Everyone stared down at the still-unconscious Jakob in disbelief. He looked small and broken, hardly someone who could have brought about such destruction.

"*Ein kleiner Junge!*" Mr. Rosenstein said, distraught. "Just a young boy! Why would he do such a thing?"

"Someone must have told him to do this," Little Johnny

said to Gooch. "A boy wouldn't do this without being told."

Jakob's eyes fluttered open. When a tiny breath escaped, Gina caught the whiff of bourbon.

"Say, kid," Gina said, smoothing his sweaty hair back from his forehead, where it mostly remained clumped up. "What gives? Why'd you bomb the drugstore?'

"Didn't expect to be caught," Jakob mumbled.

"Why did you do it?"

"My papa is still sick from what he drank here that night. Can't work. Won't work. I told you that!" He gave her an accusing look. "My mama's been through enough. Just wanted to send a message. Didn't mean to hurt anyone. "

"You didn't. You only hurt yourself," Gina replied. She looked around. "Although you caused a good amount of damage." The smell of bourbon wafted over her again. "Have you been drinking?"

"Thought I wouldn't get in trouble if I was sloshed. That's what the girl told me."

"What girl?" Gina asked. "Who told you that?"

Jakob passed out again before he could answer more questions. Mr. Rosenstein looked furious. "Some chemists recently have said that alcohol crazes drinkers," he explained. "That there are toxins in the alcohol that can make a person insane. A few killers have even been acquitted that way." The pharmacist tsk-tsked, staring down at Jakob. "I cannot believe this boy could do such a thing."

Gooch said something to the Signora that Gina couldn't catch.

The Signora looked startled. "Make sure he gets to the

hospital. The father, too. Stan, you said his name was? We'll take care of this."

"Who would bomb your store, do you know?" a detective asked them a short while later. He and his partner were both there taking notes. Gina, Roark, Benny, and Mr. Rosenstein were sitting at two tables, while Little Johnny stood by the tearoom counter. The proprietress, Mrs. Metzger, was lingering in the back, concerned but still curious. The Signora had disappeared before the cops arrived, no doubt conferring with Gooch about next steps.

Gina didn't recognize either of the policemen who were asking about the bombing. She thought they might be part of a new unit that the Chicago police had finally formed to investigate all the bombings that the city had experienced since the beginning of the year.

"Maybe the pharmacist wasn't selling them the right kind of medicine," the other officer scoffed. It seemed that they were well aware of the speakeasy below ground.

Gina glanced at Little Johnny, not knowing how to respond.

Little Johnny spoke up. "A young boy did it. Didn't understand that it was a real bomb," he said easily. "Probably did it on a dare. You know how boys are."

The cops looked like they didn't believe him. "A boy?"

"The one that was taken to the hospital. His name is Jakob," Gina said. "He was pretty upset when he realized what he had done."

The detectives scoffed. "He was more likely working for someone. Working *with* someone." He turned back to Gina.

"You seem to know this boy. You say his name is Jakob? Jakob what?"

"Jakob Galinsky," Gina murmured reluctantly. She could almost feel Little Johnny burning a hole through her for giving the cops more information than necessary.

The cop glanced at his partner. "Better check out his family. Maybe they know something about his activities."

"Oh!" Gina replied before shutting her mouth with a snap.

"Is there something you would like to add, miss?" the second detective said, giving her a hard stare. "Something you know about this child's family? Perhaps you know something else? Who might have given him the bomb, for example? It's not likely he built it himself. Even if he did, someone would have had to give him the black powder, caps, and fuse."

"We know nothing more," Little Johnny said. "We are all fine, and we thank both of you fine gentlemen very much."

It wasn't clear whether they believed him or not. The detectives stood up and shut their notebooks. "Since the damage seemed contained only to the drugstore, and only the perpetrator was injured—a child, at that—we are unlikely to bring charges against the boy's family."

"A child who caused several hundred dollars in damages. Maybe over a thousand dollars!" Mr. Rosenstein muttered. He glanced over at Little Johnny. "Of course, I defer to the good wishes of my landlady on how we might proceed. I am in her debt."

As they pulled on their jackets, Little Johnny gestured

to the tea shop proprietress. "Perhaps some pastries for the road?"

"You trying to bribe us?" the first cop asked.

"Take a lot more than a pastry," the other replied, and they both chuckled as they walked out the door.

CHAPTER 20

Gina wandered around the Third Door, unable to focus. The air still stank of smoke and stung her eyes, and it was hard for her to understand anything anyone said to her. Words were jumbled and strange. Her throat and chest were full, and she was finding it hard to breathe. Over and over she kept hearing the jangling of the pharmacy door, seeing the bomb bouncing toward her. Roark's horrified expression, his roar of *BOMB!* Roark kicking the bomb out. The collapse, the smell, the frightened screams. Her own sense of panic. And then . . . Jakob's shoe, poking out of the rubble.

Why had Jakob bombed the pharmacy? Had someone put him up to it?

She kept posing the same questions, but no answers came. Two firemen, dressed in sharp blue uniforms with shining brass buckles, walked through the speakeasy, carefully examining the walls and ceilings. Gina listlessly followed after them, not sure what else to say or do.

"Doesn't look like there's been any structural damage from the blast," one of the men told the Signora and Gooch, who had escorted the men around the main floor and all the back and side rooms.

"You might want someone to come and check the place out," the other added. "Have an engineer from Northwestern give it the once-over. Better safe than sorry!"

Unlike the cops or the Drys, the firemen really were only interested in making sure that the place was secure. Still, they weren't averse to taking the envelopes that Gooch handed them on the way out.

By eight p.m., a handful of patrons had returned to the speakeasy, but most didn't stay long, driven away either by the smell of smoke or by the grim mood that prevailed despite everyone's best efforts to the contrary. Many probably made their way to a more happening joint, where the story of the bombing had no doubt already been exaggerated beyond belief.

Mr. Kowalski stopped by and tried to ask a few questions, but everyone stayed close-lipped. "You can talk about the drugstore being bombed," Gina heard Gooch say to him in a low menacing tone, "but you're not to write about anything else."

None of the ex-servicemen had returned after the blast, Gina noticed. Like Roark, others might have gotten lost in memories of the Great War. The patrons who had decided to stay were all intrepid regulars who came for the spirits, not the gaiety, so they did nothing to lighten the already somber mood.

Ned was openly drinking from his flask as he pecked out tunes indifferently. Lulu was singing gamely, but the rest of the staff looked exhausted from the ordeal.

When Harriet arrived and heard about the bombing, she began to pout. "Rats! I guess that means no crowd tonight," she said, practically stamping her foot. Everyone ignored her.

For Gina, it was hard enough not to keep repeating the memory of the blast over and over. Unexpectedly, she felt her legs begin to wobble. As she gripped the back of a bar stool, she wondered if she might faint.

"You all right, Gina?" It was Roark, his eyes full of concern. He'd appeared out of nowhere.

"I don't know. I feel odd," she replied. "Shaky."

"You're still in shock," he said. "Sit down."

When she sat on the stool, Billy brought her over a shot of whiskey, neat. "Drink up, kid."

"I think you should go home, Gina," the Signora said, not unkindly. Gina wondered how long she'd been watching her. She tried to straighten up, but it was hard to muster the energy. The Signora continued, "In fact, I've changed my mind. We will close up early tonight. It's been quite a day. Get a good night's sleep," she told them all sternly, so that it almost seemed like a warning. "For heaven's sakes, get your clothes cleaned so the place doesn't smell like it's on fire."

Only Harriet protested, but at least she knew enough to keep her mouth shut after the Signora fixed her with a harsh gaze. She stalked out without saying another word.

"Let me walk you home," Roark said to Gina in a low voice. "Don't argue with me."

"I won't. I just need to get my things." Seeing Lulu pulling on her coat, she called, "Do you want to walk home with us, Lu?"

"Nah, I think I'm gonna see what Lucas is up to. Besides"—she gave Gina a half-hearted wink, a passable effort at good cheer—"three's a crowd."

As they moved toward the exit, Gina paused at the spot in the corridor where she and Roark had lain, stunned and gasping for breath. Roark stiffened at the memory. "It brought back something dark," he murmured. "Let's go."

Gina started to follow him out, but a noise inside the pharmacy stopped her. She opened the door a crack and peeked in. To her surprise, the store was brightly lit with large lights that had been brought in and bustling with workers putting the place back to rights under the watchful eyes of Little Johnny. Two men were relaying brick that had been blown out by the blast. Other men were measuring the window frames for new glass. The broken windows had already been removed, and the empty spaces were starting to be covered with wooden planks. A few older women wearing kerchiefs over their hair were wiping all the dust from the shelves and products. At the sight of the damage, Gina whispered a small prayer of thanks that no one had been seriously injured in the blast.

From the progress the workers had already made, it seemed like it would only take a few hours to make things as good as new. Now that she thought about it, she realized that of course the Signora would want the place secure as quickly as possible. She wouldn't want anyone breaking into the pharmacy and stealing the drugs or alcohol, and she certainly didn't want anyone breaking into the Third Door, either.

"That was quick," Gina murmured to Roark, impressed. She thought she'd recognized one or two of the workers from around the neighborhood. Never before had the Signora's long reach been so obvious.

With the alley behind them, Gina took a deep breath. The night air was crisp but not cold, and the smell of smoke had already begun to dissipate. Her steps grew slow, though, as the events of the evening began to overwhelm her again. She could feel her legs starting to tremble. "Roark, I—" she began, but before she could complete her thought, Roark had put his arm around her shoulders.

"Shhh," he murmured into her hair. "It will be all right."

Protectively, he took her other hand in his, and they began to walk in easy unison. Roark's limp seemed a little more pronounced tonight, so she kept her pace slow. For a while neither spoke. It was still early enough in the evening that many people were out and about, hurrying home from their jobs, calling to their children, thinking about fixing their suppers. Very different from her midnight walks with Lulu, where they moved quickly and quietly, trying not to draw too much attention to themselves. Roark's arm remained heavy across her shoulders.

"What are you thinking about?" Gina finally asked, as they neared her street.

He sucked in his breath. "About before," he said, looking down at her searchingly. Some of the same vulnerability she'd seen before was still in his eyes, but a slight wariness, too. "The bombing—it reminded me of, of . . . I felt like I was there again and . . ."

There was no need to finish. Gina squeezed his hand. "Thank you for saving me. I didn't even know what was happening."

"Instincts kicked in, I suppose." He looked into her eyes. "I'm just glad you are okay, Gina. That was my only thought."

My only thought. There was so much weight to those words, and she could read the pain and hope in his eyes. She didn't want to give in to the outside world.

"I'm okay," she said shakily as he stopped and drew her to him.

He tilted up her chin before pressing his lips to hers. When they drew apart, she could see he was smiling.

"What is it?" she asked suspiciously.

"It takes a bombing to bring us together. Go figure."

She leaned up and seized his face in her hands and kissed him again. "Go figure," she murmured.

When the phone rang precisely at eight the next morning, Gina answered it, fully prepared to give her cousin an earful for calling so early. Half the night, she'd tossed and turned, wondering what would have happened if Roark had not been in the drugstore at the right time. "Hello, Nancy," she said into the receiver. "What do you want—?"

Instead of her cousin, it was Aunt Charlotte who interrupted her. "I heard about what happened at *your establishment* last night." Gina could almost hear her lip curling. "What can you tell me about it?"

"I'm fine, thank you. When the bomb was tossed into the pharmacy, Mr. Roark realized what it was and kicked it back toward the door. He was in the Great War." Last night's jitters returned as the enormity of what could have happened washed over her again. "I didn't even know what was happening."

"Oh, you were there?"

"Well, yes. I thought you knew that." Gina paused. "I thought that's why you were calling. To see how I was doing."

There was a long silence on the other end. Gina wondered what her aunt was thinking. Finally, Charlotte spoke. "I am of course grateful you were not injured. Was there much damage?"

The image of Jakob's unconscious body rose in her thoughts. "Well, a kid from the neighborhood, a newsboy, was injured. Around ten years old. He was outside the drugstore when the bomb went off. He was taken to the hospital. And the whole front of the store was blasted off."

"I see." Her aunt said, tsk-tsking. Then her tone grew brisk. "Now tell me, Gina, what else do you know? Did you see who threw the bomb? Do you know who did it?"

Gina hesitated.

"Gina, are you still there? Who was it?"

The news will get out soon enough, she thought. "It was the newsboy. He's the one who did it. We found a second bomb in his bag."

"What? The child did this? Why?"

Gina thought about Jakob's mother begging her to send his father home. Jakob's father stumbling down the street, drunk. Jakob's anger when he spoke about his father's illness.

"Someone must have hired him," Charlotte declared,

not waiting for Gina to reply. "Someone ordered a hit. Who could it have been?"

Had someone hired Jakob? Gina wondered. *That just didn't make sense. Why hire a child to do something like that?*

"Gina?" Charlotte's imperious voice cut across the wire.

"I don't think Jakob was carrying out a hit, at least not like what you're saying," Gina said slowly. "He'd been upset. His father, Stan, had been one of the customers at the Third Door who had gotten really sick the same night the other two patrons had died." She thought about how Stan had groaned and held his stomach. "From what I understand, Stan hasn't been able to work, and the boy's mother has had a hard go of it recently. The boy wanted to take it out on someone."

"I see," Charlotte replied, sounding skeptical.

Gina continued, "He couldn't get into the Third Door, of course, so the pharmacy was the next best thing. He had this idea that if he got drunk before he did it, he couldn't be blamed. Unfortunately, that may have kept him from jumping out of the way in time." She wiped her eyes, remembering the sickening sensation when she'd seen the boy's foot sticking out of the rubble. His gray face when they pulled him out. And then that moment when they knew he was alive. "Although I suppose it might have helped numb him from the pain as well."

"Where do you imagine a boy like that would have gotten the materials and the know-how to pull off such a deed?"

Gina's thoughts began to race at the question. *What was it Jakob had said, before he passed out again?* "The girl," he had whispered.

"I don't know," she said, trying to soothe her muddled thoughts. "Just off the street, I guess."

"Did you talk to the Signora about setting up a meeting with us?" Charlotte asked, abruptly changing topics. "We've been rather surprised that we have not heard from you or her, for that matter."

"I'm sorry. I did talk to the Signora."

"And?"

"She says you're welcome to come in for a drink. She said she'd buy you a round in honor of Marty. Other than that . . ." Gina's voice trailed off.

"We can buy our own drinks," Charlotte replied, sounding even stiffer than before. "Perhaps after this bombing the Signora will have changed her tune."

I doubt it, Gina thought, thinking about the Signora's steel will. Still, there was no need to unnecessarily antagonize her aunt. "I will certainly let you know if she does," she replied, placing the telephone back in its cradle.

For a moment she stared at the telephone. The police had thought the bombing was a warning. Gina had assumed that the boy was just angry. *Was it possible that someone had put him up to it, to send a different kind of message?*

Gina began to tremble again. Forgoing the tea and the hot bath that she had promised herself that morning, she instead crawled back into bed, to catch a few more hours' sleep and to keep the world at bay.

The following morning, Gina walked over to the pharmacy. The place was still closed, but when Gina peered through the cracks in the slats, she could see movement inside. After she knocked on the wooden door, Benny peered out. He held up his index finger. "Just a sec," he said, his voice muffled through the door.

When the door opened, Benny gave a quick harried look up and down the street and beckoned her inside. After she had scurried into the shop, he relocked the door behind her. "Whatcha doing here, Gina?" he asked, crossing his arms.

"I just wanted to see how everything was going," she replied, looking around in wonder. A strong smell of fresh paint had overpowered the usual scent of drugs and soaps. Other than the boarded-up windows, the drugstore looked nearly as good as ever. If it weren't for the indentations and marks near the door, no one would ever have known that the place had been bombed.

"Jeepers," she said, still marveling. She pulled herself onto one of the newly shined stools at the soda counter. They were the cleanest she'd ever seen. "The place looks great."

Benny shrugged. "I suppose."

When she looked closer she could see his eyes were tinged with red. "Say, Benny," she said, feeling contrite, "how's Mr. Rosenstein doing? He didn't look so good yesterday. I guess none of us did. Is he around?"

"He was here for a while this morning, but I think he went to his synagogue to pray. The bombing reminded him of his homeland. What he ran away from."

Gina wasn't surprised he was unsettled. "Any news on Jakob?" she asked.

Benny shook his head. "Nothing. Mr. Rosenstein called the hospital this morning to find out how he's doing. No one could give him any information."

"He did? Wasn't he angry?"

"You know how Mr. Rosenstein is," Benny said. "He doesn't want to accuse anyone unfairly, no matter how bad it looks for the kid. He's a good man. Not one to jump to conclusions."

Another person would have speculated about Jakob— why he'd done it, what he'd hoped to accomplish. Not Benny. Like Mr. Rosenstein, the bombing belonged to a world he didn't want to know, didn't want to understand.

Benny pulled out one of the new glasses they'd gotten, its elegant shape designed to make Coke look cool and delicious. "At least everything seems to be working. Want a soda? I doubt Mr. Rosenstein would mind."

"Sure thing, Benny," Gina replied, watching as he placed the glass under the spigot. Then she peered closer. "Hey, wait a sec! Look at that chip on the lip of the glass. Better not use it. Could scratch your mouth."

Benny held it up to the light. Sure enough, a long scratch could be seen running the length of the glass, with a crack along the top. He pulled another glass off the shelf and then, looking disgusted, set it aside.

"That from the blast?" Gina asked, as he checked a third glass and found no damage.

"Probably," Benny replied, filling the glass with fizzy orange soda and passing it to Gina. "There are probably more cracks than we realize."

Gina gave a mirthless laugh. There were many cracks at The Third Door, and the bombing was not the only threat to the speakeasy's existence. "I have no doubt that's true," she said.

She took a sip of the drink, enjoying the sweet, bubbly

tanginess as it slipped down her parched throat. She finally felt ready to ask the question that had been plaguing her all day. "Say, do you remember that young woman who tried to steal a tube of lipstick? Said her name was Stella? A week ago Wednesday last, it would have been."

Benny frowned. "Yeah, I remember. What of it? You know, I try not to get involved in that stuff. For good reason."

"Yeah, I know," Gina said. "She threatened me."

"Threatened you?" Benny's eyes widened. He lowered his voice. "What did she say?"

"Well, she threatened the Third Door."

Benny looked up at the tin ceiling, appearing to take in the intricate lines for a moment. "I promised my mama when I worked here I would do a good job for Mr. Rosenstein. Learn a lot. Apply myself. Find a way to get to school. She was none too happy to hear about the black powder bomb last night."

"Yeah, I know." Gina had not told her papa for fear he would force her to stop working there. And then where would they be? She felt she had to prove that the Third Door was not a dangerous place to work. "I want to talk to Stella."

"You think she had something to do with it?" His brow furrowed. "Didn't she say she supplied Rinaldi's candy shop over on Fillmore?"

"Yeah. I'll go talk to them."

"You're not going alone," Roark said, appearing in the internal doorway that led to the speakeasy. Gooch was standing there behind him.

Remembering the kiss she'd exchanged with Roark the

night before caused a thrill to run through her, but his eyes were all professional now. She squared her shoulders in response, about to retort that she didn't need a wet nurse taking care of her.

He interpreted the gesture correctly, because before she could say anything, he added, "I'm joining you, and don't even try to say no."

"I'm coming, too," Gooch said. "This, the Signora would expect."

Roark shook his head. "I don't think that's a good idea. They probably know you around there. We don't want to start something that we can't handle."

Gooch gave a curt nod of understanding. "If you're not back within the hour, I'm coming after you."

With that vote of confidence, Gina unlocked the pharmacy door and held it open to Roark. "Let's skedaddle."

CHAPTER 21

Rinaldi's had a charming stone and wood façade, with a keystone indicating that the candy store had been built in 1907. When Gina and Roark walked in, a little bell jangled above their heads, sounding a lot like the bell at the drugstore. They both flinched at the sound and took a deep breath.

Thankfully, a sweet and delicate fragrance engulfed them, and Gina breathed in the aroma of candy before looking around the store in delight. Colored glass jars full of candy lined the shelves, and several barrels were heaped high with brightly colored wrapped candies. Local candies mixed in with the national brands: Charleston Chews, Life Savers, fudges and taffies, and more.

Along the side of the room were some café tables and chairs where someone might have a hot drink and a pastry. Gina's mouth was already watering as she took in the mounds and piles of sweets of all sorts. It smelled even better than the patisserie above the speakeasy, which was scarcely possible to believe.

A grandmotherly-looking woman was standing at the counter, a clean apron tied neatly around her plump form. "Welcome to my store," she said. "I'm Mrs. Rinaldi. What kind of treat were you looking for today?"

"So much to choose from," Gina said, looking around. "It all looks so delicious."

"I don't remember seeing you in here before," Mrs. Rinaldi said, smiling pleasantly. "Are you from around here?"

"Oh, not too far away," Gina murmured, still looking over the shelves, feeling tongue-tied, unsure how she could get the information she needed. Her appetite had suddenly disappeared. Suddenly she just wanted to leave, give up on the whole venture. Her shoulders sagged at the thought.

"What would you like?" Roark asked, nudging her. *Pick something*, she could almost hear him say. *Remember why we're here.* "My treat."

Her eyes flicked over the barrels overflowing with brightly wrapped candies, but then rested on the menu posted in huge letters above. The menu reminded her how women ordered tea in Mrs. Metzger's shop.

"It's a bit chilly. I'll take a hot apple cider," she said. As Mrs. Metger's patrons would, she carefully added, "With *an extra dose.*" She grinned at Roark and the pointed at the three-layer chocolate cake. "Since he's buying, a piece of that cake, too. It looks divine."

Mrs. Rinaldi studied her for a second. "Have a seat," she said, gesturing to the empty tables. "I'll bring it over in a moment." She turned back to Roark. "For you, sir?"

He pointed to the confectionary case. "Make it two ci- ders. I'll have one of those sugar cookies," he said, before leading Gina to a table by the window. "And a small box of chocolates, if you would. One of each type."

"Certainly, sir," Mrs. Rinaldi replied.

"Now what?" Gina muttered.

"Let's just give it a moment," Roark replied.

A moment later, Mrs. Rinaldi brought a tray with two mugs of steaming cider, and the cookie and cake on separate plates. Gina raised her mug to her nose and inhaled deeply, enjoying the fragrant smell of mulling spices in the cider. Taking a sip, she found the added dose of rum quite tasty.

She sank her fork into the cake and took a great bite. "Mmmm," she murmured, savoring the sweetness, then realized that Roark was regarding her, an amused smile on his face. After setting her fork down, she pushed the plate toward him. "Want some?"

"No, I wouldn't want to get between a woman and her cake." His grin grew.

At his teasing tone her cheeks flushed slightly. "Jeepers, I like to eat cake. I don't care what Doris Blake would say about me. *Lose the sweets, or lose your man.* Phfft!" She stabbed at the cake again.

"Relax, bearcat! You're not in danger of losing your man."

Gina rolled her eyes before looking over at Mrs. Rinaldi, who was carefully placing chocolates into a bright green box. "Time to ask about Stella," she whispered.

"How's the cake, dear?" the proprietress asked, having caught her eye.

"Delicious," Gina replied. "The mulled cider, too. I adore your recipe."

"I see," Mrs. Rinaldi replied, handing Roark the box, which she'd wrapped with a huge bow.

"That's actually why we're here," Gina said, trying not to speak too quickly. "*Stella* stopped by my work a little while back. Said we could reach her through you."

Mrs. Rinaldi looked at them both, then leaned over. "You can find Stella over at her uncle's hardware store," she whispered. "Ruczek's, another block south on Morgan. You didn't hear that from me."

Gina and Roark made their way over to the hardware store. The name above the door, Ruczek & Sons, was faded and a bit hard to read. Another late nineteenth-century storefront. Gina had been in the store once or twice over the years with her papa, but he preferred to buy from Gordon's Hardware, so that was her choice, too.

When they walked in, Gina breathed in the familiar smell of freshly cut pieces of wood, nails, paints, and glues. An older man, sporting a blue apron and meticulous bow tie, stood behind the counter, speaking to a customer wearing a tan coat and hat. Both men turned toward Gina and Roark.

"How can I help you good folks?" the store clerk asked, directing his question toward Roark.

"*I'm* interested in looking at the new Black & Decker quarter-inch light-duty electric drill," Gina replied, enjoying the other men's surprised looks, while Roark hid a smile. "I need to fix a few things around the house, and I thought it might come in handy. Do you have any in stock?"

The clerk gave Gina an appraising look, but bid his customer farewell and moved to help her. "Miss, please follow me this way."

As Gina was looking at the racks of tools, they heard a scuffling at the back. It was Stella trying to sneak out of the store; she had gotten caught in a pile of wooden mops in the corner.

"Stella!" Gina called out, disregarding the men around her. "Stop! I wanna talk to you! I wanna know why you did it!"

"What is going on here?" a trim white-haired man exclaimed, stepping out of a back room. He was wearing a close-fitting suit with a blue bow tie. He looked from Gina to Stella. "What is the meaning of this?"

The clerk looked sternly at Gina. His demeanor had become hard, and he no longer wore the amiable expression he'd had when they first walked in. "Explain yourself. Why are you shouting at Mr. Ruczek's niece?"

"Well," Roark began, before Gina interrupted.

"Your niece bombed Mr. Rosenstein's pharmacy!" she said to Mr. Ruczek, before angrily gesturing toward Roark. "He and I were both inside at the time! We could have been killed!"

"Mr. Rosenstein's pharmacy?" Mr. Ruczek repeated, crossing his arms. He looked at his store clerk. "I heard about that."

Gina's heart began to beat faster and she glanced at Roark. *I'm not sure we thought this through. What if Mr. Ruczek was behind the bombing? What would she do then?* As if reading her thoughts, Roark took a step closer to her, so that their arms were touching, in a silent protective way.

Mr. Ruczek was staring at his niece. "Stella? What is this all about?"

Stella's look was pleading. "Uncle Rick," she said, "she's lying. I swear it. I didn't bomb the store."

"Maybe you didn't bomb it yourself. But you gave black powder bombs to a ten-year-old newsboy," Roark said through clenched teeth. "Let *him* do your business for you!"

"He was nearly killed!" Gina said, tears skimming her eyes. "He had to go to the hospital!"

Mr. Ruczek shook his finger at his niece. "Is this true? You gave bombs to a ten-year-old boy?" His fury, though contained, was menacing.

"*She* wouldn't connect us to the Signora! Didn't want our business!" Stella cried. "I was trying to show her what's what!"

"Mr. Rosenstein's drugstore is operated by Signora Castallazzo?" Mr. Ruczek asked, putting his hand to his forehead. "Good heavens."

The store clerk sighed. "I'm afraid so, yes."

Mr. Ruczek beckoned to Stella, who slunk over. He wagged his finger close to her face. "This. Is. Not. What. We. Do!" Each word was pushed out through clenched teeth.

"I thought—" Stella began.

The clerk held up his hand, looking like he was going to strike the girl. "Shuddup, would ya?"

Stella flinched. Roark began to move forward, but Gina grabbed his arm. Things were already escalating.

She was not the only one thinking that. "Let's all settle down a moment," Ruzcek said, glancing at the clerk. The man dropped his hand. "It sounds like my niece has taken matters into her own hands. Wrongly so," he said glaring at Stella. "It seems she contributed to some damage being inflicted on one of the Signora's establishments. Is that correct?"

When Gina nodded, Ruzcek continued. "I will meet with the Signora to discuss damages. *This is not how we do business*," he said, looking angrily at Stella, who cowered at his tone. He turned back to Gina. "Miss, who was the boy that was injured?"

"Jakob Galinsky. A newsboy."

"Galinsky? That name is familiar. Stan's boy?" At Gina's nod, Ruzcek continued. "I know the family. I will see what we can do."

The man's reasonableness and sense of integrity heartened Gina. "Th-thank you sir," she said, glancing at Roark. "I guess we'll be off now."

Roark took Gina's arm, and they turned toward the exit.

Ruzcek stepped in front of them. "Before you go, let me give you a small gift," he said. "For bringing this *matter* to my attention in such a *neighborly* way."

"Uh," Gina replied, again taken aback by his response. She had no idea what to say.

His clerk held up the drill. "The young lady was interested in this Black & Decker. Seemed real knowledgeable, too."

"An excellent choice," Mr. Ruczek said, tying it up quickly in some brown paper and twine. "Please. Take this tool as my gift to you. A sign of my good faith. Please give my best regards to the Signora, and let her know I should very much like to discuss this situation with her."

When Gina hesitated, Roark picked up the package

from the counter and tucked it under his arm. "Thank you," he said, handing Gina the box of chocolates he'd purchased from Rinaldi's. Then, speaking to her under his breath, he added, "Time to get out of here."

"Bring on the giggle water!" a well-dressed man shouted from the balcony of the Third Door, to general cheers from the patrons below.

"Now you're talking!" they shouted, raising their drinks. For a Wednesday night, the place was already crowded, pulsing with excitement and energy. News of last Saturday night's bombing had spread, and rather than people being afraid to come back, scores of customers had already descended on the speakeasy. The bombing had made the place even more thrilling, a place of curiosity and daring.

As the man descended the stairs, she could see it was George, with a gorgeous woman clinging to each arm. Just then Ned began to play "Tiptoe Through the Tulips," causing George to tiptoe down the steps in an exaggerated way, everyone watching him to laugh. Behind him were two other couples, the men hooting and hollering in excitement, the women with their elaborate headdresses waving and blowing kisses, as if they all expected to be the life of the party. They'd clearly already had a round or two at another establishment before they arrived at the Third Door.

George gave an imperious wave to Billy Bottles as the group reached the floor and moved to a few side tables. "Hotsy-Totsys all around, my good man!" he called, eliciting a general cheer from his entourage. "I feel like a million bucks!"

The men clapped his back in a sporting way while the women tittered into their hands.

"I'm feeling a bit squiffy already," one of the women said, giggling. She kept squinting as if she were used to wearing glasses.

Lulu glided over to the group. "Seven Hotsy-Totsys, sir? I'll bring them right over."

"Smokes, too! We need some good cigars. Gina, over here!" George called, causing all his friends to cheer again.

"You're a merry bunch," Gina commented as she held out her tray. Their high spirits were infectious. "Something good happen?"

"You betcha! Stocks went back up again! The rally happened! We're in the money again! Cigars tonight—we'll have three El Productos, and the girls will have—well, whatever you girls smoke. Marlboros?" George took a couple of staggering steps and tossed a few dollars into Ned's tip jar. "Let's get this joint swinging, Neddy baby! I'm feeling on top of the world!"

Obliging, Ned began to play a quick, toe-tapping song that got everyone up on their feet. George and the other men began to swing the women around, and within a few minutes they had downed their first cocktails and called for another round.

When Gina brought over the next round of drinks, George was holding court. "I wasn't sure if the rally was going to happen, you know? All our clients were calling us, demanding answers. We didn't have any answers! I wasn't sure what to expect." His words were starting to slur, and his grin was growing wide and dopey. "The stocks rebounded, thank heaven. All those dips that kept happening this month and last, I'll tell you, even I was a little worried. Usually Dan was the one—" He broke off, a shadow briefly darkening his face, before his grin returned.

"So everything is stable again?" Gina asked, setting his drink down.

He frowned. "Well, nothing is ever 'stable.' Hey, we're back on top, baby!"

"Wanna tell me what happened?" William Morrish said to her, a little while later. He was sitting in what Gina now viewed as his customary spot.

"Oh, you mean the bomb? We're all okay," she said, placing his whiskey tonic in front of him.

"I heard you were there when it happened." His voice sounded strained.

Gina glanced at him. He looked a little more ruffled than usual. She shrugged her shoulders. "I really am all right."

"That's swell," he replied sounding distracted.

Questions bubbled up in Gina's mind then, threatening to overspill. *What are you doing here really? Why were you watching Fruma that night?*

As George ordered another round sometime later, Gina could see that the alcohol was starting to hit him hard. His words were growing increasingly difficult to understand, and he was getting more rowdy and handsy with the women around him.

When Gina returned with the drinks, George stood up, leaning unsteadily against the high-backed chair. "Say, you

wanna have a date later?" He glanced at his female companions, who were slumping in their chairs. "Well, maybe not
tonight, a different night."

"Oh, no, I don't think so, " she said, looking around,
hoping that the Signora and Gooch hadn't heard her. She
certainly had no wish to be scolded again.

"Well, in case you change your mind." He pulled his
business card out of his wallet and dropped it on her tray
with a five-dollar bill. "You'll know where to find me. I
could take care of a girl like you real nice."

Five dollars! She tucked the bill away quickly and
glanced at the card. *George Abbott. Stocks, Bonds, Provision, Grain,
Investments. Carter, Davis & Company. 701-707 The Rookery. 209
South LaSalle Street. Telephone Wabash-3808.*

Still, she didn't want to give him any ideas. "I can take
care of myself, thanks."

"Aw, be nice," he said, reaching to embrace her. "That
fiver should buy me at least a kiss, don't you think?"

"Buzz off, pal," she said, attempting to break free of the
arms encircling her waist.

"Party's over, fellow," Gooch said sternly, appearing out
of nowhere. "Let the lady go. You're leaving."

With a quick tug, Gooch had pulled George to his feet,
removed the glass from his hand, and then captured his
arms behind his back.

"What are you doing?" George sputtered.

"Kicking you out."

George was too drunk to put up much of a fight, although Gina could see the sad awareness cross his face when
he realized that his friends were not going to help him.

"Bye, George," they called, the women blowing him kisses. "Thanks for the drinks!"

If it hadn't all been so pathetic, Gina would have laughed at George's hangdog expression as the bouncer marched him away across the speakeasy floor. Once upstairs, Gooch and Little Johnny would unceremoniously dump the bum into the alley.

She leaned against the piano, rubbing her arm where George had gripped her.

"You all right, toots?" Ned asked.

"Oh, sure. I'd have wrangled myself free in no time. Nothing I couldn't handle."

"That's what Gooch is for. Don't forget it."

"Yeah, sure." Gina surveyed the room, looking for empty glasses and the telltale signs that someone might be waiting on a smoke. The people who'd been fawning over George earlier were now snickering about his unceremonious exit.

"What a pip!" one of the women said.

"Yeah, but his cash was just fine. I'll miss it dearly," another replied, eliciting gales of laughter from the others. When Ned started playing the Charleston, most of them dashed out onto the dance floor. In her hurry, one of them knocked over a bar stool, which Gina went to right.

Alma was still sitting there, tapping her fingers on the table. "Hey, Gina," she said. She looked tired.

"Everything hunky-dory?" Gina asked. "Ready for another round?"

"Sure," Alma replied, giving a helpless wave toward the women dancing the Charleston. "I don't know how my friends haven't keeled over. George bought them quite a few cocktails, and they're still raring to go."

"I don't know either," Gina replied, following Alma's gaze. The women were doing some high kicks now, while the men watched them appreciatively. "I'll be back with your drinks soon."

After putting in the order, Gina began to switch out ashtrays and wipe off tables. When she got to where George had been sitting, she noticed something on the floor. It was a fairly expensive pair of spectacles. She chuckled when she saw them, remembering George placing them in his vest pocket earlier. Must have fallen out at some point. *Serves him right*, she thought. *Especially after being so handsy with me.*

She picked them up. On the other hand, George might need them, and it wasn't like he'd be allowed back inside the speakeasy for a while. Gina sighed. Maybe she could still catch him if he hadn't gotten too far. He'd only left a few minutes ago.

As she passed by Lulu, she said, "Cover for me, will you? There's something I need do real quick."

She hurried up the stairs, spectacles in hand.

CHAPTER 22

Little Johnny and Gooch were standing by the exit leading to the alley, exchanging a few words in low voices. Unlike the chandelier-lit speakeasy, the corridor was not well lit, and there was still a lingering aroma left by the bomb and the fire. When they saw her, they grew alert.

"What is it?" Johnny asked. "Do you need us?"

"You hustled that guy out quick!" she called out, as she moved down the corridor.

Gooch looked her over. "Don't you worry, Gina," he said. "He won't give you any more trouble."

"I know he won't," Gina said. "Unfortunately, he dropped his spectacles. Mind if I check the alley? I thought I might still catch him." Seeing their scowls, she added, "I don't think he'll try anything."

The ringing of a little bell caused them all to turn. That meant one of the bouncers was needed back down in the speakeasy and the other one had to stay at the door.

"Make it snappy," Little Johnny said, opening the green door. "Don't go far. If you don't catch him, then it's his loss."

Gina stepped out into the alley, the fog closing in on her almost immediately. As the door shut behind her, she shivered. Even though she knew that Little Johnny was probably watching her through his peephole, the familiar surroundings of the alley had taken on a menacing feel. The two electric lights were dimmed by the fog, and a third light gave off only a dull red glow. The light was intended to be welcoming, to let patrons know the Third Door was open for business, but right now it gave her a vague sense of warning.

As she peered up and down the alley, she saw George with his hand against the wall, trying to steady himself. He was muttering to himself, and a few of his drunken bits and phrases floated toward her. "Can't believe those guys. Taking my drinks. Why, I oughta—"

Gina was about to bring him his spectacles when a movement in front of her caused her to step into the shadows. A chill ran up and down her back. Someone else was there, watching George. She couldn't quite see the person's face or figure, despite the soft red glow of the speakeasy bulb. The person's furtive movements made her own heart beat furiously. *Why is this person watching George? Is it a mugger?* Then, in the dim light, Gina saw the glint of metal. *Is that a gun?*

She clapped her hand over her mouth, trying to keep herself from screaming. The figure shifted, as if listening for something.

Gina froze, clutching George's spectacles to her chest.

Then a man on the street called loudly to George, and the figure stepped back into the shadows, waiting. Gina waited, too. Another man appeared beside the first, and they said something in joking tones that elicited a great boisterous laugh from George.

"That gin joint's a total dive," she heard him say, his voice easily carrying in the still night air. "Their drinks are bad, and the floor show is worse. I know a good gin joint on Maxwell."

The figure shifted, dropping the gun down. She still couldn't tell if it was a man or a woman. *Should I scream for Little Johnny?* Gina wondered. *Is George about to be attacked?*

Oblivious to his plight, George continued. "Plus, I've got lots of jack to burn! Wanna join me? My car's just around the corner." George started singing, and the other two men gladly joined in. Soon the sounds drifted off as they moved down the street toward George's car.

Straining her eyes, Gina watched to see what the figure would do. Just then the Third Door opened again, and a laughing couple came out, breaking the silence. Gina opened her mouth to scream for Johnny, in case the couple was set upon. But the gun and the figure disappeared from view, and the couple passed by in peace.

Gina sat up straight. She didn't know what had woken her, but she had not been able to shake the image of the figure in the alley. She'd been thinking about it all night. *Had someone been watching George in the alley? Had she really seen a gun?*

Finally, she telephoned Nancy, as she tried to sort through her restless thoughts.

"What is it?" Nancy asked. "You woke me up. I was on the late shift."

Gina filled her in on what had happened in the alley the

night before. "Don't you think that's strange? If it were an ordinary thug, he'd have held up the couple who came out a few moments later. But this person left when George did."

"Hang on," Nancy replied, the sleepy thickness finally disappearing from her voice. "Tell me this again."

Gina explained again, then asked, "Do you think we should tell George that someone was watching him? That he might be in danger?"

"Nah, why? He's the sort who's probably always getting people in a lather. Could have been anyone. Besides, you don't know for sure what you saw."

"You're probably right." She hesitated. "Still, it was odd."

"Well, what do you want to do?" Nancy asked. Gina could practically see her cousin, arms folded, toes tapping.

"I'm going to call George. Tell him someone was watching him. Besides, I have his spectacles. He'll want them back."

"All right," Nancy said. "Let me know what he says."

"Will do," Gina replied, hanging up. As she replaced the telephone in the cradle, a curious sense of satisfaction stole over her, knowing that *she* had ended the conversation for once.

Gina stared at the card that George had given her, flipping it this way and that, before finally dialing the number. As it rang, she thought about what to say. *Hi, George, it's me, Gina. The ciggie seller who had you thrown out of the Third Door last night.*

That would never do. She hung up before the switchboard operator picked up.

Twice more, she did the same thing, dialing the number and then hanging up before she reached the operator.

"Get a grip, Gina," she told herself, forcing herself to stay on the line as the operator took the call.

"How may I direct your call?" the operator pertly asked.

Gina gave her George's office extension and waited to be connected.

A crisp-sounding woman took the call. "I'm sorry. Mr. Abbott is not taking calls. He is out sick today."

Was there a slight note of exasperation in the secretary's voice? It was hard to tell. Then, without asking if she could take a message, the woman hung up the phone.

Gina hung up, too, a bit shocked by the woman's rudeness.

How odd, Gina thought. "Out sick?" she said out loud, feeling unsettled. "Something's not right."

"What's wrong, dear?" her papa asked, fiddling with the radio dial. "Anything I can help you with?"

"Thanks, Papa," she said, kissing the top of his head. "I just need to figure something out."

CHAPTER 23

"I can't believe you're afraid of elevators," Gina grumbled to Nancy as they reached the fifth floor of the Rookery in the Loop. Two more long and winding flights to go. Her calves were already aching. It didn't help that she'd been wearing her pumps again, instead of donning something sturdier and hideous, like the boots her cousin was wearing. She'd taken them off around the third floor and was holding them in her free hand. "We'd be there by now."

"Hey, if you'd heard witnesses describe how they'd seen people's limbs get cut off when the elevator that they were on slipped between floors, you'd feel the same way," Nancy snapped. "Those are the ones who emerged from those cages alive! The stairs are much safer. Trust me."

"I suppose," Gina conceded. They rounded another corner and began to mount the next flight, her hand holding tight to the railing as she continued to pull herself up step by step in her stockinged feet. "So what am I going to say to him anyway? 'Hello, Mr. Abbott, here are your spectacles and I think someone was watching you? Maybe wanting to kill you?'"

"Exactly," Nancy huffed.

Gina pulled out the business card that George Abbott had given her at the speakeasy. She'd tried calling again, but no one had answered at all, even after the switchboard had connected her to his office. Was George all right? Or was he still out on a bender? Given the state he'd been in when she'd last seen him, anything was possible. Maybe he'd been fired. Or maybe something had happened to him. She thought again about the furtive figure in the alley, the memory making her shiver.

"Funny thing that the secretary hasn't answered the phone," she said, pausing to take a breath.

"Maybe she's out sick, too," Nancy replied, each word punctuated by a sharp intake of breath.

"The whole thing is odd, don't you think?"

"No odder than you wanting to talk to Mr. Abbott. Didn't you say that he was thrown out of the Third Door because of you?"

"Yeah, but I'm telling you," Gina said, facing the stairs again. "Something is really off here."

At last, they reached the seventh floor. Breathlessly, Gina pushed open the stairwell door that led into a long corridor of offices. As she slipped her shoes back on her aching feet, the first thing she heard was the harsh sound of multiple ringing telephones behind the closed doors up and down the hallway. The sound grew louder as they made their way down the empty corridor. They reached a glass door marked

701–707, with CARTER, DAVIS & COMPANY in fancy white lettering. Below the firm's name were the names of all the partners and associates.

Gina pointed to George Abbott's name on the door. "I guess he does work here." She took a deep breath. "Okay, here we go!"

The wooden door opened into a luxurious office suite, with three empty desks in the middle of the reception area, and a set of closed office doors just beyond. There was also an empty waiting area, full of expensive-looking chairs, lamps, and sofas. On every desk, there was a ringing telephone with no one to answer it.

What in the world?

"Hello?" Gina called. She and Nancy exchanged a puzzled glance. Where was everyone? "The door was open," Gina said. "Is the office closed?"

She called "hello" again, this time a bit louder, thinking one of the office doors might open.

To her surprise, a gray-haired woman with an untidy bun emerged from behind one of the desks. The name plate on the desk the woman was standing behind read "Mrs. DeVry."

Had she been hiding? Gina wondered. *What else had she been doing behind the desk?*

The woman blinked rapidly, as if she were trying to focus. Her spectacles hung from a chain around her neck. In her hands she gripped a pad of paper and a pen. "What do you want?" She sounded more confused than rude.

"Mrs. DeVry, ma'am, we're here to see Mr. Abbott," Gina replied, stepping toward her. "We have something important to discuss with him. I called a few times, and"—here she gestured toward the ringing phones—"no one picked up." She looked around at the empty suite. "Mrs. DeVry, what is going on?"

Mrs. DeVry unclasped and clasped her hands. "None of the associates are here. Haven't you heard?"

"Heard what?"

She put her hand to her head. "The stock market is crashing! They're all at the Exchange, praying for a rally. Well, they should be praying." She made a disheartened gesture toward the ringing phones and piles of memos. "I was told to stop taking calls." Her voice cracked. "I don't know how to make the ringing stop. Do you?"

Mrs. DeVry looked shrunken, pitiful. Without a word, Gina disconnected the telephone on the woman's desk, then the ones at the other two empty desks. The ringing in the men's offices could be heard, but at least the sound was more muted now, less strident. The silence was remarkable. Even Gina felt it. Mrs. DeVry sagged back in relief.

"They are all at the Exchange right now?" Nancy asked, glancing at Gina.

The secretary nodded. "Pray for us all." Tears slipped down her cheeks as Nancy and Gina beat a hasty exit from the office.

"We're going to the Stock Exchange," Gina told Nancy, stopping before the ornate brass elevator doors in the middle of the corridor. "We *are* taking the elevator down." She pressed the button for emphasis.

To her surprise, Nancy did not object, although she did

step into the cage quickly and kept her eyes tightly closed as the elevator operator brought them back down to the ground floor.

"The Exchange is that way," Nancy said, when they stepped back out onto the street. "Three blocks or so."

Even before they reached the outside of the Stock Exchange building, pandemonium on the streets was evident. Thousands of people were milling about, some with tears on their faces, others looking fiercely determined.

Paper was flying everywhere—strips of tape from the stock ticker machines, as well as other documents that appeared to be shredded stock certificates. Newspaper boys were calling out the headlines of the special afternoon editions.

"Millions of shares sold in New York!"

"Investors seek to save what they can!"

"Ticker tape lags behind!"

Amid the chaos a rattily dressed old woman stood silently, holding a giant sign in her hand. Gina shivered when she read the words. BEHOLD! THE END IS NEAR!

Nancy tugged on her arm. "What a crowd! How will we ever find George?"

"He'll be inside," Gina replied. "Maybe we can find our way in."

It took them a while to push through their way through the crowd. Around them were the voices of confusion, fear, and despair.

"Why aren't the banks helping us?"

"Where is the Federal Reserve in all this?"

"I don't understand what is happening," an older woman wailed. "Why are the prices going up and down like this?"

"There's going to be a rally, Mother, " another woman replied, full of self-importance. She smoothed her fashionable coat. "It's been up and down all day."

"Why don't I have money to buy when everything is so cheap?"

"Doubt there will even be any stock market left, if this keeps going like this."

Near them, an elderly woman fainted, and several people gathered around her. Not everyone was there to help her, though.

"Get these women out of here!" an elderly gentleman grumbled. "That's the third namby-pamby gone down in the last hour!"

"Keep moving," Nancy grunted, her grip on Gina's arm tightening. "We don't have time for this."

When they finally approached the doors, they found themselves blocked by police and guards everywhere.

"I see a way in," Nancy said, practically dragging Gina through the chaos. She said a few words to the beleaguered policeman, and he waved her on with an indifferent flick of his baton. He didn't seem to care, the press and stress of the crowds having done him in.

They passed onto the trading room floor alongside the brokers, traders, bankers, and other men in fancy suits. Others in the room had clearly snuck inside, adding to the general sense of confusion.

Nancy and Gina made their way through the grand room, with its majestic columns and walls papered with exquisite green and gold wallpaper, to the trading room floor. Right now, no one was interested in the glamour of the room, as the stock market's sudden crash was wiping people out left and right.

The Exchange's floor was muted and subdued, a stark contrast to the flurry they had experienced outside the building. Most people were transfixed by the big black boards at circular tables around the rooms, staring as the abbreviated names of stocks and their prices were posted by nervous-looking clerks holding reams of ticker tape. A few people holding notepads were trying to write down the numbers on the big board. Most just had their arms folded tightly across their chests, or their hands stuffed in their pockets, waiting for specific stock numbers and prices as they were posted. All around, people's faces were glum, mouths downturned, jaws slack, eyes widening as desperation set in. When people did mutter something to those standing around them, their comments reflected a darkly bitter humor as they grew more aware of their terrible sinking fortunes.

"They just took twelve hundred dollars from me!" Gina heard one man say to his companion. "All that I had! From now on, I guess I'll need to work for my money!"

"Heaven forbid!" his friend replied. "I had sixteen hundred dollars in the bank. Then I drew it out and bought Simmons on margin!"

"Oh, Simmons," the first man said, giving a shallow bark of laughter. "That one's down the toilet."

"Yeah. I think I've got about five bucks to put back in the bank."

An older gentleman chuckled, the grim sound like a death rattle. "I just put a few hundred dollars into the stock market. Earlier this month, I sold some real estate. Trying for the big money. Lesson learned. Never again. Good-bye, stock market." With that, he put his tan hat firmly on his head and walked out the door of the Exchange, a throwback to a more genteel response to tragedy.

Gina grabbed Nancy's arm. "Look, I see him!"

George Abbott was up on a small stage, speaking into a telephone. Gina and Nancy pushed their way toward him. George had set down the phone and was staring numbly at the big board, shock and dismay written all over his face.

A man in a rumpled suit had climbed up next to him. He was mopping his flushed and sweaty face with a handkerchief. They had just gotten close enough to hear when the man said to George, "Maybe I should buy one of the good stocks?"

George turned to stare at him. "Don't you dare! You heard the boss! They are going to kill and stuff anybody who buys anything today." His voice was grim. "The short sales are where the profits are at."

"You believe that?" the man replied, looking incredulous.

"I have to!" he replied.

Just then, there was an explosive sound. Gina flinched, and a few people screamed.

"Shooting!"

"Bombing!"

Some people began to flee toward the exits, while others craned their necks, looking for the source of the disturbance.

Gina was among the first to realize that a press photographer standing nearby had just used his flashbulb, the sound tearing through the hall like a bomb. He looked a bit sheepish over the distress he had caused. "Sorry," he said lamely to anyone who was listening. Frowning, the people turned back to the board or staring down at slips of paper in their hands. As quickly as the panic had begun, it stopped.

George mopped his forehead with a soggy handkerchief. Seeing the gesture reminded Gina why she was there. "Mr. Abbott," she called, "I need to talk to you!"

He turned and looked at her. "Oh, it's you," he said, his instinctive charm emerging despite the shock and strain he was under. "Look, doll, I'm sorry I grabbed you at the Third Door. Your guys made it perfectly clear. I won't cross that line again. Everything hunky-dory now?"

"I wanted to talk to you. It's important."

"Look, I'm busy, doll," he said, sounding serious. "No time for hanky-panky now."

"I'm not here for that," Gina said, ignoring Nancy's side-eye.

"Well, no time for business questions either. Keep the good stocks, dump the bad. That's all I got."

"Aren't they all bad right now?" Gina asked, watching a woman wipe her eyes with a tissue.

"I don't have time for this." He started to turn away. Nancy nudged her.

"Wait! Mr. Abbott, please! George!" At the sound of his first name, George turned back around.

"I've got your spectacles," she said.

For the first time, George grinned. "Well, thanks, darling," he said, reaching for them. He breathed on the glass and wiped them off on his vest before slipping them back on.

"I've had a bad time of it, not being able to read the board. Although maybe that's been a good thing."

"Also, I think someone was watching you when you left the Third Door," Gina said. "I got a bad feeling about it. I thought maybe the person wanted to hurt you."

"What——?" George started to say, but he was interrupted by a man shouting something at him.

"Simmons dropped another fifty!"

"Hold! Hold!" George shouted, flailing his arms. He looked down at Gina. "Look, I can't deal with this right now. Come find me later."

"Come to the Third Door tonight," Gina replied. "I'll tell you everything."

George glanced at the huge clock on the wall and groaned. "Ugh. Twenty minutes to go till the closing bell. It's too late for a rally." He mustered a wry grin. "I'll be needing a stiff drink. Or two. Or three. Or hell, I'll drink every bottle of rum in the place. Of course, you'll probably have to buy it for me, because I'll have just lost everything." He repeated the word. "Everything."

Gina looked around the great room again, oppressed by the funereal feel. People were clearly grieving the loss of their money, their earnings, their livelihoods, their future.

"I'll be there when I can," he said.

CHAPTER 24

"This place is a morgue," Lulu whispered to Gina when she walked into the Third Door a few minutes before six o'clock. A few people had already drifted in, some looking like they'd been crying, most just looking stunned and dismayed. There was none of the customary gaiety or laughter—no joy at all.

"Corpse Revivers all around," Jade said to Gina and Lulu under her breath. "These people have got no life in them."

"How much did we lose?" everyone kept muttering to each other.

"There will be a rally tomorrow," others would reply, trying to reassuring themselves. "Black Thursday will soon be just a dreadful memory."

"We'll get it all back soon enough."

"For now, let's just drink and forget everything."

"Everyone will come to their senses over the weekend."

"Bottoms up!" This last brought about wry laughter all around, inducing a sense of fake cheer and joviality among a few. Most continued to sit sullenly, staring into their drinks or murmuring frustrated comments to their companions. More straight alcohol than usual. Lots of absinthe. Still plenty of frothy concoctions to help dull the pain of the day.

Ned was playing pieces she'd never heard before, pounding the piano keys with the whole force of his body, his entire torso involved in each moment. Rather than jolly, happy-go-lucky tunes, he was playing something horrible and discordant, each note and chord jarring and grotesque. Definitely not something anyone would want to dance to. Yet somehow it matched the mood in the room perfectly.

"What in heaven's name is that?" Gina asked.

"'Piano-Rag-Music,'" he replied. "By Igor Stravinsky."

The Signora came out and stared at him, one eyebrow raised. "Ned. Please."

Chuckling grimly at the rebuke, Ned switched to a jazzier number. When he nodded at Jade, the singer stepped forward, wearing a shimmering black gown. As she began to croon, her sultry voice spoke stirringly of loss and despair. The murmured conversations began to cease as patrons turned toward her, listening to her words far more intently than usual. Instinctively, Ned began to slow down the tempo, so that each soulful note from Jade punctured any veneer of good cheer. By the crescendo, some patrons looked stunned, tears running down their cheeks.

Roark came in and seated himself at one of the empty tables in the corner, instead of heading into the back room with the ex-servicemen. He winked at her, and she came over. "Gin and tonic?"

"You got it," he said. "Our friend George arrive yet?"

Gina had called Roark from a walnut telephone booth outside a drugstore after she and Nancy had left the Stock Exchange, filling him in. He hadn't been happy that she'd sought out George Abbott, even though he'd accepted her explanation. "No," she said. "I wonder if he will."

"He will if he thinks you're here waiting for him." There was a tinge of jealousy in his voice.

She scowled. "I'm not *waiting* for him."

Nancy came down the stairs then and, seeing them, walked over and plopped herself into a chair across from Roark. "He here yet?"

"No."

"I hope you don't mind, I asked Captain O'Neill to join us."

Gina stared at her. "The captain? Really?"

"Relax. He lost a lotta dough on the market today, and I invited him for a drink. He's not a Dry. Don't think anyone really cares about that right now anyway."

Sure enough, Captain O'Neill and another cop came in, both dressed in civilian clothes. Without speaking, they each reached for one of the small bowls of peanuts placed on the tables, crunching the salted snack with gusto.

Gina thought that for sure Ned would start playing "The Laughing Policeman" as soon as he saw the coppers, but he didn't. Perhaps he could see that the policemen, like everyone else, were ready to drown out the losses of the day in cocktails. Did they expect the city to be quiet tonight? She thought that was unlikely, but it was hardly her place to say.

The Signora herself brought over two glasses of finer

wine. "Here you go, *Mr.* O'Neill," she said, emphasizing the word "Mr." "On the house. It's been a rough day. We'll do what we can to take the edge off."

The younger policeman looked startled, seeming about to jump to his feet. Captain O'Neill rested his hand on the man's arm, effectively keeping him seated. "Thank you, Signora Castallazzo," the captain said, and, after the Signora turned away, downed the glass in two gulps.

Around seven o'clock, George finally wandered into the Third Door, a far cry from the triumphant rooster he'd been the last time he'd entered the joint. He looked a mess, even worse than when she'd last seen him at the Exchange.

"Where's that ciggie seller? Gina!" he called out as he descended the stairs. "She promised me a drink. On the house. I need it bad!" He pulled a leather-covered flask from his vest pocket. "I finished my own supply of bourbon twenty minutes ago."

Gooch hustled over, a deep scowl on his face. "Hey, didn't I kick you outta here the other night?"

"That was when I was rich. Now I'm poor. Poor as dirt. You wouldn't kick a man when he's down on his luck, would ya?"

"I might," Gooch replied, reaching for his arm. Seeing this, Gina scurried over to intervene.

"Come sit here," Gina said hastily, linking her arm in George's. "It's all right, Gooch. He's gonna behave himself tonight. Right, George?"

George gestured toward the bar. "Anything you

say, toots. I'll take a sidecar. May be the last I have for a while."

She escorted him to a table near where Nancy and Roark were seated. "Nice and cozy here. I'll be back with your drink in a moment."

When she returned, he took a long sip, then stared at her. "All right, doll, give it to me straight. What's all this about someone following me? Trying to kill me?" He was slurring his words—whatever was in his flask was already doing him in.

"Someone was watching you in the alley after you left the other night," Gina said. "I think they had a gun. Someone has it in for you, I'm thinking."

George laughed, with only a trace of bitterness. "Unfortunately, you'll need to be much more specific," he said.

"We were hoping you'd have something more to tell us," Nancy said, swiveling on her stool.

"Hey, what's this?" George said. "I remember you from earlier."

"Just drink your drink and try to answer our questions," Roark said.

George began to shift uncomfortably. "Listen, I gotta use the little boys' room. I'll try to sort this out when I get back." He gave Gina a wan smile. "It would be great to have my drink freshened. Then I can run through the list of people who want to kill me, which has certainly grown after today."

Gina watched George cross the empty dance floor toward the men's room and then continued her customary sweep of the room. Her eyes fell on Alma sitting at the end of the bar, a half-finished cocktail in front of her. *She's been here a lot,* Gina thought. *I never asked her whether she might have seen anything that night.* Idly, she watched Alma for a moment as she smiled along with the others around her. A moment later she stood up and moved across the dance floor, probably to powder her nose.

"Say, Ned," Gina said to the piano man. "See that woman over there? Alma? She seems to be here a lot, but never with the same people."

"What of it?" Ned said, running his fingers energetically across the keys. "You think she's a quaff?"

She shook her head. Alma seemed too mousy, too nondescript, to be a lady of the evening, nothing like the sort that Gooch and Little Johnny would escort out when they spotted one. Most knew enough to enter the joint in pairs. She'd only seen Alma leave alone. She was sort of a sad person, Gina thought, remembering how she'd found her crying in the ladies' room over the recent deaths of her father and Fruma.

"Well, we've got all kinds here," Ned said, banging the keys for emphasis. A despondent chord arose from the piano. The Signora gave him a warning look, and he began to play a quicker tune. It was all to no avail, though—the mood in the room was low, and no one felt much like dancing.

Gina turned her thoughts back to George, wondering what else she might ask him about. He'd been gone for a while now, and a thought came to her and she decided to go after him. She left the speakeasy floor on the way to the restrooms. Sure enough, he was standing in the corridor.

"Hey, George, could the person have been one of your clients . . . ?" Gina began to ask, trailing off midquestion as she took in the scene in the corridor in front of her.

George was standing by the door of the men's room, his hands halfway in the air, a stupid smile on his face.

Alma was standing there between them, and Gina could see she was holding a small pistol in both hands, pointed squarely at George's chest.

"Alma!" Gina shouted. "No!"

Alma looked at her but waved the gun in George's direction. "This doesn't involve you, Gina. Just turn and walk away. I promise I'll even kill him out in the tunnel—yes, I know about that dirty tunnel out of the speakeasy. I won't make you clean up this mess."

"What's going on?" George mumbled, a dumb smile crossing his lips. Clearly muddled by drink, he did not seem to grasp the threat before him. "You ladies fighting over me?"

Both Alma and Gina rolled their eyes at the man's arrogance.

He blinked, trying to focus. "Well?"

Alma waved the gun more deliberately at him. "See this, Georgie? It's a pistol. Best used in point-blank situations, like this. My father, whom you killed, showed me how to fire a gun, so I know exactly what to do. Just so you understand, I'm going to kill you," she said, smiling in a way that bared her teeth. "I'm going to enjoy it, too."

George looked startled, and the first flicker of fear crossed his alcohol-addled features. "W-what? Kill me? What do you mean I killed your father? I didn't kill anybody. You got the wrong guy, lady."

"Oh, no, I know I got the right rat. Already got the other rat."

The other rat? What did she mean?

Gina started to back away down the corridor but stopped when Alma caught her. "You know, I've changed my mind," Alma said. "I don't want to kill you, but I will if you scream. Come here, next to Georgie."

Gina did as she was told, her heart pounding, hoping someone on the speakeasy floor would notice her absence and come find out what was going on. Maybe there was a way to alert Nancy or Captain O'Neill, or the younger cop who was out at the table getting wasted.

Keep her talking, Gina thought. *Maybe I can stall for time.* She didn't want to think what would happen if Alma was able to manipulate her into the tunnel. She might get away with it all.

"Alma, when you say that he killed your father, what did you mean?" Gina said, striving for as pleasant and soothing a tone as she could muster. "What happened to him?"

"This *rat*"—she pointed to George—"and the other one, *Daniel,* convinced my father to put all his savings into stocks, back in September." Tears began to fill her eyes. "Why'd you do that? He just wanted something to retire on! Instead, he lost everything! Do you have any idea what that type of loss would do to a man?"

"Oh, the small drop back in September," George said, his forehead creasing as he struggled to think through what she was saying. "That was the first of the drops. I guess we should have seen this one coming." He looked lost in thought. "The market can be volatile," he said, trying to explain, taking on a slightly pedantic tone as if speaking to a client. "Fluctuations happen. Not my fault. Even what happened today. Not my fault."

Alma hissed at him. "It was, too!"

"Not my fault!" His tone turned petulant. "You get it? That loss was not my fault."

Tears began to slip down Alma's face in earnest now. "You're the one who doesn't get it. It is your fault—why can't you see that? My father lost his livelihood, his hard-earned money, and his self-respect. You wouldn't help him and"—she gulped—"now he's gone!"

"What h-happened to him?" Gina asked, even though she had a sense of what Alma would say.

"He ended up throwing himself off Navy Pier!" Alma cried. "He drowned in Lake Michigan."

"I didn't make him invest," George complained. "I didn't make anyone do anything. Why does everyone keep blaming me?"

"You talked him into it!" Alma exclaimed. "I know you did. You and your *pal*, Daniel!"

Everything clicked for Gina then. "*That's* why you poisoned Daniel! Revenge for your father. Is that right?"

Alma did not say a word, her fury-filled eyes still fixed on George. She seemed unaware that Roark and Nancy had appeared behind her. Roark put his finger to his lips, and Nancy gestured for Gina to keep talking.

"Will you admit it, Alma?" she asked.

Behind Alma, Roark counted with his fingers. On the

count of three, Nancy and Roark tackled Alma together, bringing her to the ground. The gun went off, and George screamed, a high-pitched wail.

"Oh, no!" Gina cried, seeing him slump down the wall in pain.

George stared down at his arm and began to bawl as the blood started to show on his blue silk shirt. Gina rushed over to George's side as Nancy successfully wrangled Alma. Others began to move. Gina could see Lulu standing there.

Roark came over to examine the man's wound. "Flesh wound," he said, sounding relieved but also a little disgusted by the sobbing man's overreaction. "We just need to bandage it. You'll be all right."

Gina looked around for something that could serve as a bandage. "Lulu, hand me your scarf!" she called to her friend.

With wide eyes, Lulu silently unwrapped the bright turquoise embroidered scarf from around her neck. She watched as Roark wrapped it tightly around the wound on George's arm. "Oh, no," she murmured.

Gooch and Little Johnny pushed forward then, followed by the Signora and Captain O'Neill.

"What is going on?" the Signora demanded, looking around. Captain O'Neill and the other cop had pushed their way through as well.

"This woman—Alma—poisoned Daniel Roth, and tried to kill Mr. Abbott just now," Nancy explained, pointing at the murderess. "They had encouraged her father to put all his money in the stock market back in September, and he lost everything in the earlier drop."

"What's your full name, miss?" Captain O'Neill asked Alma, who had shrunk a half size. Gone was the woman Gina had seen earlier, a menacing presence standing tall in her fervor. Now she looked like a defiant mouse, although startled by the trap around her.

"Malone," George said, sniffing. The gunshot wound appeared to be sobering him up. "Alma Malone. I remember now. Her father was one of my clients. I didn't know anything about his death."

Nancy frowned. "*Why* did you kill Fruma Landry?" she asked Alma, who remained tight-lipped.

Gina closed her eyes for a moment. "You were sitting at the bar, near where Billy Bottles prepares the drinks. You didn't mean to kill Fruma, did you?" she said, working it out. "You poisoned the men's drinks and—"

"That idiot kept letting Fruma drink them," Alma hissed, pointing at George. "It was frustrating. Dan would drink his, but George kept giving his drinks away to that silly girl."

"I did," George replied, still slumped against the wall. "I remember that."

"There was another mix-up with the drinks," Gina said, continuing to sort through the movements of the evening. "You'd slipped some poison into at least one other sidecar. You thought it was intended for George or Dan, but instead I took it over to Mr. Morrish. He sent it back." Gina pondered. "I set down that drink on the counter near Stan Galinsky, who drank it, thinking I'd given it to him. He's been sick for days."

The Signora spoke up then. "I talked to Mr. Galinsky's

family. He'd only suffered that first night. But a melancholia took hold of him, keeping him in bed, unable to do his day-to-day work."

"That pathetic man should have been home with his family," Alma said. "I was just glad I got Daniel at least." She waved her hands dismissively. "It wasn't so hard to poison them. Every time one of those drinks was served, I'd stir in a dose."

The wanton nature of the poisoning caused everyone to stare at her in horror. Alma tossed her head. "It's hardly my fault that other people ordered the same drinks. How was I to know?"

"You must have been pretty angry when George didn't die," Nancy said, trying to keep Alma talking. "That's why you wanted to kill him the other night!"

"We need the police! Why hasn't someone called them yet?" George sputtered.

"This is Captain O'Neill," Nancy said, pointing to the off-duty captain.

"And this is Officer Doyle," Captain O'Neill said to him, indicating Nancy. "She's the one who figured everything out."

"Well," Nancy said, glancing at Gina, who shook her head after a meaningful look at the Signora. She didn't want the proprietress knowing about her role in the investigations.

"This woman tried to kill me," George sputtered. "And she just admitted to killing my friend Dan. And that other woman. What was her name again?"

Even Nancy looked disgusted. "You mean the woman you went home with? Her name was Fruma Landry."

"Well, whoever she killed," George replied, indignant. "This woman needs to be arrested!"

Captain O'Neill said to Nancy, "Why don't you call it in, Officer Doyle. Signora, may we use your telephone? We'll need a paddy wagon to cart the accused off to Harrison Street station."

"Certainly," the Signora said, welcoming him into her private salon.

"Captain O'Neill, this means Adelaide is innocent," Gina called. "She was just high and stupid when she put the necklace on her dead flatmate, but she's innocent."

Captain O'Neill touched his cap, acknowledging her statement. "Looks that way. I'll see about having the charges against her dropped."

As they led Alma away, she began to laugh, deep hysterical laughs. "I hope you enjoy the *fluctuations* of the market! I'm hoping you lose everything! I may go to prison, but I'll still be laughing at you!"

George buried his head in his good hand, a shell of his blustery, cocky self. Alma's laughing was all they heard as she was escorted to the paddy wagon waiting out on the street above.

CHAPTER 25

Even though twenty-four hours had passed since they'd all begun to drown their sorrows, the Third Door patrons still seemed to be going through the motions. There was still a faint sense of hope that the stocks would rally, although grim whispers about "depression" could be heard.

Fewer people than usual were there, and most who did come were only drinking, not dancing. Around seven, Gina was surprised when Fruma's ex-fiancé, Vidal Bartucci, descended the speakeasy stairs, accompanied by Mr. Kowalski, the reporter from the *Tribune*, and another man. Earlier, Gina had called both men to let them know that Fruma Landry's murderer had been caught and that Adelaide had been released from jail, cleared of all charges. She certainly had not expected them to come to the Third Door, let alone be together. A story about Alma Malone had already run in the *Tribune*, with Kowalski's byline. However, the three men took a table in the corner and beckoned her over.

"Thanks for the telephone call yesterday," Vidal said to

Gina. "It means a lot to me, to know that Fruma's murderer was caught." He wiped away a tear. Gina studied him. His regret and sorrow seemed sincere. "I just wanted to let you know about something I recently learned. Probably seems unimportant, given what's going on with the stock market and all that, but I thought you would both find this interesting."

"What is it?" Gina asked, looking expectantly at the other man, whom Vidal had yet to introduce. "Want a drink?"

"No thanks," the other man replied. "I've got to head to the airport in an hour. Special chartered flight to DC later."

"Allow me to introduce you to Captain Melvin, known to his friends as Ace."

The reporter and Gina looked at each other. "I think I know where this is going," Mr. Kowalski said.

"Tell them what you told me," Vidal said to Captain Melvin.

"Sure thing. Off the record?"

The reporter frowned but jerked his head in consent.

The pilot continued, "Back in mid-August, a young woman chartered a plane to Joliet airport because she wanted to jump out of it. Her name was Fruma Landry. She wanted to set a world record, she said."

Gina leaned back against a stool as she listened. Captain Melvin continued, "I have to admit, I didn't believe she'd do it, and I may have told the airplane mechanic that." He wiped his brow. "Look, I shouldn't have taken her money. We're not supposed to charter private flights under the table. Another flight had been canceled, and she offered to pay double the expenses. I couldn't let that opportunity pass."

"Well, what happened?" Gina asked. "Did Miss Landry jump out of the plane?"

"She sure did!" the pilot exclaimed, looking pleased. "I've jumped out of plenty of planes myself, and I checked all her equipment."

"It was true?" Mr. Kowalski said suspiciously. "Why didn't you tell anyone? Didn't you know about the kerfluffle in the papers? The claims that she had made the whole thing up?"

"No. I was out of the country for a while, flying some planes over in France for some U.S. diplomats there. I didn't know anything about it. I hadn't given her my name, so that's why she couldn't name me."

"And you're coming forward now because——?" the reporter said.

The pilot shrugged. "I thought I'd clear Fruma's name, even if just with you three. I thought that such a spirited girl deserved better than what she got."

Gina nodded, a sense of regret that such a lively spirit had been so wantonly extinguished. She raised an imaginary glass. "To Fruma," she said, and the others followed suit.

Over the next three days, Chicagoans everywhere continued to pray for the stock market to rally. There was a brief respite on Monday, although there were many strange signs and fearful happenings that kept people from gaining much confidence or sense of optimism about the market.

Particularly odd were the reported sightings of clouds

of blackbirds and starlings that had swirled around the financial district of New York. "A bad sign," the Chicagoans whispered to each other. "A bad omen."

Then suddenly it was all over. On Tuesday—Black Tuesday—everything sank completely. Even the most optimistic among them were beaten and forced to surrender their sense of hope. No possible rally. No reprieve. Just a grim new reality and a sense of foreboding about what lay ahead.

Gina was there when handfuls of patrons starting filing into the speakeasy at the end of the day, looking deadly serious. George stopped by to see if anyone wanted to buy his Duesenberg on the cheap, but he soon left. There was no gaiety that evening, false or otherwise. The stories patrons shared were grim. Stockbrokers and investors in New York who had jumped out of their Wall Street offices to their death. Millionaires committing suicide. A few Chicago bank executives missing, feared dead. The word "depression" was no longer a whisper.

"What do we do now?" Lulu asked.

The Signora looked pale. "We go on as we can, until we can't."

"Miss!" an older woman called to her on her way into Mr. Rosenstein's drugstore the following afternoon. It was Mrs. Galinsky, Stan's wife. As before, a tiny girl in tattered clothes gripped her skirts, and Jakob stood sullenly behind her. She pushed him forward. "My boy has something to say to you."

"Miss Ricci, I'm sorry I bombed the store," he mumbled, shuffling his feet.

"I should think so! You'd better not do anything like that again!" Gina said. "You could have been killed. Or killed someone else!"

Mr. Rosenstein opened the door then, regarding the family. He must have seen them through the window. "You, boy, you are all right now, *ja?*"

Jakob nodded, not looking him in the eye. His mother poked him, and he spoke his words of apology again.

The pharmacist gave a curt nod to acknowledge the boy's contrite and forlorn words. He waved at the shop behind. "Everything is fixed now, as you can see."

"Have you returned to the *Tribune?*" Gina asked, noticing that the boy did not have his faded satchel slung across his chest.

Both mother and son looked sorrowful. "They sacked me," Jakob said.

"Stan said he's sworn off drink," Mrs. Galinsky said, looking proud. "The foreman let him return to work, thank God. He's been home earlier than he's been in years!" Then the brightness of her smile dimmed as she looked over her children, clad in raggedy and dirty clothes, their poverty obvious to behold.

Mr. Rosenstein coughed slightly and straightened his bow tie. "Jakob," he said. His voice was stern. "You come to the store tomorrow after school. I will pay you to wash dishes and sweep the floor. There will be no lollygagging, no sleeping on the job. You understand me?"

Mrs. Galinsky gasped and clapped her hands together in mute thanks. Jakob straightened his shoulders and looked directly up at Mr. Rosenstein's face. "Yes sir! You can depend on me, sir."

That evening, William Morrish stopped by the Third Door. She hadn't seen him since the night Alma was arrested for the murders of Fruma and Daniel. "What have I missed?" he asked, taking a sip of his whiskey. "Any more poisonings? Shootings?"

Gina shook her head and turned to go, then turned back to him. "You know what I've been wondering? Why were you watching Fruma that night?"

"Was I?" He smiled slightly. "That sounds like the question of a jealous woman."

"Phfft," she said. "Hardly. But don't deny it. I know you were watching her."

He shook his head. "No, I was there for you."

"What do you mean?"

He took a long sip of his drink. Then he spoke with the air of someone giving up a long-held secret. "I work for Charlotte and John Doyle."

"My great-aunt and -uncle?" When he just shrugged, she began to piece it together. "They wanted the Signora to hire them to protect the Third Door."

"She wanted nothing to do with it, as you might surmise." He swirled his glass. "I was there that day to learn more about what threats the Third Door was facing. She turned me down flat when I spoke with her."

"Why did Gooch and Little Johnny let you come back, then?" Gina demanded. "You were there the very next night."

Here he smiled. "That's because I told them I was sent by the Doyles to protect you."

"I don't need your protection."

Roark came in then. He frowned when he saw them, but he didn't come over. William chuckled. "No, I don't think you need my protection. At least not right now." He downed the last bit of whiskey. "I won't be coming back, unless you invite me."

Gina placed the empty glass on her tray. He stood up. "I'll still be around, though. If you ever need me, come to Maisie's."

"Maisie's?" she asked. "The ice cream parlor? Why there, for heaven's sake?"

He put his finger to his lips. "I own the place. But that's a secret just for you to know." Seeing Roark heading over, he touched her hand. "Come anytime. Even just to make that guy jealous."

Later that evening, Gina and Roark left the Third Door together. Even though it was almost midnight, the streets were full of zozzled people, openly drinking from flasks. The police just watched them walking around; no one was being arrested. The world was upside down.

"Harriet's left," Roark said. "Finally. For Hollywood."

"Oh yeah?" Gina said, stopping. "Has she gone for good? I thought she wanted to work at the Third Door."

"I think she was just yanking your chain," he said. "I don't think she ever intended to work here. At least not for long."

Gina considered this. She remembered the way Harriet had spoken. Maybe things would have been different if Roark had welcomed her back the way she'd hoped.

"She left me a present," Roark said.

"Oh yeah? What?" Gina asked. *What do I care what Roark's wife gave him? Why is he smiling like that?*

"She signed the divorce papers before she left."

Gina looked up, her heart starting to beat quickly. Roark's face was inscrutable. "She said that I'd regret it when she's raking in the big bucks."

"And will you?"

"Gina! As if you have to ask." Turning to her, he took her face in his. "Now I can do this."

Leaning down, he kissed her thoroughly. This kiss was different from what they'd experienced after the bombing. Urgent, but not frantic. Hopeful. Her hands went around his waist as if they belonged there. Only as the wind picked up and an old newspaper caught itself around her leg did they reluctantly separate.

As she reached down to disentangle it, the wayward page reminded her fleetingly of Jakob, the ex-newsboy. Jakob had done every task Mr. Rosenstein had asked of him, and more. A small bright light in an increasingly dark and worrisome world. She shivered, though, when she glanced at the headline. U.S. ECONOMY CONTINUING TO WORSEN. WORLD BRACING FOR IMPACT.

Roark took the paper, crumpled it up, and tossed it into a nearby rubbish bin. "Enough of that," he said. He drew her hand through the crook of his elbow, and they continued to walk. "There's a fight at the Coliseum on Monday night. Would you—and your papa—like to join me? It'd be an honor to bring Frankie the Cat."

Now was not the time to think of the world's troubles. She smiled up at Roark. "Tell me all about the fight. My papa will want to know everything."

AUTHOR'S NOTE

I set both *Murder Knocks Twice* and *The Fate of a Flapper* in 1929 Chicago for the sheer drama associated with that location and period. It was the last year of the glamorous (and highly problematic) roaring twenties and was marked by two pivotal events—the St. Valentine's Day Massacre in February and the great stock market crash in October. By reading every edition of the *Chicago Daily Tribune* from 1929, I also learned about the more than one hundred bombings that occurred in Chicago that year alone. The Lake Shore Athletic Club really was bombed that year, as were ice cream parlors, drugstores, banks, private homes, and many other types of stores. There are even stories of some locations being bombed twice in a single day. There's no clear answer to why there were so many bombings that year. However, the ability to make bombs was a skill servicemen had brought back from the Great War and, as such, became an intimidation method of choice during the 1920s, particularly with the rise of organized crime as well as frustration with fluctuations in the stock market.

I was also struck by how common death from alcohol poisoning was during Prohibition, a fact that informs the backdrop of this story. By some estimates, over ten thousand individuals across the United States died from alcohol poisoning, with the number of annual deaths dramatically ticking upward after 1927. As author Deborah Blum has explained, in 1927 the U.S. government deliberately "denatured" alcohol used for industrial purposes by adding dangerous substances, rendering it highly dangerous to drink. Prohibition agents began to crack down on Chicago-area chemists who were being paid by bootleggers to chemically test alcohol before it was distributed.

Additionally, I was fascinated to learn more about the events leading up to the stock market crash, including what happened in that last fateful week of October. While reports of executives throwing themselves out of skyscrapers have long been exaggerated, certainly there was much desperation and a general numbness among those directly affected. *Tribune* reporters described the silence of Black Thursday in the Exchange as stock prices dropped, as well as the gallows humor that ensued. Some of my dialogue was drawn from those journalists' accounts.

I also drew on the newspaper to help inform my characters. For example, while Fruma Landry is a fictional character, she was inspired by the stories of two real Chicagoans— Leta Wichart, a twenty-two-year-old stunt woman who accidentally leapt to her death while filming a motion picture in Hollywood, and twenty-year-old Mary Daly, who claimed that she had jumped out of a plane at 31,000 feet, passed out, and drifted for eleven hours before setting down several hundred miles outside Chicago. Her story, unlike Fruma's, was immediately questionable, as she claimed that she somehow never lost hold of her notebook and pen, periodically writing impressions and poems as she passed over farmlands and towns.

Other characters were also inspired by real historic figures. Nancy Doyle was loosely inspired by Alice Clement, a police matron who in 1913 became the first female detective in Chicago and one of the first in the nation. The character of William Morrish emerged from a compilation of mugshots taken of Chicago gangsters and descriptions of gamblers I'd come across in the *Tribune*. Lastly, Stella, my fifteen-year-old bootlegger, was based on a real teenager named Stella Rzegocki who had been arrested for delivering alcohol to a candy store.

ACKNOWLEDGMENTS

I am very fortunate to have a wonderful group of family and friends who have supported and encouraged me while writing this book.

I would be remiss if I did not first thank those friends who actively supported my cocktail research. The amazing Alexia Gordon actually helped me figure out what kind of cocktail a woman might be drinking if she threw that cocktail onto the dress of another woman, in order for the contents of said cocktail to be seen on said dress. She even calculated distance between drink and dress and material of dress—scientific research at its finest! Lisa McCaw helped me make several Prohibition-era cocktails, and it was from her that I learned the hard way, as Gina did, that one must shake a cocktail *before* adding club soda. Other friends helped with important cocktail research as well, including Gretchen Beetner and Brian Paetow, who just know a ton, and Kristopher Zgorski who suggested Hotsy-Totsy as a character's drink of choice. I am grateful to Sharisse and

Dennis Grannan for telling me some great stories about 1920s Chicago gangsters over drinks.

I am also very grateful to my friendship with Lori Rader-Day and Erica Ruth Neubauer—our many conversations about writing and life (again, often over drinks!) keep me encouraged and inspired. I am also so appreciative of other friends who help keep me balanced through the ups and downs of this crazy writing endeavor. These include Teri Bischoff, Maggie Dalrymple and Steve Stofferahn, Denise Drane, Jamie Freveletti, Julie Hyzy, Jess Lourey, Nadine Nettman, Patricia Skalka, and Helen Smith. I am also appreciative of my good friends from Sleuths in Time, Sisters in Crime Chicagoland, and Mystery Writers of America, especially those from the Midwest chapter. I am thankful to the good folks at ArrivaDolce, my favorite coffee shop in Highland Park, who let me write for hours at a time in a peaceful and cheerful environment.

I really appreciate too the hard work and care that the wonderful people at Minotaur have taken with this book, especially my amazing editor, Hannah Braaten, Nettie Finn (whose name I really wanted to use for a character, but I already had Neddy Fingers), and India Cooper, my copy editor. As always, I am very appreciative to my agent, David Hale Smith, for his ongoing encouragement and friendship.

I am thankful to my parents, James and Diane Calkins, as well as to other members of my family, including Becky Calkins, Vince Calkins, Monica Calkins, Steve Wagner, Jadyn Wagner and Avi Wagner, Robin Kelley, and Angie Betz for your love and support over time.

Additionally, I'd like to thank my two boys, Alex and Quentin Kelley, for being so wonderful and amazing. I'm proud of them every day, for the light that they shine and the joy that they bring.

Last, but never least, I'd like to thank my dear husband, Matt Kelley, who is an unmovable rock and unending source of love and support. I find that he acquires new executive titles with every book I write—in addition to being Alpha Reader, Chief Continuity Expert, and Finder of Verbal Tics, he also served as Decipherer of World Series Box Scores, helping me translate what was happening between the Cubs and Athletics and putting it into dialogue. You're darb!

ABOUT THE AUTHOR

Lisa Bagadia

SUSANNA CALKINS, author of the award-winning Lucy Campion series, holds a PhD in history and teaches at the college level. Her historical mysteries have been nominated for the Mary Higgins Clark and Agatha awards, among many others, and *The Masque of a Murderer* received a Macavity. Originally from Philadelphia, Calkins now lives in the Chicago area with her husband and two sons.

"A THRILLING SERIES."

—Victoria Thompson, bestselling author
of *Murder on Trinity Place*

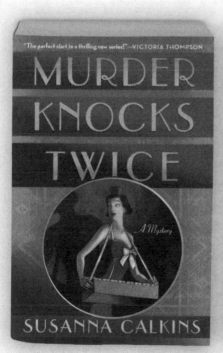

ST. MARTIN'S GRIFFIN

A 2019 Agatha Award Nominee for "Best Historical Mystery"!

After nine months as a cigarette girl at the Third Door, one of Chicago's premier moonshine parlors, Gina Ricci feels like she's finally getting into the swing of things. The year is 1929, the Chicago Cubs are almost in the World Series, neighborhood gangs are all-powerful, and though Prohibition is the law of the land, the Third Door can't serve the cocktails fast enough.

Two women in particular are throwing drinks back with abandon while chatting up a couple of bankers, and Gina can't help but notice the levels of inebriation and the tension at their table. When the group stumbles out in the early morning, she tries to put them out of her head. But once at home that night, Gina's sleep is interrupted when her cousin Nancy, a police officer, calls—she's found a body. Gina hurries over to photograph the crime scene but stops short when she recognizes the body: it's one of the women from the night before.

Could the Third Door have served the woman bad liquor? Or, Gina wonders, could this be murder? As the gangs and bombings draw ever closer, all of Chicago starts to feel like a warzone, and Gina is determined to find out if this death was an unlucky accident, or a casualty of combat.

Praise for THE FATE OF A FLAPPER

"Written with wit and an understanding of the tensions during one of the most volatile times in history…will give readers insight into the world of Prohibition and what the human spirit is capable of in desperate times."
—*PUBLISHERS WEEKLY*

"A fun romp…with lots of 1920s atmosphere." —*BOOKLIST*

Praise for MURDER KNOCKS TWICE

"The perfect start to a thrilling new series." —VICTORIA THOMPSON

"The secrets are as heady as bathtub gin in this smart 1920s mystery that will keep you guessing." —DEANNA RAYBOURN

"Peppered with memorable characters and rich historical details, *Murder Knocks Twice* is sure to have readers asking for another round." —ANNA LEE HUBER

"A page-turning romp through Prohibition-era Chicago! You're in for a wild ride." —RENEE ROSEN

COVER DESIGN BY DAVID BALDEOSINGH ROTSTEIN

COVER ILLUSTRATION BY BRADLEY CLARK

MINOTAUR BOOKS
ST. MARTIN'S PUBLISHING GROUP
120 BROADWAY, NEW YORK, NY 10271
PRINTED IN THE UNITED STATES OF AMERICA
www.minotaurbooks.com

US $17.99 / CAN $24.50
ISBN 978-1-250-19085-7

51799 >

9 781250 190857